more
than
words

ALSO BY JILL SANTOPOLO

The Light We Lost

more than words

Jill Santopolo

G. P. PUTNAM'S SONS   NEW YORK

PUTNAM

G. P. Putnam's Sons
Publishers Since 1838
An imprint of Penguin Random House LLC
penguinrandomhouse.com

Copyright © 2019 by Jill Santopolo

Library of Congress Cataloging-in-Publication Data

Names: Santopolo, Jill, author.
Title: More than words / Jill Santopolo.
Description: New York : G. P. Putnam's Sons, [2019]
Identifiers: LCCN 2018041586| ISBN 9780735218307 (hardcover) |
    ISBN 9780735218321 (epub)
Subjects: | GSAFD: Love stories.
Classification: LCC PS3619.A586 M67 2019 | DDC 813/.6—dc23
LC record available at https://lccn.loc.gov/2018041586

International edition ISBN: 9780593083659

Printed in the United States of America
10 9 8 7 6 5 4 3 2 1

Book design by Amy Hill

For my father
1949–2015

more
than
words

prologue

HE'D IMAGINED THE BABY WOULD BE A BOY. A SON TO take to ball games, to watch his favorite movies with, to teach to drive stick. A son who would slay the Jabberwock with him, who would pick up his own sword and fight the manxome foes alongside his old man. The way *he* had. A son who would continue his legacy, the family's legacy. An heir.

Standing with his baby girl in his arms, her head resting in the crook of his elbow, he felt the need to say he was sorry. To apologize for imagining her a boy. Because from the moment she was born, the moment he first saw her, it was as if a seed had been planted in his heart. It quickly rooted there, and now, three days later, he felt it growing, filling him with pride and love and determination.

"Nina," he whispered to the fragile baby in his arms. "I will raise you to be strong. I will raise you to be powerful. I will raise you to be fearless."

His daughter stared at him, her eyes blue like his, her cheeks round and pink. "And I will protect you," he said. "Until the day I die. That's my pledge to you."

The baby reached her hand toward him, touching his chin with her fingers.

The pact was sealed. The deal was made. And Joseph Gregory would spend the rest of his life trying to keep that promise.

1

SOMETIMES NINA GREGORY GOT LOST IN THE ELASTIC-ity of time. When she was concentrating on something with a singular focus, time seemed to stretch, like a rubber band pulled taut, until—snap!—the sound of a cleared throat or a car horn would make time feel normal again.

She was lost there now, putting the finishing touches on the speech her boss, Rafael, was going to give at tonight's campaign fund-raiser. "You're in the Nina zone," her college roommate, Leslie, would have said if she were there.

Then, just as Nina got to the last sentence, her phone buzzed, bringing her back to the present. It was Tim.

On a call that's running over. Probably be about 20 mins late tonight. Sorry!

No worries, she typed back. *I'll be there.*

Can't wait to see you quickly appeared on her screen.

Nina smiled. *Same*, she wrote.

Tim's answer was a smiley face and a thumbs-up emoji.

When Tim was on forever-long conference calls with the

start-ups he worked for, he would scroll through emojis, sending strings of them to Nina, summarizing his day in cartoon images. Getting those texts always made Nina laugh. Deciphering them reminded her of the rebus puzzles the two of them used to solve together as kids, when they shared the backseat of her father's car, before they knew their futures would twine around each other.

As she was responding to Tim's text with her own emojis, Jane, the campaign's communications director, leaned on the edge of Nina's desk. "Big favor," she said, twisting her micro braids into a bun. "Would you be okay staffing tonight's event on your own? Mac and I need more time to hammer out the details of Rafael's position on charter schools before I prep him for that New York One interview."

Nina didn't usually staff events. Most speechwriters didn't. But she happened to be going to this fund-raiser because her closest friend from high school was hosting it. Actually, Priscilla was hosting it because Nina had asked her to, though she'd made sure no one at the campaign knew that.

"No problem," Nina said, shifting her attention to Jane. "I'm sure I can handle it. Just tell me what I need to know."

As Nina hit print and e-mailed herself the speech as backup, Jane gave her a crash course. "Mia's running advance for the event, so you don't have to worry about the logistics. All you have to do is introduce Rafael to donors with information that he can use to start a conversation. I've got the guest list along with their photos and what we know about them—I'll text it over. But you could probably manage without the list anyway."

Nina nodded.

"Make sure he always has a drink in his hand—a weak one," Jane continued. "He likes vodka soda with a twist of lime." She was ticking the pointers off on her fingers. "And make sure no one monopolizes too much of his time. Mia will have the gift bags set up—so you don't have to worry about that either. She can help if you need anything."

Nina nodded again. "Got it," she said.

"I promise, it's not hard," Jane answered, pushing herself off Nina's desk.

"Don't worry," Nina said, gathering her bag and her blazer. "We'll be fine."

She grabbed the speech and walked into the hallway. Rafael was waiting right outside the elevator bank, his tie perfectly straight, his gray suit jacket folded neatly over his arm.

"So it's just you and me, huh?" he said as Nina stopped beside him, buttoning her blazer.

"That's what they tell me," Nina replied. She looked up and he smiled.

The *Daily News* had written about Rafael's smile twice, calling it "high-wattage" and "compelling," part of "Rafael O'Connor-Ruiz's Charm Offensive." Nina could understand why. There was something about his smile—the unselfconsciousness, the way his eyes crinkled, how it showed both rows of his teeth—that made it impossible not to smile back.

"I think we can manage," he said, running his left hand through his thick black hair.

Until last fall, Rafael had been an immigration lawyer, defending New Yorkers who were facing deportation. And then he and his wife divorced, he took a leave from his firm, and he announced in January that he was going to run for mayor of New York City. That was four months ago. Nina had been his fourth hire, after Jane, Mac, who was the campaign manager, and Christian, who ran the fund-raising outreach.

"I have complete faith in us," Nina answered.

The elevator came just as her phone buzzed with a text from Jane.

"Our car is outside," Nina said to Rafael. "Jane said to tell you the driver's name is Frank. He took you home last week and is a Yankee fan."

"Frank," Rafael repeated. "Yankee fan. Right. I remember him."

Rafael had made it very clear during his first meeting with his senior staff that he wanted to know the name of every single person he came in contact with during the election cycle, so he could address them properly when he said hello and thank you. He wanted everyone to feel valued, no matter their job.

"Do you know how annoying that's going to be?" Mac had grumbled, when the meeting ended.

But Nina loved that Rafael had made that request. It reminded her of her father, actually, who knew the name of every bartender, housekeeper, and bellhop who worked at the Gregory hotels.

"Did it ever occur to you," Jane had said to Mac then, "that you should probably know these people's names anyway?"

Nina had hidden her laugh behind a cough, but since that first meeting, she found herself siding with Jane over Mac whenever there was a side to take. And she liked that Rafael seemed to, as well.

2

"SO THIS FUND-RAISER," RAFAEL SAID TO NINA AS
they rode the elevator down twelve floors. "You know the hosts?"

Nina nodded. "Priscilla Winter and Brent Fielding. Pris and
I went to school together from kindergarten through twelfth
grade. Her family made their money in steel, but now they're in
biotech. Brent runs a hedge fund. He grew up in Boston."

The elevator doors opened, and the two of them walked out
of the lobby toward the waiting car.

"Frank!" Rafael said, when he saw the driver standing at the
car door. "Great to see you again. Thanks for being so prompt."

"Of course, sir," Frank said, opening the door for Nina before walking around to the other side to open one for Rafael.

Nina looked around the backseat. Water. Tissues. No candy.
Her favorite drivers were the ones who brought butterscotch.

As they pulled into the New York City traffic, Nina shared
her phone's location with Mia so their progress down the city
streets could be tracked, and then handed Rafael the printout

of the speech. As he memorized, his lips moved, his hands gesticulated. It was like his own kind of performance art.

Nina leaned back in her seat, watching him practice her words. With his broad shoulders and the cleft in his chin, he looked like Hollywood's idea of a politician. Handsome, charming. He was brilliant, too. Nina loved translating his ideas, his passion, into the precise words that would fire up his audience. But behind his polished façade, behind his megawatt grin, he was an enigma. "What are you thinking?" she sometimes wanted to ask him.

Her phone buzzed again. Nina looked down, expecting a note from Jane or another emoji-filled text from Tim. But it was her father.

The woman holding the professorship your grandmother endowed at Smith is retiring and there's a reception in six weeks. They asked me to make a speech, but I don't think I should plan that far in advance. Would you RSVP yes in my place, Sweetheart? I'll forward you the e-mail.

Nina read the words. And then read them again. Benign as they might seem, they felt like a vine tightening around her chest, making it hard to breathe. *I don't think I should plan that far in advance.*

Every moment of every day she tried to forget that her father was sick. Again. That the doctors had said there wasn't anything they could do this time. She'd hated seeing him go through chemo three years before. But then, at least, there was hope, the chance that they'd still have days sailing their boat on the Atlantic Ocean, nights drinking scotch on the rooftop of their hotel on Central Park South. Now there wasn't. Which was why Nina tried to forget about it the best she could.

But when he sent texts like this, forgetting was impossible.

The squeeze in her chest became a sting in her eyes. *Shit.*
Nina never let herself cry anymore. Not in front of anyone. Not
even Tim. She thought about emotionless items to keep her
feelings in check. *Forks. Light bulbs. Pebbles.* But though she
battled against them, she couldn't stop her tears this time. She
looked around the car. There was no way to escape. Nowhere to
be alone. Nina sniffed quietly, hoping Rafael wouldn't notice,
as a tear snaked its way down her cheek.

He looked up from his phone.

Nina turned away, hiding her face from him. *Mom,* she
thought, sending a message into the atmosphere, *please help me
out here. Please keep me strong and focused. Fuerte y centrado. Fuertrado.* She'd been talking to her mom in her mind since she was
eight, when she was really at a loss. Usually it helped.

"What is it, Nina?" Rafael asked in a soft voice she'd never
heard before. "Are you okay?"

She closed her eyes, tilted her head back as if gravity could keep
her tears at bay. But they seeped out from under her closed lids.

"Hey," he said. "Is it something I can help with?"

Nina took a deep breath. She tried again. *Paper napkins. Plastic spoons. Wooden toothpicks.* Her mind was clearing. She opened
her eyes and blotted tears with her fingertips. "I'm sorry," she
said, turning to face him. "It's my dad."

For a moment, Rafael didn't speak. He just put his hand gen-
tly on hers, as if to say: *I'm here. I understand.* It wasn't something
she'd expected. Nor was the callused skin on his fingertips, tough
like a guitar player's. There was so much they didn't know about
each other. Still, the warmth of his fingers made things better.
She gave him a brief smile.

"I really am sorry about that," she said, fumbling in her purse
for a tissue. "My father just texted, asking me to step in for him,

to give a speech because he isn't sure if he'll be able to, and—it caught me off-guard."

"I was a mess when my father was sick," Rafael said. "I'm impressed with how well you've kept it together these past few months."

Nina knew his father had died of congestive heart failure five years before—she knew his whole biography—but she'd imagined him handling that heartbreak with the same pragmatism he seemed to have used to get over his divorce. In the months she'd known him, Rafael had been all facts—and passion about how he could make the city better. But emotions—those had been locked away, kept secret. Or maybe just saved for people outside the office.

"I hate being a mess," she told him.

He nodded sympathetically.

"Something like this," he said, slowly, "it makes you see the world through a different lens. I think it's hard not to fall apart when your view of life is shifting."

She looked at him, amazed. He'd put into words a feeling she'd been trying to explain to Tim for weeks. "It's part of every decision I make now. I try to forget about it, but it's there, sharpening my focus, narrowing my choices."

She finally found a tissue and used it to dab at her eye makeup. Then realized there had been a box of them sitting in the car door all along.

"My sister was pregnant when my father was dying," Rafael told her. "And she told me that every decision she made about my niece—from her name to what her nursery looked like—was filtered through the idea that my father might not be around to meet her. It's why my niece's name is Emilia."

"Your father was Emilio," Nina said.

Rafael nodded. "My sister always loved the name Tiffany. If my father hadn't been sick, I'm sure my niece would have been named Tiffany. It's just one small example, but—" Rafael shrugged. "I'm sorry you have to experience it," he said. He took her hand in his again and squeezed, the pressure saying, without words: *I get it. I've felt it.* His eyes said so, too.

"I'm sorry you had to go through it twice," she said, thinking about his ex-wife.

"My mom's still around," Rafael answered.

Nina smiled. "I know," she told him. "I meant with Sonia. Someone else in your life who disappeared, who you lost."

Rafael looked at her for a beat, as if weighing her words, as if weighing his own. "I hadn't thought about divorce like that before," he said. "But you're right. The grief, the shock, the un-tangling of emotions. It's not all the same, but a lot of it . . . you're right."

"I guess both of our perspectives on life are changing right now."

"I guess so," Rafael said, and he squeezed her hand once more.

3

BY THE TIME MIA MET NINA AND RAFAEL IN FRONT OF the Norwood Club, the warmth that had flowed between them had cooled. But something had changed. When they got out of the car, Rafael waited for Nina so that they walked up the stairs side by side. She felt less like his staffer and more like—well, she wasn't sure quite what—like a colleague or maybe even a friend.

A tiny blond woman holding a glass of champagne threw her arms around Nina as they walked through the oak doorway.

"Pris!" Nina said, laughing. "It's great to see you, too."

"Everything okay?" Pris whispered into her ear. "I heard your dad hasn't been in the office very much this week."

"It's all fine," Nina lied, hugging her friend back. "He's been working from home."

"Oh, good," Pris said. "I'll tell my dad. He has an empty spot at a charity poker tournament on Wednesday and was hoping your dad could join."

Nina nodded and turned to Rafael, who'd been quietly watching the two women. "Pris," she said. "This is Rafael O'Connor-Ruiz. Rafael, Priscilla Winter." Then she remembered Jane's rule. "Priscilla and Brent are about to head off to Cannes for the film festival."

Rafael stuck out his hand. "Thank you so much for hosting this fund-raiser," he said, his face lighting up, that megawatt grin in place.

Priscilla smiled back. "Oh, our pleasure!" she said. "When Nina tells us a candidate is worth supporting, we listen."

Nina cringed. She'd been unmasked. Rafael looked at her and raised an eyebrow but then turned back to Pris. "So tell me about this trip to Cannes."

Brent joined Priscilla, and the two of them chatted with Rafael, while Nina flagged down the waitress and ordered herself a Sauvignon Blanc and Rafael a vodka soda, heavy on the soda.

She walked over to some of the other women there, people she knew from the board of the New York City Ballet, which she and Pris both served on.

"When are you going to see the Balanchine?" Maggie Lancer asked, after hugging Nina hello. "I hear it's just fantastic."

"Tim and I have tickets next month," Nina said. "But I heard that *Romeo and Juliet* this summer is going to be even better. Zachary's dancing Romeo."

"Zachary is stunning," Maggie said. Then over Nina's shoulder, she saw a couple walk into the room. "Oh, Hayley's here! I have to talk to her about our dinner plans next weekend."

As Maggie walked away, Nina cast her eyes back toward Rafael. A small crowd had gathered around him, and they were all laughing at something he'd said. There was no denying his presence, his ability to draw people toward him. But at the same time, it looked to Nina like her friends were treating him as the night's entertainment. It made her slightly uncomfortable.

She was just about to walk toward him when she felt arms wrap around her and lips on the top of her head. Nina took a deep breath. Redken shampoo. Shea butter soap. Sandalwood shaving cream. Ever since he started shaving, Tim smelled exactly the same, a mixture of those three scents. That was one of the most comforting things about Tim; he was such a creature of habit. Nina could predict what she'd find in his refrigerator on any given day. She could even buy his clothes: Brooks Brothers slim-cut jeans in indigo denim, striped button-downs, V-neck sweaters, and navy blazers where he stuck his spearmint gum— always Eclipse, where you popped the white square through a thin piece of silver foil. There were never any surprises with Tim, and that was so much of what she loved about him.

Nina turned into Tim's embrace and fit there perfectly, tucked right underneath his chin.

"Sorry I'm late," he said into her hair.

She tilted her head and rose on her tiptoes to give him a kiss. "Barely late at all," she said. "Don't worry about it."

"Thanks." He squeezed her shoulder with one hand as he waved a waiter over with the other. "Just wine tonight?" he asked her.

Nina shrugged. "Technically I'm working," she said. "Want to meet my boss?"

"Of course," he answered. "I've heard enough about him."

Once Tim placed his order and said hello to a few of their friends, she led him toward Rafael, who was now in a conversation with Priscilla and one of Brent's work friends.

"Tim!" Pris exclaimed as they got closer. She gave him a hug and a kiss on the cheek.

"Rafael," Nina said. "This is my boyfriend, Tim Calder. Tim, my boss, Rafael O'Connor-Ruiz."

The two men shook hands.

Pris looked at Nina standing next to Tim and grinned. "I predicted this," she told Rafael. "Back in high school, I knew the two of them would end up together. It's just . . . it's like they were born to be a couple."

"Oh?" Rafael asked.

"Our fathers were college roommates," Nina explained, just as Tim said, "We grew up together."

"And Tim's dad is the CEO of Nina's dad's company," Priscilla added. "So they're basically like family already."

Rafael smiled at them, but it wasn't his *Daily News* grin. "It must be nice to be with someone who knows everything about you."

Nina looked up at Tim. He probably did know everything about her. Or at least as much as one person could ever know about another. She wondered if Rafael's smile had dimmed because he hadn't felt that way about his ex-wife.

"Have you met the Lancers yet?" Nina asked him. "They were big donors during the presidential election."

"Point me their way," he said, and this time his smile reached across his whole face, though Nina was beginning to realize that there was a difference—small but perceptible: sometimes that smile was genuine, and sometimes it was just for show.

As Nina guided Rafael in the Lancers' direction, he threw a quick look over his shoulder at Tim.

"Your boyfriend seems nice," he said to Nina.

"Thanks," she said. "He is."

· · ·

LATER THAT NIGHT, back at Tim's place, as Nina was brushing her teeth with the electric toothbrush he had gotten her, she thought about that word: "nice." It was a perfectly fine way to describe someone—complimentary even—but it was tepid. Flat. That was how Rafael saw Tim. She was surprised by how much it bothered her.

4

NEW YORKERS IN NINA AND TIM'S CIRCLE BRUNCHED
on Sundays. It was a citywide tradition. A cultural touchstone.
And the Sunday brunch at The Gregory on the Park was leg-
endary. Nina's grandfather had personally crafted the menu
when he opened the hotel in the early 1930s. It was four courses.
Decadent. And served with champagne. Tourists knew that if
they wanted New York City's finest afternoon tea, they went to
the Palm Court at The Plaza. And if they wanted the finest
Sunday brunch, they went to The Grove at The Gregory on the
Park.

When Joseph Gregory took over the hotel in the 1980s, he
decided to add a Saturday brunch, too. The first one was on the
third Saturday in January 1989. Nina had been three, Tim had
been five, and they'd sat with their parents at the front table
near the door and greeted guests as they arrived. The guests
loved getting to eat brunch in the same room as Joseph Gregory, which Nina now ascribed partially to people's fascination
with wealth, and partially to her father's public persona; he was

the affable millionaire who was just as happy chatting with the Yankees' owners as with their fans. Nina knew that wasn't entirely true, but it was what everyone thought. It was their truth.

It had been such a hit that her dad decided he would attend brunch the third Saturday of every month after that first one, except for in July when he was in the Hamptons. Nina and her mother had gone with him, until her mother died. Then it had been Nina and her dad until Nina went off to college, when Tim's parents, TJ and Caro, joined him. Now, Nina and Tim came when they could.

Tim loved sitting at the head table, waving at the kids who walked in, nodding at the adults. Nina didn't. Ever since she came back to the city after college, she'd felt uncomfortable at these brunches—dressed up and on display. But she knew it was good for business—and important to her father—so she never complained. Except to Leslie, who encouraged her to rebel by showing up one day in ripped jeans. Nina never had, but she thought about it often.

When she and Tim walked into The Grove that Saturday, a room filled with the same wrought-iron sconces and intricate crown moldings her grandfather had picked out, Nina's father rose from his chair. He knew the room, knew where to place himself for the best effect, and stood directly in a beam of light, so it looked like he was glowing. Nina walked over and hugged him tightly. She was dimly aware of cell phones flashing in their direction, but mostly she inhaled the scent of his cologne— the tobacco, leather, and thyme that seemed to capture the essence of who he was.

"Joseph Gregory, Thrilled to See His Daughter for Brunch," her father said, captioning the photos the guests were taking, writing the headline for the story. It was a game he'd invented when

Nina was a kid, coming up with both the best and worst possible headlines that would describe any given moment of their lives— a way for her to understand consequences and repercussions. But since his cancer returned in January, he'd stopped offering up the worst headline. She hugged him harder, not caring that they were putting on a show for the guests. "Love you," she said.

"More than words," he answered, his rejoinder for Nina's entire life.

As they sat, Joseph at the head of the table, Nina on his left next to Tim, TJ and Caro across the way, Nina tuned out the conversation for a moment to take a mental picture of the tableau. She wanted to remember this. Her father presiding over the family that he'd willed together through friendship.

"How's the campaign going?" he asked her.

Talking politics with her dad was always tricky. Nina had heard a conversation that he'd had with TJ once about her job. "She's going through an idealistic phase," he'd said.

It had made her reevaluate what she was doing, wonder if everyone else thought she was being ridiculous, working for a politician instead of joining the Gregory Corporation right out of business school. But she decided that even if he was right, she wasn't going to change her mind.

Working in politics made her feel like an agent of change in a way that working in the hotel business never could. Volunteering for the New Haven mayor's reelection campaign in college, Nina had fallen in love with speechwriting. She'd sat in on policy discussions and then tried her hand at synthesizing the ideas into just the right words, finding a way to change minds. It was a challenge, a game with high-stakes results. And she and the mayor's team had won. Business never gave her that kind of high.

"It's going well," she said. "We're neck-and-neck with Marc Johnson."

Her father took a sip of coffee. He'd donated to Marc Johnson's campaign for comptroller four years before. "Well, you tell me when he's a sure thing."

Nina smoothed her napkin onto her lap. "Absolutely," she said.

Joseph Gregory only endorsed winners, regardless of party or previous donations.

"But I'll vote for him in the primary no matter what," he added.

"Yeah?" Nina asked, surprised.

"Of course," her father said. "It'll look good for us if you chose the winner."

Every time the Gregory name was associated with a success, it gathered power, cemented its meaning in people's minds. That was something her grandfather had always said, something her dad repeated: *Names have meaning. And you're nothing without your name.*

"Well, fingers crossed," she said, taking a small roll from the overfilled bread basket. "So, anything exciting happening at the hotel this week?"

"We're about to exchange the calla lilies for roses," Caro said, looking around at the vase upon vase of flowers filling the restaurant. She managed all the events at both Gregory hotels, which included the seasonal changing of flowers at The Grove and the downtown hotel's restaurant, The Garden. In the fall there were chrysanthemums, winter brought snowdrops, spring was calla lilies, and summer was roses. Nina's grandmother had made the first arrangements herself, but now there was a florist that Caro had hired. The flowers were replaced each week, early Friday morning, before the restaurants opened for breakfast.

She turned to Nina. "Would you like to come watch?"

Nina had loved watching the flowers change with her mom when she was a kid. Thousands of them, filling the restaurant with their scent and color. It seemed like a ceremony, the welcoming in of a new season—and was overwhelmingly beautiful. "That sounds fun," she answered. "I haven't come in ages."

"Oh, wonderful," Caro said. "Can I steal you for breakfast afterward?"

Tim cleared his throat. "Ahem," he said. "What about me?"

Nina nudged his shoulder playfully. "Are you afraid we're going to talk about you? You know, your mom and I do have other topics of conversation." Caro had always been there for Nina. She'd been the one who talked to her about what it would be like the first time she got her period and taken her prom dress shopping—both times. And Caro had made sure that Nina was on birth control before she went to college, even though it meant an argument with Nina's dad.

Caro tucked her graying blond bob behind her ear. *Nantucket blond*, she started calling it, once the color began shifting toward white. "Of course you're welcome, Timothy," she said. "I'll see you both at six A.M. on Friday."

"Wait, it's that early?" Tim groaned. "You can't change the flowers at, say, eight?"

Nina started to laugh. TJ was shaking his head. "Son," he said, "what are we going to do with you?"

Her dad, who had been watching this whole exchange with a smile playing across his face, started to chuckle. But then his chuckle turned into a cough that wouldn't stop. Nina's laughter faded.

"Dad," she said, quietly. "Did you bring that inhaler?"

He nodded, then looked around the room. "Can't do it here," he coughed. "Be back."

He got up and, still trying not to let his coughing fit show, walked out the door of the restaurant, toward the bathroom.

TJ stood up. "I'll see if he needs help."

Caro, Tim, and Nina sat in silence. Nina felt like she did in the car with Rafael. Like there were vines wrapping around her rib cage, like she couldn't breathe. Caro looked at her, reading the situation perfectly.

"Girls' trip to the restroom?" she asked. Then, softly, as if she hated saying it, but knew she had to, "No tears in front of the guests." It was something Nina's father had reminded her often as a kid, but he hadn't needed to for years.

Nina shut her eyes for a moment. She quelled the panic. Quelled the fear. And just like she did when she was eight, in the months after her mother died, she willed her heart to be unbreakable. They were putting on a show, and in this show, the heiress did not cry. Nina opened her eyes again.

"I'm fine," she said. "The next time Kristin walks by, could someone flag her down? I'd love a refill on my coffee."

Nina turned, but she wasn't looking for Kristin. Her eyes were on the door, waiting for her father to come back to brunch. Her heart wasn't unbreakable. Not even close.

5

AFTER BRUNCH, NINA HADN'T BEEN INTERESTED IN the fun things Tim had suggested they do. "I'm sorry," she said, standing outside the hotel. "You do something fun. I'll just . . . go home and . . . I don't know. Read a book or something until I have to get ready for the art opening tonight. I'm not feeling particularly fun right now."

"I want to help," he said, twirling his finger around her hair, so for a moment it sat in one spiral down her back. "Just tell me what to do."

But the truth was, she didn't know. She took his hand, looking across the street at the trees, at the flowers in full bloom, at the horse-and-buggies waiting for passengers. There was some comfort in being here with Tim, in feeling his fingers woven between hers.

"Let's go to the park," Nina said.

They crossed Central Park South in the sunshine and walked through the Artists' Gate.

As they veered onto the loop, a breeze ruffled Nina's skirt.

"I'm sorry I'm such a downer. I just . . . feel like there's this darkness hanging over everything."

"Even when you're with me?" Tim asked.

Nina sighed. The clip-clop of hooves echoed behind them, and Nina turned to watch a dapple-gray horse coming up the drive, pulling a white carriage with a family inside. This wasn't about their relationship. She hoped Tim wouldn't take it that way. "Always," she said.

He swallowed, and then his expression shifted to the mischievous one she knew well. "Nothing will cheer you up?" he asked. "Not even a carousel ride?"

Nina's mouth quirked into a small smile. She'd dragged Tim with her to the Central Park carousel more times than she could count. But she shook her head. "I don't really want to be cheered up," she said. "I just . . . can you stand in the darkness with me?" She'd been reliving the car ride with Rafael over and over in her mind these past weeks, trying to figure out why it had made her feel better. And that was what it had been: He'd stood with her in the darkness and made it feel safe. It was what she'd needed then. It was what she needed now, too.

"Remember when we went skiing in Park City?" Tim said, as they kept walking, bikers and joggers zipping by them.

Nina nodded. She knew what he was going to say. She'd been eleven and terrified.

"We couldn't see more than a few feet in front of us."

Nina nodded again. She'd panicked. He'd panicked.

"Even though we were scared and didn't know what was going to come next, we went slowly, and stayed together, and we got down the run."

Nina looked at him.

"We'll get down the mountain, Nina," he said. "But there's no use worrying about how. Your dad is still okay. We'll deal with things as they come. For now, for old times' sake, how about we see if a ride on the carousel will make you smile? Will you try? For me?"

She let out a long breath. "For you," she said.

He steered her toward the center of the park, into the bright sunshine.

"I just want you to be happy," Tim said. Then he bent over and kissed her. And she tried to forget everything, to lose herself in his kiss like she had four months before, the first time she'd felt his lips against hers, but she couldn't do it.

6

IN HIGH SCHOOL, ALL OF NINA'S BREARLEY FRIENDS wanted to know what was going on when Tim took her to the Interschool Prom when she was a sophomore and he was a senior. And then two years later, they were sure something was going on when he came back from Stanford for the weekend and she took him. But nothing was happening then. At least not on Nina's end. Tim was the person she always counted on, leaned on, looked up to. But he wasn't the person she daydreamed about kissing.

Pris had asked what was going on between them again when Tim visited Nina in college, traveling across the country to spend the weekend with her in New Haven. But Nina had thought of him as a friend then, too. He was the one she called when she was feeling homesick, the one who cheered her up. But he wasn't the person whose name she doodled in her Spanish notebook, who made her feel tongue-tied when she ran into him in the dining hall.

And then back in January, Tim had stood with his hand

around Nina's waist as her father told the press that his cancer was back, that he'd eventually be stepping down as chairman of the board. As her father said those words, Tim held Nina up, held her close.

"Who will be taking over as chairman?" a reporter asked.

"I'll keep my position as long as I'm able," he replied. "And then my daughter will take over for me, the way I did for my father. This is still a family company."

Nina took a deep breath. It was real. It was going to happen. Before business school she'd made a deal with her dad: She would work in politics until he needed her to take the helm of the corporation. She'd figured she'd be ready by then. She'd be able to continue the family legacy after she'd solidified her own. But she hadn't even gotten ten years. Not only was she going to lose her father, she was going to lose the life she'd imagined for herself. The future she'd expected would be hers.

"You okay?" Tim whispered in her ear at the press conference.

If it were anybody other than Tim, she would've said yes. "No," she answered, truthfully.

This wasn't just a company, it wasn't just a hotel—it was her family, it was her father, her grandfather, it was everything they ever gave up, every compromise they ever made, every risk they ever took to solidify their place in New York society. And now it would all rest on Nina. She wasn't ready.

"Then let's go," Tim said. He pulled his phone out of his pocket, acting as if it were vibrating. He held it to his ear and furrowed his eyebrows. Then he tapped her shoulder and, still pretending someone was on the other line, motioned for her to come with him.

They ducked into an empty conference room.

"Well, that was shit," he said.

"It was worse than that," Nina responded. "It was like a thousand people watching while you take a shit."

Tim raised his eyebrows, surprised to hear her swear. "Well, then it's a good thing we got you out of there."

Nina couldn't help it. She laughed, glad Tim was with her. Glad he'd orchestrated their escape.

"My dad said we're going to your dad's for dinner tonight." He went to the counter and made them each a cup of espresso.

"Yeah," Nina answered. "He said he wants to be surrounded by the people he cares most about."

Tim sat down and put Nina's cup in front of her. "Well, you don't have to twist my arm. Are you cooking?"

"With Irena," Nina said. "Between the two of us, we're making all my dad's favorites."

"So Kobe steak?" Tim tipped back in the chair, lifting the front two legs off the ground. He looked so relaxed, Nina thought, so comfortable. He'd always been that way. So comfortable in his skin. She admired it, wondered, sometimes, what it would be like to feel that way, too, not to watch her words, control her emotions, evaluate her actions the way she knew her father expected. She wondered what she'd be like if she hadn't been raised that way—so disciplined, so aware.

"Mm-hm," Nina answered Tim. "And a lemon meringue pie, and string beans with almonds, and honey corn bread."

"Delicious," Tim answered back, tipping the chair forward again. "Can't wait."

WHEN NINA LEFT AFTER dinner that night, Tim did too, and they got a drink at Weather Up, the cocktail lounge right near her apartment, and then another. And went to sit by the river. And soon they were talking about life and love and the future, their breath making puffs of smoke in the cold night air. And then Nina was crying, and Tim was holding her, and maybe it was the alcohol, or maybe it was just the time it was meant to happen, but Tim kissed her, and Nina relaxed against him, and he tasted like the past and the present and the future all at once.

By the time Priscilla called to ask what those photos from the press conference meant, Nina and Tim were finally dating. "You two were meant for each other," she'd said. And maybe it was true.

7

SINCE JOSEPH GREGORY RELAPSED, CARO CALLED NINA more.

"Hi, darling," she said, late Sunday afternoon, the weekend after the brunch. "I'm down at the Seaport hotel checking on a few catering concerns."

"Is everything okay?" Nina answered. She'd been reading a new speech out loud in her living room, dropping her voice to see how the words would sound in Rafael's register.

"It's all fine," Caro said. "But since I'm down your way, how about a walk along the river?"

Nina was one of the few people in Caro's life who didn't mind taking long walks with her. Caro built them into her schedule, but TJ thought it was an inefficient use of time.

Nina put down the speech she'd been reading. "Sure," she said, glad for the break. "I'll see you soon."

The two women planned to meet in the lobby of The Gregory by the Sea. Just after her grandfather died, when Nina was

two years old, her dad had opened the second hotel by the seaport and named the rooftop bar Nina's Nest. You could see all
of New York Harbor from there. It was one of Nina's favorite
views of the city.

WHEN NINA GOT TO THE HOTEL, she said hello to the staff and
then waited in front of the framed spread of her parents from
People magazine hanging next to the elevator bank. In one of the
photos they were both laughing, her mom's dark brown hair
loose and sweeping across her face. Nina wondered if that was
how her mom had looked when she caught her father's eye in
Barcelona. He'd been enjoying paella and a glass of wine on the
beach, just as Nina's mother was finishing her doctoral thesis on
the depiction of the female body in Spanish literature. He'd always said that she'd been so beautiful reading on the beach—
serene, ethereal—that he'd had to invite her to join him.

The media loved the story: New York's most eligible bachelor
falling in love with an unknown woman from Colorado while
on vacation. Their wedding was held in the ballroom on the
thirty-second floor of The Gregory on the Park and was covered
in the *New York Times*, the *New York Post*, *Newsday*, *New York
Magazine*, and the *Daily News*. Shorter pieces even made it into
the national magazines. The pieces were scattered throughout
the two hotels in frames. Nina had once drawn a map detailing
where they each hung, her parents' love story made into her very
own treasure hunt.

She remembered the first time she'd ever seen the *People* magazine spread. She'd been five years old, and the piece had been
published as part of the coverage on the opening of the rooftop

bar at The Gregory on the Park. Her dad had named the bar Los Tortolitos, Spanish for *the lovebirds*, something her parents had been called in the Spanish press, and jokingly adopted for themselves. Nina had needed her mom to read the article's title to her. "Los Tortolitos: A Love Story for the Pages," she'd said, when Nina brought her the magazine, "and then underneath it says, 'Don't you wish your man looked at you the way Joseph Gregory looks at Phoebe?'"

"I do, Mommy!" Nina told her.

Her mother laughed and picked Nina up. "When you're older, you'll find someone who loves you like that, but not for a long time." Nina wondered if that was how Tim looked at her now.

"NINA, DARLING," CARO SAID, crossing the lobby and shaking Nina out of her reverie. She was wearing white tailored pants, a boat-neck sweater, and a pair of flats. There was a silk scarf around her neck. She was dressed down, since it was a Sunday, but dressed down for her was dressed up for most people.

"My parents looked so happy together," Nina said to Caro as they started walking along the water, her mind still on the magazine spread.

"They balanced each other out well," Caro said.

Boats were pulling into New York Harbor, and Caro paused to watch one drop anchor.

It was funny. When Nina was dating other men, she talked to Caro about them. Asked questions, wanted her opinion—not necessarily on the men themselves, but on what to say, on how she felt, on how to navigate both their emotions and her father's. But now that she was dating Caro's son, she didn't feel like she could talk about it with her. At least not directly.

"What do you think is the most important thing, the one thing that makes your relationship with Uncle TJ work so well?" Nina asked.

A foghorn sounded in the distance, and Caro turned. "Honesty," she said. "I've always told TJ that we can handle anything that comes our way as long as we're honest with each other. Then we can be partners. A team. Face the world with a unified front. I know I can trust him, always."

Nina nodded. She wondered if Tim felt that way about her. That he could trust her with everything. He definitely used to. He shared his triumphs, his dating disasters, even his most secret failures, like the mistake he'd made at work the previous year that cost his company an investor. He'd barely been able to give voice to it. She knew she told him everything—all about her jobs, her boyfriends, her embarrassments and fears. And then she realized with a start that she hadn't told him about her conversation with Rafael in the car before the fund-raiser.

She wanted to ask Caro if she thought that was a problem, but instead she said, "When you and Uncle TJ started dating, did it feel . . . exciting? Did it . . . make your heart race when he touched your shoulder?"

Caro laughed. "Watching him walk down the street made my heart race," she said. "I'm glad you and Tim have that, too."

"Right," Nina said. Caro tilted her head slightly, as if she needed to see Nina's expression from another angle.

"You two are happy?" she asked.

"We are," Nina said, as both women moved away from the

pier and started walking down the path. "Now, what was going on today with the caterers?"

Nina wished she could confide more in Caro, but right now that seemed impossible. And Nina wished, for probably the millionth time in her life, that her mother were still alive. But that was impossible, too.

8

WHEN NINA GOT BACK TO TRIBECA AND PUT HER KEY
in the elevator that led to her loft, she dialed Leslie. She needed
a dose of her best friend: Just hearing Leslie's voice made Nina
feel stronger, more able to handle what was being thrown her way.

"Les!" she said, when her friend picked up the FaceTime
call. "Where are you?"

"Cole's soccer game," Leslie said, flipping the phone around
so Nina could see the field. "Why do we make four-year-olds
play soccer? Half of them can't even kick the ball when it's two
inches in front of them."

Nina squinted and saw Cole, his dark curly hair flopping as
he ran. "Well, he looks like he's having fun at least," she said.

"He basically just runs back and forth from one side of the
field to the other," Leslie told her. "And we pay for this. He
could run in the backyard for free."

Nina laughed. "Do you need to get back to the game?"

"Not at all." Nina saw Leslie standing up, telling Vijay she'd
be right back, and walking down a set of bleachers. "I'm glad you

gave me an excuse to get up," she said as soon as she was in the privacy of a little grove of trees. "Those benches could use some cushions. How's everything going? Campaign? Your dad? Tim?"

"It's all going . . ." Nina stood at the floor-to-ceiling window in her living room and looked past her phone, out at the cobble-stoned Tribeca streets below her. "I just got back from a walk with Caro. I miss my mom, Les."

"Oh, Neen," Leslie said, sitting down on the grass, leaning against the trunk of a tree. "It sneaks up on you, doesn't it." Leslie's mom had died when she and Nina were in college, and other than Rafael's surprise moment of empathy, she was one of the only people Nina felt could truly stand with her in the darkness.

"She died almost twenty-five years ago," Nina said, wishing she were there, next to her friend, her back against a neighboring tree. "I used to think at some point I'd stop missing her. But I don't think I ever will."

Nina remembered going with her mom to Columbia University when she was very young, sitting in a small office filled with books, her mother's students asking Nina how old she was, what her favorite color was. And her mother urging her to answer "en español" after she'd answered in English.

"She's got your cheekbones," other professors would say.

Or: "She's got your freckles."

It was true—those were the two features that Nina and her mother shared. Otherwise, Nina looked like her dad. Her hair was light brown, the way his used to be, and silky. Her eyes were dark blue, like his, too, and the two of them had matching dimples and up-turned noses. Whenever people saw them together for the first time, their eyes would shift back and forth, as if matching feature for feature, checking to see where they diverged.

Nina sometimes wondered if she'd look more like her mom if she wore her hair shorter. But her hair was so much lighter . . . There must've been someone in her mom's family who had light hair, too, though Nina didn't know who. She didn't have albums from her mom's childhood the way she did from her dad's, his great-aunts and -uncles and distant cousins, most of them still living in England and Wales, making appearances at various parties throughout the years.

"Yeah, I don't think you'll stop," Leslie said, pulling Nina back to the moment. "But maybe that's a good thing. If you miss her, it means you remember her. It means she's still here."

"I guess," Nina said. "But does that make it any easier?"

Leslie paused for a beat. "I didn't say it was easy." Nina saw her friend stand up suddenly.

"Oh, no way! My son just scored a goal. Yeah, Cole! Way to go, buddy!"

Nina smiled. She heard all of the parents cheering in the background. "You should go. Tell him I say congratulations."

"I will," Leslie said. "And I'll call you later. I love you, Nina. Miss you."

"You too," Nina answered.

Nina grabbed her bag and decided to take herself out for frozen yogurt with rainbow sprinkles—something she used to do with her mom. Maybe this was an afternoon for remembering.

9

THE NEXT WEEK, IT STARTED TO FEEL LIKE SUMMER. June was here. It was warm enough that women were outside in sleeveless dresses for the first time since last September. The sun was shining, the sky was deep blue, and there was just enough of a breeze to make the day feel alive. Nina usually made do with the coffee that Jane brewed at campaign headquarters but decided to stop for an iced coffee on the way to work.

She paused at the crosswalk while cars drove by in front of her and lifted her face to the sun, closing her eyes for a moment to listen to the horns and the car engines and the chatter that gave New York City its vibrant energy.

Campaign days were getting longer, and she knew the caffeine would help carry her through—at least for the next few hours. Lost in her thoughts, she walked smack into the person who was coming out of the coffee shop. They both paused, stunned for a moment by the collision, and then Nina looked up. It was Rafael.

"Fancy meeting a woman like you in a place like this," he said, putting his hand on her arm to steady them both.

"We caffeine addicts need to stick together," she told him. They hadn't touched since the car ride to the Norwood Club nearly a month before, and his hand on her arm brought an unexpected blush to her cheeks.

"Amen," he answered, letting go of her and raising his paper cup in a toast. "I've got a triple shot of espresso in here. Hey, I just found out those Lancers you introduced me to are planning to throw me a fund-raising dinner. Christy's going to add it to my schedule this morning. Any chance I could prevail upon you to come along? You're good at that whole thing—you make the introductions seem so natural."

"Sure," she said. "Happy to. Has the date been set?"

"I don't think so. I'll tell Christy to make sure you know as soon as she does."

Nina nodded. "Okay," she said.

Rafael's hand hovered above her shoulder and then dropped at his side. "Okay, great," he said. "Thank you. It'll be fun." And he smiled at her—his genuine grin.

As Rafael walked out the door and Nina got in line, she couldn't stop thinking about how her body had responded to his fingers on her arm. Did touching her make his heart race, too? Was that why he'd almost put his hand on her shoulder? Was that why he'd decided not to?

Nina pulled her phone out of her bag. *Just saying hi,* she texted to Tim. *Hope you had fun at the game last night.*

She'd have to be careful.

10

IT TURNED OUT THAT THE LANCERS' DINNER WAS THE same evening as the event at Smith for the retiring professor.

"I don't understand why you're so annoyed about this," Tim said, as he and Nina got ready to go to work the next morning. He was at her sink, wrapped in a towel from the waist down. Nina watched his pectoral muscles twitch as he ran the beard trimmer across his square chin. "You don't even like Maggie Lancer all that much."

It wasn't that, though. It was the fact that it wasn't her choice.

"I just . . . I hate that I couldn't say no," Nina said, as she clipped her grandmother's pearls around her neck, the ones she'd inherited the day she was born. "Is that bratty? I sound bratty."

Tim turned the beard trimmer off and shrugged, his freckled shoulders rising just slightly. "There's a trade-off," he said. "Money comes with strings. This is one of your strings. How about . . . we can have, I don't know, three or four or even five kids and then we can ask them to make these speeches for you. Or . . . I can do them, if you don't want to."

Nina looked up at Tim's familiar smiling face. She imagined little kids with his red hair and her blue eyes. She'd never make them fulfill obligations like this.

"Our kids can choose what they want to do," she said, more seriously than she intended, then pulled her hair out of the way and turned around. "Will you zip me?"

He obliged.

Nina continued talking. "No strings attached. Not from me. I'm doing this speech because my dad asked me to, but next time, maybe I can send something for someone else to read."

Tim had walked into the bedroom and was buttoning his white collared shirt; his jeans and sport jacket were laid out on the bed. "I bet you can," he said. "It's not a bad position to be in, you know, being asked to give a speech because your family endowed a professorship."

Nina looked at Tim again. She knew she was extraordinarily lucky—in so many uncountable ways. She always tried to remember that—how millions of people would trade places with her in a heartbeat. But still, in that moment, she wished that she and Tim could swap. That he could be the one to take over the Gregory Corporation, and she could be the one who was Caro and TJ's child, with no expectations except success in the field of her choosing. But it didn't work like that. She was a Gregory. And that meant there were some responsibilities that were hers and hers alone.

11

THE NEXT MONDAY NIGHT, NINA HEADED TO HER
dad's for their weekly *Jeopardy!* and dinner date. Like Tim, Joseph Gregory was a creature of habit, and, especially after her
mom died, Nina found comfort in the predictability. When she
was a kid, they would have Chinese food together at least once
a month on Monday nights, and they still did. As Nina walked
to the Chinese food restaurant, she said hello to Janusz, who'd
been working in the pharmacy on Columbus since Nina was in
high school, and waved through the window at Penny, who had
been ringing people up at the diner across the street since Nina
was in lower school. Visitors often criticized New York City for
feeling impersonal, too filled with people to make any lasting
connections, but Nina had found the opposite to be true. The
blocks around her father's apartment seemed like a small village. The pizza place, the fruit stand, the dry cleaner, the clothing boutique. Nina thought, not for the first time, that New
York City really was made up of hundreds of different worlds,

each right next to another. She wouldn't go to a pharmacy five blocks away any more than she would go to one in New Jersey. Carrying the bags of Chinese food, Nina headed into her father's building.

Earlier that year Priscilla's parents had moved out of the apartment she'd grown up in, and Pris had been sadder about it than Nina had expected. "It's my whole childhood!" she kept saying. "It's gone!"

"It's not gone," Nina had reassured her. "Your memories are there, no matter where your parents live."

But ever since then, Nina had felt extra fond of this building, the place she learned to walk and talk, where she lived with people who watched her grow and mature. In Manhattan, a building like this was a community, a small town in a big city— and everyone here, staff and residents, had played a role in turning Nina into the person she'd become.

When she got up to 21-B, she walked into the gallery and called out to her father. "Dad!" she said. "I'm here! Where are you?"

"In the dining room," he called back. She noticed that his voice sounded weaker than it used to. And his words were punctuated by a cough. But only one.

Nina walked through the great room, which was broken into different sections with rugs and furniture; one area had couches, another a table and chairs, and another was filled with bookcases and a love seat. Pieces from her grandmother's art collection hung on the walls.

Through the great room was the kitchen, and then the dining room. Their housekeeper, Irena, had set the table with Nina's grandmother's gold-rimmed china and put a vase full of daisies in the center of the table. Six months after Irena had started working for the Gregorys, when Nina was in sixth grade, Irena had told her a story about her two sons who were in middle school, too, in Brighton Beach. Nina had realized then that when Irena was at her house, she wasn't home with her own kids. After that Nina had started telling Irena she was going to have dinner with friends after school, so Irena could go home early. Sometimes Nina actually did go over to Priscilla's place on the Upper East Side, or Tim's a few blocks away. But sometimes she spent the afternoon at the Met, doing her homework in the Temple of Dendur and then having an early dinner in the Trustees Dining Room on the fourth floor. They didn't usually serve dinner on weekdays, but the chef made an exception for her, their secret.

"YOU THINK WILL'S GOING to win again?" her father asked, as he opened up the television cabinet he'd had installed specifically for their Monday night dinners. He'd been talking about Will all last week, the bartender from Texas who'd been on a winning streak. "I bet you a lollipop he does."

Nina unpacked the food and spooned it into the dishes Irena had laid out on the table. They'd been betting candy on the results of the game show for as long as they'd been watching it together.

"I don't know," Nina said. "Most champions don't even get to day four. The chances he makes it to day five are slim. How about a Hershey bar he doesn't?"

Nina's father laughed. "Playing it safe, I see. You're not taking into account the Ken Jennings principle that some people are just smarter and can keep a streak going for a while."

Nina put the empty cartons in the take-out bag and tossed

them into the kitchen trash. "Ken Jennings is one in a million," she said.

"Maybe Will is, too," her father replied, picking up his soup spoon.

Alex Trebek came on the screen, and Nina and her father ate and watched, until one of the contestants chose the Daily Double.

"Three Tootsie Rolls she misses this Daily Double," her father said. The category was circus equipment, and the Daily Double was behind an $800 clue.

"No way," Nina answered. "Two Hershey's Kisses she gets it. She's answered three questions right in this category already."

Joseph Gregory shook his head. "But she hasn't gotten one $800 clue yet. Her knowledge is limited to the $600 level."

Her father insisted that *Jeopardy!* clue amounts were tied to difficulty, though Nina wasn't quite sure that was the case. He used the analogy in real life, too, when assessing people. Nina wondered sometimes what level he thought her knowledge was limited to, but she was afraid to ask. For her whole life, whenever Nina did something that her father found unimpressive, he would tell her: *You're smarter than that.* Those words always made her try to be better, to work harder, to think things through. But they hurt, too. And made her wonder if she really was smarter than that, or if her father was expecting her to be at the $2000 level, but she was only at $1600.

"I believe in her," Nina told her father.

She took a bite of her moo shu vegetables as the contestant, a woman named Zoe, wagered all her money on the Daily Double.

And then a video clue filled the screen. "A version of this apparatus was developed by the same man who popularized the one-piece outfit acrobats wear while performing on it," the person hosting the video said.

"What is a tightrope," Zoe answered.

Nina and her father groaned. "What is a trapeze!" they both said at the same time.

"I'm sorry, the correct answer is what is a trapeze," Alex Trebek replied. "And the man who developed it was Jules Léotard, who popularized the one-piece leotard."

"We really should audition," Nina told her father, covering up her disappointment that he'd been right. Zoe missed the question.

He laughed quietly. "No question we'd win if they let us play as a team," he said. "And I think you owe me some Hershey's Kisses."

Nina smiled, even though her heart ached. "Just add them to the balance sheet," she said. Her father kept meticulous track of who owed whom which candy; the last time they'd paid off their candy debts was when Nina left for college. *Jeopardy!* Mondays had been put on hiatus until she'd moved back for business school at Columbia. The newest balance sheet had been going for ten years now.

"Acrobats are remarkable," her father said, as he watched Zoe choose the next clue.

Nina thought about what it would be like, flying through the air, unfettered, ungrounded, and she shuddered. "I couldn't ever do it," she said.

"My careful Nina," her father replied. "You should face your fears, though."

She sighed. It was something her father had been telling her all her life. "You can't be a good businesswoman if you're risk averse," he'd say. And maybe it was true. But sometimes being afraid seemed smart. Besides, he was the one who'd made her fearful—fearful of what people would think, fearful that she'd disappoint him, that she wouldn't live up to his expectations.

"You know," he said. "I've always tried to protect you."

When Nina looked over at him, his face was more serious than she'd expected. "I know, Dad," she said.

"Whatever comes," he said, "I hope you'll remember that."

She wondered what he meant, but then the moment passed, and he was wagering a Hershey bar on a $1000 clue. Nina wrote it off as her father being her father, worrying what people would say about him after he was gone. But she couldn't help the impression she got that he was trying to tell her something more.

12

EVER SINCE THAT CAR RIDE TO THE NORWOOD CLUB, ever since they'd bumped into each other at the coffee shop and his touch made her blush, Nina had been self-conscious around Rafael. When they were in the same room, she found herself hyperfocused on what he was doing. She noticed tiny things, like how he sometimes bit his lip when he found something funny. How he ran his right hand through his hair, just above his ear, when he was about to say something controversial. And how his eyes often slid to hers in a meeting, as if asking for confirmation on a decision he just made.

But they hadn't been alone again, until they found themselves together in the elevator in mid-June.

"I think we got an express," Rafael said, as they passed floor after floor without stopping.

"Rare during lunch hour," Nina replied. And then she cringed. *Rare during lunch hour.* What a stupid observation. If she weren't so self-conscious around him now, she would have said, "I've always wondered why someone hasn't figured out the technology to create a smart elevator that knows when all the floor space has been taken up."

And then Rafael probably would have told her about a scientist he brought over to the United States on an H-1B visa who was working on something similar. And they would've had the kind of conversation Nina loved. But instead, there was dead air between them.

"So where are you headed?" Rafael asked, breaking the silence.

"Probably the salad place," she answered, looking up at him. "I haven't decided. What about you?"

"Well, my lunch meeting was canceled last minute," he said, leaning casually against the elevator wall. "And I snuck out before Jane could give me something else to do. So I figure as long as I stay away from the office, I can get a quick breather. The diner seems appealing." He paused and ran his fingers through his hair. He was going to say something controversial. "Any chance you want to join?" he asked.

Nina knew she shouldn't. She had work to do. But there was something about being near him. . . .

"No pressure," Rafael added. "I know you've got a lot on your plate."

The elevator stopped at the lobby.

Rafael stepped aside so she could exit first.

"I'd love to," Nina found herself saying. "Thank you."

The two of them walked to the diner at the end of the block and grabbed two seats at the counter.

"Isn't it nice to eat at a counter?" Rafael said, after they'd both ordered. "I just put in a breakfast bar in my apartment. Sonia hated the idea, but I love it, eating up high like this."

Nina was surprised he'd brought up his ex-wife. But maybe

he felt safe talking about her with Nina in the same way she felt safe talking about her dad with him. She wondered if she could ask more, ask why they'd gotten divorced. The rumor was that one night they went out for dinner and a helicopter ride around Manhattan to celebrate their third anniversary, and the next morning, she told him that she wanted out, that she hadn't been happy for a long time. In looking at him now, Nina couldn't figure out what about Rafael could make a woman unhappy.

"It *is* kind of nice," she said. Though it meant they were next to one another instead of across a table. More of a chance for their elbows or thighs to accidentally touch.

"I'm sorry you won't be able to make it to the Lancers' event," he said as their food arrived. "How's your dad doing?"

Nina shrugged. "He's mostly okay," she said. "But I keep noticing things. Small things. And I know there are going to be more and more of them. That it'll snowball until . . ." Her throat felt full. She wouldn't cry in front of him again. Especially not in the middle of a diner.

Rafael had picked up his sandwich, but put it back on his plate, uneaten.

"Do you read poetry?" he asked her.

Nina swallowed the lump in her throat. "Not much," she said. "But a little. When I was a kid, I memorized Lewis Carroll's 'Jabberwocky,' for my dad."

"*He took his vorpal sword in hand; Long time the manxome foe he sought—*" Rafael quoted.

"*So rested he by the Tumtum tree and stood awhile in thought,*" Nina finished.

Rafael laughed. "You're full of surprises," he said.

You too, Nina wanted to say. But instead she just smiled. "Why did you bring up poetry?"

"Well," Rafael answered, stretching out the word. "I took a couple of poetry classes in college, and I've come to think of life like poetry. It's my own theory, but it makes me feel better about things."

"What do you mean?" Nina asked, hoping that whatever he was about to say would be comforting.

"I think of people like poems," he said. "Maybe someone's a haiku, or a villanelle, or a cinquain, a sonnet—our length and form are predestined, but our content isn't. And each form has its own challenges, its own difficulties, and its own beauty. Your father's poem is coming to an end, but that doesn't make it any less beautiful or worthwhile or important."

Nina felt her eyes brim with tears and blinked hard. Instead of letting them out, she picked up her grilled cheese and took a bite, focusing on its flavor, how it felt on her tongue.

"Did you pick poems for people at the office?" Nina asked, after she'd swallowed, her tears gone.

"Hm, not really," Rafael said, taking a bite of his own sandwich. "But I think Jane is probably a limerick. A bit of rigidity, but also funny and irreverent and predictably unpredictable."

Nina laughed. "What about Mac?"

"Lineated prose poem," Rafael said. "Intense and compact, but freer than most poetry. Kind of outside the box."

"I like this," she said, though she might have come up with something else for Mac, something that captured his arrogance and impatience. "Does it work for everyone?"

"If you think long enough, you could probably make a case for everyone being some kind of poem," he said.

"Even me?" she asked, the words slipping out before she realized that they could be dangerous.

"Even you," he answered, looking directly at her, his dark

eyes sparkling. *This man is dangerously charming*, Nina warned herself. "I think you're a sestina."

"I'm afraid to ask why," she said, continuing the conversation against her better judgment.

He laughed. "It's nothing bad. Sestinas are complex and intricate. You are, too. Or at least that's how you come across."

She took another bite and chewed slowly. "What about you?" she asked.

"I think it's hard to poetry-analyze yourself," Rafael said, "but I might be a ghazal. I like the idea of the couplets being emotionally autonomous. Not everything I feel in one part of my life permeates all of it."

"So you're a poem that compartmentalizes?" Nina asked. The description actually felt true to her.

Rafael laughed. "I guess that's one way to look at it."

Nina realized then she wanted to know what his other compartments were like.

13

JULY FOURTH WEEKEND, WHICH WAS ALSO NINA'S birthday weekend, arrived before she knew it. Overriding Mac's objections, Jane gave the okay for Nina to take the long weekend off. "Rafael said it was fine," she told Nina as she left headquarters with her weekend bag. "He said to tell you he hopes you enjoy your birthday with your father. Oh, and he told me to give you this." Jane handed Nina a book of poetry: *The Incredible Sestina Anthology.*

Nina took it and smiled. "Thanks," she said. "And tell him thanks, too. I really appreciate the gift. And the time off. I hate asking for special treatment, but—"

"Stop it," Jane said. "Go. Take a swim in the ocean for me. Read your poetry. I didn't know you were into poetry."

Nina looked down at the book in her hands. She remembered him telling her she was intricate and complex. "I think it's Rafael who's into poetry," she said.

"Well, enjoy," Jane said, shooing Nina out of the room.

. . .

TIM AND HIS PARENTS were heading out to the beach, too, and they picked Nina up so they could all go out together.

"Do you think your dad's going to let us sleep in the same room?" Tim whispered to Nina once she was settled in the car. They were in a black SUV with two rows of seats behind the driver, TJ and Caro in the first row, Nina and Tim behind.

"No chance," Nina whispered back.

"Even though he loves me?" Tim asked.

"Even though he loves you," Nina said. "I'm still his little girl." Though the truth was, she hadn't asked. She wouldn't, not after what happened when she'd brought her college boyfriend, Max, to the house, and, drunk on love and her desire to be an adult, put his bag in her room. Her father had pulled her into the study and told her, in no uncertain terms, which room Max would be sleeping in that weekend. It was the biggest fight they'd ever had. And marked the beginning of the end of her relationship with Max. And changed her relationship with her father, too. She started to weigh her words before sharing them, to leave out the details he might not like.

Tim wrapped his arm around Nina, and she leaned into him. "Then we'll have to sneak out," he said quietly, right into her ear. "Expect a knock on your door tonight. Or maybe I'll throw seashells at your window."

Nina laughed.

TJ turned around. "What's so funny back there?" He and Caro had been answering work e-mails for most of the ride.

Nina and Tim exchanged a look. "Oh," Nina said, grasping for an answer, "Tim was—"

"Checking to make sure she's still ticklish," he finished.

"Right," Nina said. "Apparently I am."

TJ looked at Nina and Tim and then at his wife. "Oh, really," he said, leaning toward Caro.

"Don't you dare," she said, a hint of playfulness in her no-nonsense voice. Then she laughed as TJ lunged toward her. "They're both crazy," she said to Nina.

"Completely nuts," Nina agreed.

They all were laughing now, but as much as Nina felt like part of it, she also didn't. She looked at Tim and TJ and Caro and felt a flash of jealousy that their family was there, whole and intact, while hers was nearly gone.

14

WHEN THEY ARRIVED AT THE HOUSE, THE BACKYARD grill was already going, and Nina's dad was sitting next to it, giving instructions to Carlos, the nurse he'd brought with him to the beach after his doctors balked at him being out there alone. Nina grabbed Tim's hand when she saw that. Usually it would've been Joseph himself grilling the steaks, holding a drink.

As it got dark, Joseph suggested a nighttime ride on the boat, the *Mimsy*, which her father had named after the first line in "Jabberwocky." "I heard someone's setting off fireworks tonight over the ocean," he said. "For your birthday, Sweetheart—though I prefer when they do it on the actual day." It was their old joke that the July Fourth fireworks were for her. Since the Fourth was a Tuesday this year, she knew they'd be going off all weekend.

Nina remembered the fireworks displays when she was little, when she, her dad, and her mom would all take the boat out together after dinner, and Nina would pretend that the loud booms didn't scare her, because she didn't want to miss the light show. But her father had known, somehow, and every time a blast went off, he'd tickle her or try to make her laugh. He knew to chase away her fear without her having to tell him about it.

"You captain us tonight," he said to Nina, tossing her his captain's hat—the one she'd bought him a dozen or more Father's Days ago. She put it on her head. It was slightly too big, but once she stuffed her ponytail inside, it fit just fine.

"Lookin' good, Captain," Tim had said, quickly kissing Nina when their parents weren't looking.

THE BOAT RIDE WAS SHORT-LIVED because Joseph started shivering. Even with a blanket around him, he was cold.

"Sorry, Sweetheart," he said to Nina, when they were back on the beach. "I know how much you like your birthday fireworks out on the water."

"It's okay, Dad," she said, leaning against him. "We can see them just as well from here."

Joseph Gregory wrapped both arms around his daughter, and they stood like that, draped in the blanket, watching the lights explode in the sky.

"I nearly forgot your birthday present," he said, after a moment, pulling a box out of his pants pocket. "Early, like the fireworks."

Nina laughed and took the long, narrow box.

It was from his favorite jewelry store, the one on Main Street in East Hampton. She untied the ribbon and opened it. Inside was a tennis bracelet made of sapphires. She ran her fingers across the stones.

"It's the same setting as the diamond bracelet I had made for your mother," he said. "I thought you could wear them together. It'll be a good way to remember us both."

"It's beautiful," Nina whispered. She laid her head against her father's chest and let his shirt absorb the silent tears that leaked through her lashes.

"When we get back to the city," he said, tightening his arm around her back, "we should go over the financials for the corporation. There are some things you need to know before you take over."

"Sure," Nina said, clearing her throat, concentrating as hard as she could on keeping her voice steady. *Seashells. Jellyfish. Seaweed.*

And then a firework went off, bursting open above the water, and Nina raised her head to watch.

15

THAT NIGHT, AFTER THEIR PARENTS WERE ASLEEP, Nina and Tim snuck back down to the beach. Nina was in shorts and a sweatshirt, her feet bare. Tim was dressed the same way.

"Remember the summer I was afraid of the ocean?" Nina asked him. The wind was blowing her hair, and she and Tim were pressed against each other for warmth.

"I would've been afraid, too, if I'd gotten clobbered by a wave like you did."

She'd been ten and wouldn't even put her toes in the water for weeks, until her father decided that she needed to get over her fear. So she, Tim, and her father had stood in a line, holding hands, with Nina in the middle, jumping waves together.

"I will never let go until you're ready," Nina's father had told her. "But we won't stop until you can jump without us."

By the end of that weekend, Nina had made peace with the ocean again. But she'd never again felt quite as safe as she did that day between her father and Tim, with both of them holding her tight.

"Did I ever thank you for helping me that day?" Nina asked.

"I don't remember," he said. "How about a thank-you kiss, just to cover your bases?"

Nina rose up on her toes and kissed him, tasting his minty toothpaste, feeling his beard against her chin.

"I love you," Tim said, when they broke apart.

"I love you, too," Nina answered.

Then he tugged her toward the pool house, which had a sauna on one side of it. "There's some privacy in here," he said, locking the sauna door behind them in the dark, but not flicking the switch to turn on the heat. They were in a small cedar room with a wooden bed covered in a towel and a foam pillow, outlined in dim moonlight that came in through the window. "Not sure how comfortable this will be, but there's no chance our parents will find us."

Nina climbed onto the wooden bed, brushing the sand from her legs. "I think it'll do," she said quietly, loving how secret this rendezvous felt.

Tim climbed on with her and kissed her, their bodies facing one another. She ran her fingers along the delicate curve of his ear and then down the line of his jaw, where his beard ended.

"Oh, Nina," he said.

He reached for her, sliding his hands into her shorts, and she moved against his fingers, feeling herself relax. Then she wrapped her fingers around him and stroked, matching his rhythm.

"Now?" he asked.

She could feel how hard he was getting, how much she wanted him.

"Yes," she said. She slipped her shorts and underwear off, and lay on her back, his favorite way to make love.

Tim hovered above her and slid inside. Nina closed her eyes

and felt him, Tim, her Tim. He moved more slowly than usual, his knees against the wooden slats of the sauna bed. Nina liked it better this way; it gave her the time she needed to luxuriate in the feeling of him against her, until, "I'm going to—" she said, and Tim bent down to kiss her as an orgasm rippled softly through her body. He orgasmed, too, and then rested his head on her chest.

Nina ran her fingers through his short auburn hair. It still amazed her that life had led the two of them together like this.

It had felt so strange, at first, to go from best friends to something more. She'd spent so long putting Tim in the friend box that relocating him to the boyfriend box felt like a redefining of terms as uncomfortable as calling orange juice *milk*. It had been weird to see how his face changed when he'd climaxed the first time they were together. He looked like her Tim, but not. It was a new expression, and it had unnerved her. Now she was used to it. Used to calling him her boyfriend. Used to the expression on his face when he came, how it transformed him into someone new. Their relationship had become something different. And Nina was grateful for it.

So grateful that she tried to forget about the question Leslie had asked her months ago, the one she couldn't figure out an answer to: *Why do you feel like you have to get used to it?*

16

NINA'S FATHER HAD PLANNED TO COME BACK TO THE city for brunch on the third Saturday in August, but he wasn't feeling up to it the day before and decided to stay put.

"You just want to get in a little more beach time," Nina teased, attempting to make light of the moment. "I see what's going on."

Her father had mustered up a laugh, but both of them knew what was going on. They just didn't want to acknowledge it to each other.

The next morning, Caro called.

"Darling," she said, when Nina picked up her phone at the campaign office. Tim was golfing at Chelsea Piers, and then they were supposed to meet at the Boat Basin on 79th Street just after noon. Tim's friend Sebastian, his fiancée Julia, and a few other couples including Priscilla and Brent were planning to spend a few hours on Sebastian's sailboat for his birthday, before Nina went back to work. "TJ and I are still going to The Grove for brunch, but you know that the guests come each month to see your father, not us. I know Timothy said the two of you were planning to have lunch on Sebastian's sailboat. I hate to ask, but is there any chance you could eat with us instead? Your father didn't want me to call you. To be honest, Nina, I think he'd hoped you'd offer. But . . ."

Nina sighed and tried not to feel stung by Caro's words. She should have offered. She'd known it when her father called. It was her job now, but something had held her back. "Of course," she said, blocking off the third Saturday of every month in her calendar as she spoke. "I'll tell Tim he can still go on the boat, but I'll see you and Uncle TJ there."

"Oh, wonderful," Caro said. "And I was thinking, in September . . ."

"Already in my calendar," Nina said. "October, too."

"See you soon, darling," Caro said. Then she paused. "I know this isn't easy. But you know you won't have to face it alone."

Nina had to clear her throat before she could say, "Thanks, Aunt Caro. I'll see you soon."

17

NINA'S DAD CAME BACK TO THE CITY FOR GOOD THE next week at his doctor's request, earlier than he'd planned. The thing Nina found the most troubling was that he acquiesced without a fight.

But instead of worrying about that, instead of focusing on how wrung out her heart felt, how dark a place she could spiral into, Nina focused even more intently on the campaign. Marc Johnson was polling well. They were in for a fight.

"We can do this," Jane said, every morning, reminding the staff, reminding herself.

Nina truly believed in Rafael. She admired his determination, the way he inspired her to be the best version of herself, to think harder, to push her mind further. Being around him was intoxicating—which was why she tried to keep her distance. Alcohol was dangerous when you consumed too much of it. When it was the thing you always wanted, the thing you were ashamed to find yourself dreaming about.

In those weeks, it seemed like every time Nina looked across the room she would find Rafael's eyes on her. While he was talking to Christian or reviewing talking points with Jane.

She wondered if it was on purpose, or if that just happened, his gaze moving toward hers. She imagined it was out of his control. And she wondered how often her gaze slid over to him, without her realizing, too.

18

IT WAS NEARLY ONE IN THE MORNING THE NIGHT BE-
fore the primary. The hum of the office had disappeared, though
Nina could still hear car engines and squealing tires through the
open windows in the main area, where all the desks were
jammed next to one another. The city never slept, and neither, it
seemed, would Nina or Rafael. They were alone together in a
conference room, putting the final touches on tomorrow's potential speeches—alone for the first time since their lunch at the
diner. Nina caught his eye across the conference table and then
quickly turned away.

As much as she'd refused to admit it, she knew their attraction had been growing slowly over the past months, like tem-
perature rising barely perceptibly, half a degree at a time. But
those tiny invisible increments added up to something enor-
mously detectable. Nina wondered if they'd reached that point.
And if they had, if she could continue to ignore it—pretend
that the sweat didn't exist, that she still needed her jacket. Nina

felt like she had to. If she didn't, it would mean that so many pieces of her life, carefully balanced upon one another, would come tumbling down.

She kept forcing herself to think about Tim. About what it felt like when they walked hand-in-hand through Manhattan and how soft his lips felt against hers when they kissed. About how easily they fit together—their lives, their families, their expectations. About how comfortable she felt in his arms. But there wasn't this—this pull that drew her to Rafael.

She'd been so strong, so careful all summer. But tonight she was finding it hard. Tonight, when she caught a glimpse of how worried he was, of how much he wanted to win, all she wanted to do was comfort him the way he'd comforted her about her father. To rest her hand on his.

Rafael cleared his throat. "You want a Coke?" he asked, pulling two dollars out of his wallet and standing up, scraping the legs of the chair across the linoleum floor as he did. "I don't know if I'll be able to get through the next three minutes without another infusion of caffeine."

"I'm good," Nina said, shifting her eyes back to her computer screen, though she was more than a bit tired. She needed to get this done. She needed to get away from the temptation. She felt like Eve, staring at a forbidden apple. Or was the apple a kiss and Rafael the serpent? Or was *she* the serpent? "I'll give version B one more pass, and when you get back from the vending machine, maybe you can try it out loud again?"

"Absolutely," he responded. "But I hate version B."

Nina smiled. "I know. I hate it too."

Out of the corner of her eye, she watched Rafael walk across the conference room. Even at one A.M., after he'd exchanged his button-down shirt and suit jacket for a T-shirt and hoodie, his face unshaven and his hair a mess, Nina felt her body trying to point itself in his direction. Carisuapo, Nina's mother might have called him—a combination of the words *carismatico* and *guapo*. Charismatic and handsome. Though if Rafael said it, it would sound more like caliuapo. Nina had gotten used to his Cuban accent—the dropped *s*, the *r* that sounded more like an *l*. As she sat there, watching him walk down the hallway, she found herself trying to figure out how he would pronounce other Spanish words. Difrutal. Depue. She pictured the shape of his lips as he spoke.

Nina closed her eyes and took a deep breath, trying to reset her mind. No more Rafael. No more lips. *Tim*, she thought, picturing his face in her mind. His hazel eyes with their reddish-blond lashes. His smile when she walked into a room. Her mind cleared, Nina focused on the speech, her eyes zipping across the computer screen, her fingers dancing on keys. This was just work. Nothing more.

Nina rolled her neck from side to side. She needed a run. She needed a massage. All this time bent forward over her laptop had tightened her shoulders. She tried to imagine Tim's hands kneading her muscles, to see if her mind could convince her body the massage had already happened, but somehow it was Rafael's fingers she saw. His manicured cuticles, the soft dark hair that climbed from his wrist toward his pinky. Involuntarily, she shivered. *Stop it*, she told herself.

Nina rolled her neck once more, carefully pushing thoughts of massages out of her head, and went back to her screen.

"I brought you a present," Rafael said, walking back into the conference room a few minutes later and dropping a bag of M&Ms on Nina's side of the table. His voice was resonant in the quiet room. He'd unzipped his sweatshirt and she could see the T-shirt underneath. It read *Pluto: Never Forget*.

"Thanks," Nina said. "Nice shirt."

Rafael beamed at her. She couldn't help but smile back. "I was hoping you'd like it," he said.

Nina could feel herself blush. She was in Rafael's mind when he changed that night.

"It doesn't take much, Palabrecita, does it?" Rafael's smile somehow turned sweeter.

"What did you just call me?" Nina asked, feeling her blush deepen.

"Palabrecita," he answered, leaning against a bookshelf as he drank his Coke.

"Poor little word girl?" Nina roughly translated the word, a mash-up of *palabra* and *pobrecita*, she figured. Her mother would have liked that. She used to call Nina *intelinda*, a combination of *intelligent* and *beautiful*.

Nina invented her own word combinations, but this was the first time Rafael had added to her invented dictionary. She hadn't even realized he'd known about her portmanteaus. She usually just shared them with Jane and Jorge, who was in charge of the Get Out the Vote messaging.

Rafael nodded at her definition. "Poor little word girl indeed. I've kept you here late tonight. I just took a spin around the office and literally everyone else has gone home. Even Rocco."

"The janitor?" Nina asked.

Rafael nodded. "And he usually stays pretty late."

Nina rubbed her eyes, surprised her contact lenses didn't feel more like sandpaper. Though the main room had windows, the conference room they were in didn't, so it was hard to know what time it was when you were in there—her contact lenses were usually her only indicator of exactly how long she'd been awake. "I don't mind," she said. Though she should. She reminded herself how perfectly her life and Tim's meshed together. How nice their future would be—each running their own company, summering at her grandparents' place in the Hamptons, dinners with his parents, ski holidays in Alta, little redheaded children who would eventually inherit the hotels but would work in the corporation only if they wanted to.

"Well, good. I don't mind either," Rafael said, that unreadable look back in his eyes.

Then he came up behind her to read the screen over her shoulder. Nina swore she could feel the heat radiating off his body. She tried closing her eyes, but it didn't work this time. Neither did imagining Tim welcoming her to his place at night with a hug. *Milkshakes. File folders. Banana peels*, she thought. But none of those tricks changed how close Rafael was, how nice it would be to lean back and rest her head against him, to feel his hands on her shoulders. The image of him giving her a massage popped back into her mind and she felt goose bumps rise on her arms. *Mom*, she thought, *please help me if you can. Fuertrado.*

"Maybe you don't need to read this one out loud," Nina said, looking at her screen.

Rafael's face was so close to hers, it wouldn't take much for their foreheads to touch, their noses. Their lips.

"Won't it be bad luck if I don't read it?" he asked, his face still inches from hers, his breath tinged with the sweetness of Coca-Cola. "If I don't prepare to lose, then I will. If I prepare to win, I won't."

Nina laughed, the tension between them slackening as she did. "Are you really that superstitious?"

Rafael straightened up and ran his fingers through the hair just above his right ear.

"What?" Nina asked. "What are you thinking about hiding?"

Rafael shook his head. "It's like you're a mind reader. Did you major in telepathy in college or something?"

"Poli sci," Nina answered. "But I wish they'd offered telepathy. Or telekinesis. I've always wanted to be able to move things with my mind."

Rafael smiled at Nina again. "Poli sci. That's right. I remember your résumé. You minored in Spanish literature. And then got an MBA."

"That was for my dad," Nina said. "I'd wanted to do a master's in Spanish lit. As a way to connect with my mom . . . or to connect with her memory. Maybe I wanted . . ." It was getting late. Nina was tired. She didn't usually talk about her mom so easily with anyone other than Leslie. It made her wish for things she could never have. But Rafael was . . . Rafael. She could see why he was spectacular in a courtroom—it was the same reason he was good at a fund-raiser or in front of a crowd. There was something disarming about him; it made her want to trust him with everything.

"Maybe you wanted what?" he asked, sitting on the edge of the table, his dark brown eyes focusing in on her.

"Maybe I wanted you to tell me about how superstitious you are," she answered, her tired brain back in action, deflecting, defending.

He looked at her for a long moment, his eyes gentle. It seemed like he understood she'd revealed a piece of herself she wasn't quite comfortable sharing. She raised her eyebrows, waiting for him to answer.

Finally, he knelt down next to her. "I can't believe I'm going to show this to you." He pulled his T-shirt away from his neck, matching her reveal with one of his own. "Look in my collar. Right near the tag."

She looked at the soft skin at the nape of his neck, and then quickly shifted her eyes to his collar. Pinned to the fabric with a gold-colored safety pin was a black stone dangling on a short chain. "What's that?" she asked.

"An azabache," he said. "My abuela pinned it on my shirt the day I was born. I haven't gone a day without wearing it since. It's supposed to keep away the evil eye."

Rafael let his shirt go and turned around.

"Do you believe it does?" she asked, curious.

"My abuela did," he said. "And I . . . I don't know. I mean, nothing truly terrible has happened in my life so far, I guess. And there have been a lot of good things." He looked at her in a way that made Nina wonder if he counted her as one of those good things. "Can I definitively say that it's not the azabache?"

Nina thought about that. And thought briefly about the fact that he didn't count his divorce as something truly terrible. Or his father's death. "I guess you can't," she answered. "Unless . . ."

Rafael put up his hand. "I know what you're going to say. Unless I took it off and saw if my luck changed without it pinned to my collar. My college roommate suggested the same thing years ago. I'm not willing to try that. Especially not on primary day."

Nina laughed. "I agree," she said. "Today is not the day to experiment with luck. And honestly? It can't hurt, right?"

"Plus it makes me feel like my abuela is with me," Rafael added, standing up. "But if she were here, she'd tell me to read version B. Not to tempt fate."

Every new thing Nina learned about Rafael made her want

to ask questions about his past, his family, his childhood—not the kind of questions she asked as a speechwriter, but the kind she'd ask of a close friend.

"Then let's not tempt fate," she said. "But it's closing in on two. Are you sure you want to stay this late? You can always give it a read in a few hours, after we've slept and showered and changed."

Rafael looked at Nina again with an expression she couldn't quite figure out. It was a combination of emotions, really. Puzzlement? Longing? Apology?

"Why wouldn't I want to stay?" he asked.

Nina bit her lip. There were so many answers, but she didn't want to get into any of them. Not when Rafael was leaning over her shoulder again, his breath hot and sweet against her cheek, making her shiver just slightly. "Forget I even asked," she said. "Let's hear it."

And while Rafael began to read, Nina ignored the thrill she got from hearing her words from his lips. *Hotelier's Daughter Fired after Secret Relationship with Candidate Revealed*, Nina thought. *Joseph Gregory's Daughter Cheats on Longtime Beau with Boss.*

Her father was always so proud of their family's reputation. And she was, too. *Scandal* and *affair* weren't the words she wanted to be her contribution to the Gregory legacy. There weren't any skeletons in their closets, no poorly treated employees, nothing to tarnish their name or their corporation.

She couldn't be the one to change that. Especially not now.

19

THE FOLLOWING NIGHT THE WHOLE CAMPAIGN STAFF was gathered around the TV. The polls had just closed, and they were waiting for the reports. The numbers were looking good, up in some neighborhoods they hadn't been expecting—news that had Jorge doing his version of a touchdown dance.

"Rafael's really going to win the primary," Jane said. "And if he does, ninety-ten says we're working on the campaign of the very first Latino mayor of New York City."

"I was a true believer from the beginning," Mac told Jane. "Everyone said I was nuts to take this campaign manager job, but I knew."

"The way you know about a good melon?" Nina quipped.

Mac looked at her funny. Jane laughed.

"She's quoting from *When Harry Met Sally*," Jane explained.

"Oh," Mac answered. "I didn't know people like you watched normal movies."

Nina looked at him askance but didn't say anything.

"Are you serious?" Jane said. "Nina's totally normal. She just wears shoes that cost more than my rent. And uses seasons as verbs. But other than that, she's like that magazine spread *'Heiresses are just like us!'*"

Nina had friends—like Priscilla—who wore their parents' money like a badge of honor. But once Nina had heard about the loans that Leslie had to take out to go to college, she felt a little bit ashamed of how easy she'd had it. Working outside her own bubble gave her perspective. It was another reason she liked being part of the campaign. She looked down quickly at her Manolos. Maybe she wouldn't wear them to the office again.

"*Summer* and *winter* are perfectly acceptable verbs," she said, covering up her feelings with a smile. "I deal in verbs, I should know."

Jane laughed again. Mac still looked uncomfortable. Nina wondered if her expression had mirrored his before she'd switched it. Then she felt her cell phone vibrate in her pocket. She pulled it out and turned away from the group. "Your dad?" Jane asked softly, her expression immediately worried. Nina marveled at how open Jane's face was all the time, her every thought telegraphed for the world to see. You always knew where you stood with Jane.

Nina shook her head while reading the message. "Tim," she said, relief in her voice. "Wishing us luck and asking how the numbers look."

Jane grinned. "The best friend, now so much more. I could place a feature on the two of you anywhere," she said.

"You and any other comms person worth their salt," Nina said with a smile. "But we're not features kind of people."

As Nina laughed, she thought about Jane's words. Tim was more, but he was less now, too. She couldn't tell him about the feelings she was battling against at work. The way she was drawn to Rafael, even though she didn't want to be. How she'd been thinking about Rafael's breath on her cheek all day, about the soft skin of his neck. Before, she would have told Tim. But now she'd lost her confidant, traded that relationship for one she wasn't convinced she liked better. Or perhaps one she was trying to convince herself she did like better. Leslie's question rang in her mind: *Why do you feel like you have to get used to it?* Every answer she came up with seemed wrong.

Nina looked around the rest of the office and caught Rafael looking back at her just before he picked up a remote control, increasing the volume on the television. All conversation stopped as everyone stared at the screen.

"We have breaking news in the race for Gracie Mansion," the anchor was saying. "With ninety-two percent of the votes counted, we can officially say that Rafael O'Connor-Ruiz has won the primary!"

The campaign headquarters exploded with shouts and cheers. Mac started high-fiving everyone. Jane hugged Nina. Champagne bottles were popped. Jorge started doing his touchdown dance again.

Nina looked back over at Rafael, to flash him a thumbs-up, and saw him walking toward her.

"Congratulations," she said. "Felicitaciones."

His grin was wider than she'd ever seen it. "May I thank you with a hug?" he asked. "I couldn't have done it without you. And I mean that seriously."

Nina willed herself not to feel anything as she opened her arms, holding Tim's smile in her mind. "Of course," she said. "And you absolutely could have done it without me."

For the very first time, the warmth of Rafael's entire body pressed against hers. His heartbeat thumped when hers did.

Time stretched—until she heard the click of a cell phone camera.

"Rafael O'Connor-Ruiz embraces speechwriter Nina Gregory in celebration of his win!" Samira shouted. "Tweeting now!"

Nina pulled away. "Do you still feel good about tonight's speech?" she asked, her body tingling from being against his. "We have another few minutes before they'll expect you out front, if you want to change anything."

"I feel great," Rafael said, reaching out and squeezing Nina's forearm.

Nina took a deep breath and smiled. But her heart was racing. In that moment, Nina realized that if she wasn't careful, the future she and Tim had planned could disappear in an instant. She was falling for her boss.

20

THE NEXT MORNING, AFTER A RUN ALONG THE HUD-
son, Nina left her apartment in Tribeca and took a car uptown.
Rafael had told everyone to take the day off. Nina wanted to
spend it with her father. She planned to have Tim join them for
dinner as a nice surprise. Her father didn't need to donate to
Rafael's campaign. He didn't even need to approve of her job.
He just needed to be there. To be alive. To stand sentry between her and the fear that bit at her heart whenever she
thought about what it would be like when he was gone.

When Nina got up to 21-B, Carlos opened the door.

"How's he doing this morning?" she asked, dropping her bag
on the bench in the entry gallery.

"It hasn't been the greatest day," Carlos said. He never su-
garcoated things. Nina appreciated that.

She braced herself as she headed into her father's suite of
rooms.

"Dad?" she said, as she knocked on his door. "Dad? It's me."

She heard a groan and pushed open the door in alarm. Her father's teeth were clenched and his back was arched under the blankets.

"Carlos!" she yelled.

"There are lollipops," her dad said through his teeth. "Please, Sweetheart."

Nina saw the painkillers in a prescription bag from the pharmacy on her father's dresser. She brought one to him and quickly unwrapped it, as Carlos entered the room.

"What—?" he said just as Nina's father took the lollipop from her with a trembling hand and quickly put it in his mouth, shifting it against his cheek. The next few moments seemed like hours, as Nina watched, feeling entirely helpless as her father's face contorted with pain and then relaxed again.

"You didn't tell me it was this bad," she said, quietly.

He looked at her, his blue eyes glassy. "I didn't want you to know," he said. He took her hand and laced their fingers together. Carlos slipped out.

"I'd thought we could take a walk in the park, but . . ." Nina looked around the room. "How about we work on that crossword we started a few days ago, if you haven't finished it? Unless there's something else you want to do?"

"The crossword puzzle is good," he said, his voice barely above a whisper.

As they worked on the puzzle Nina marveled at how, even filled with pain and the drugs to block it, he was still quicker than almost everyone she knew. She felt her eyes fill.

"I love you, Dad," she said to him. "So much that it hurts sometimes."

"Oh, Sweetheart," he said, slowly. "These days, my love for

you hurts all the time. I feel like by getting sick like this, by dying, I'm somehow letting you down. I didn't mean for this to happen."

Nina crossed the space between her chair and her father's bed. She bent down and hugged him carefully; he felt so fragile. "Of course you didn't," she said. "And you've never let me down."

"I want you to listen," he said. "I don't know how long I have, and there are some things I need to make sure you know. I've been thinking about this all week."

Nina sat on the edge of his bed. "I'm here, Dad."

"You know your grandfather always said that you're nothing without your name." Nina could hear the strain in his voice, the way there was just enough air in his lungs to make it to the end of the sentence. "When you take over the business, remember that. Everything you do, it's not just for you. It's to honor me, to honor your grandfather. We created something that will live on after we're gone, and it's your job to take care of it. You know how important that is to me."

"I know, Dad," Nina said. All her life, her father had talked to her about the Gregory legacy. What her grandparents had done to build it, to secure it. How her grandfather wanted the Gregory name to mean success and luxury, and how her grandmother wanted it to mean elegance and culture. That was why she started her art collection and joined the board of the Met. Nina's father built on what both his parents had done. He grew his mother's collection, expanding it from its home in the Hamptons to his apartment and the lobbies of the Gregory hotels. And he stepped into her spot on the board of trustees at the Met after she died. Later, when he took the helm of the Gregory Corporation, he expanded on his father's success, too, and added power to their family's legacy, innovation. Nina wasn't sure yet what she'd contribute, but she felt the weight of it. The weight of the pride her father felt in being a Gregory. The gravity of the mission he felt he was giving her.

"Have you read through the financials yet? The envelope I gave you last week? Did you bring it with you?"

Nina sighed, feeling a squeeze in the pit of her stomach, the one that came from disappointing her father. "I haven't had a chance yet, Dad. I'm sorry. It's at home. The campaign's been crazy."

He was quiet for a moment. "In that case, I just want to say: If you find anything . . ." Her father faltered.

"What do you mean, Dad?" Nina asked.

He shook his head. "It's nothing." He looked so defeated. "We can talk after you go through the numbers."

"Should I be looking for something?" she asked. She wondered if this was a test. If he'd put something in there so he'd know she could do the job. His way of making sure her intelligence was at the $2000 level.

"We'll talk this weekend," he said. "Sooner rather than later, okay?"

Nina's stomach squeezed harder. "The doctor said you'd be okay until January," she said. "We've got so much time to talk." She kept telling herself that. She had to keep telling herself that.

"It's not an exact science, Sweetheart. You're smarter than that."

It stung. Those words always stung.

"And there's one more thing." He tightened his grip on her hand. "I don't want you to be here, at the end of your life, and regret anything."

"Do you?" she asked, the squeeze in her stomach still there. "Regret anything?"

He moved his head in such a way that Nina couldn't quite tell if he was nodding yes or shaking it no. "I just wish . . . I wish I'd had more time with your mother. I wish—" he said, and then stopped.

"Me, too," Nina whispered, so quietly she wasn't even sure if her father had heard her.

He took another deep breath, his face set like he was about to say something important, essential. "You know," he said. "Timmy loves you."

"I love him, too," Nina said.

"When we spoke last night, he asked me . . . well . . . I don't want to ruin anything. TJ and I had always hoped this would happen."

Nina blinked. Did that mean what she thought it meant?

Joseph Gregory reached out and grabbed his daughter's hand again. "I'm so happy you'll have someone to take care of you. Someone who can look out for the company. Someone who understands us."

Nina nodded, too surprised to respond. She and Tim had only been dating for eight months. But her parents had gotten engaged nine months after they'd met. Nina wondered what her mother had thought about her and Tim when they were babies. Did she think they were meant to be together, too, from the time they were born? Or would she have pushed Nina to explore the world and see who she met on the beaches of Barcelona or Rio or Tel Aviv? Not follow the safer path.

"I'm sorry, Sweetheart, but I'm a bit tired," Joseph Gregory said to his daughter. "I just . . . feel weak today." *Cansabil*, Nina thought. Tired and weak. The word came easily, with her mother already on her mind. "How about picking out a movie? It'll be like old times. You can watch a movie in my room until you fall asleep, and then . . ."

"And then you'll carry me into my room so I can wake up in my own bed," Nina finished, so aware that her father could never carry her anywhere now. He was clearly aware of it, too. She saw him brush a tear off his cheek with the back of his hand. Ignoring that, Nina put in *The Princess Bride*. The two of them had watched it together countless times, dissolving into laughter at the lines *Anybody want a peanut?* And *Have fun storming the castle!* Lines that perhaps weren't funny to anyone else but had once made her dad laugh so hard that the club soda he was drinking bubbled out of his nose.

Another line they liked—*I hate for people to die embarrassed*—took on a more somber note now. She half paid attention to the movie while her father fell asleep. Then she left the room, the movie still running—the Ancient Booer doing her thing.

Nina wished she'd brought those financials with her today. Then when her father woke up, she could tell him she'd read through them. They could talk about whatever it was he wanted to, and she wouldn't have to see disappointment on his face. After everything he'd given her, the least she could do was not disappoint him during his last months on Earth.

21

WHEN TIM ARRIVED, NINA WAS IN THE KITCHEN, SUR-
rounded by cookbooks. Cooking relaxed her. At least in the
kitchen she was in charge. After catching Nina up on what her
sons were up to and her new grandtwins were doing, Irena had
left to change the bed linens. Nina had gone through the cookbooks looking for soup recipes. She figured that while she was
cooking dinner, she could make her father broth if nothing else.
And she could make him enough for the next few days at least.
Maybe more, if she froze it. How much more would he need?

Nina hadn't taken a psych course since she was nineteen—
but in the recesses of her mind she remembered something
about how knowing the outcome of a particular event made
people more comfortable. It was why New York City had installed those time clocks on most of the subway lines. The trains
didn't come more frequently, but passengers could see when
they were supposed to arrive, and knowing that they had to wait
four or seven minutes made them less agitated. They were able

to plan. Their faith in the transit authorities increased. The whole city was slightly calmer during rush hour. It was a smart psychological move.

Nina wished she had a time clock for life. If she knew she had a month left with her father, she would act one way. Two months would be something else. Three months. Four. She knew it probably wasn't much longer than four months, but if it was, it would change her approach.

In our ignorance, we are at a loss, she thought. *Without the facts, there's no way to create a solid path.* But the truth was, she had no idea how much time she had left either. Perhaps all her planning, all her father's planning was for naught. For all she knew, she could die tomorrow.

"Hey," Tim called, as he let himself in. Nina heard his voice echoing down the hallway. "Smells good in here." When he walked into the kitchen, he wrapped his arms around Nina. "Mm, you smell good, too, like raspberries. It's been too long."

"I missed you, too," Nina said, resting her head briefly on Tim's chest. She felt relaxed around Tim. Calmer. Like her blood was pumping at the right speed when he was there.

Then she rose up on her toes to reach the spices in the cupboard. "I got it," Tim said, as he pulled down the onion powder she'd been reaching for.

"Thanks," she said. "Want to tell me about your day, while I cook?"

"Not much to tell," he said as he watched her boiling and chopping and seasoning, following the recipe with precision. "I think the investors are interested. Darren, you remember him— the investment banker who's helping us secure funding? He asked if we wanted to have dinner next week."

"I could probably make that happen," Nina said, checking the recipe before adding the peppers to the stir-fry. "It'll depend on the campaign, though."

Tim walked up behind Nina and slid his arms around her, cupping her breasts in his hands. "I'm going to be so happy when that campaign is over," he said, kissing her neck. "I'll get so much more time with you."

Nina wriggled out from Tim's grip. "Tim! We're in my dad's apartment!"

"What?" Tim said. "It's not like he's going to catch us."

Nina froze. Tim saw it.

"I'm sorry," he said. "I'm sorry. I'm sorry. I didn't mean that."

"It's fine," Nina said, and kept stirring the vegetables. But it wasn't fine. Not really. Even though she was living through her father's illness with Tim. And even though they'd been friends forever, he didn't get it. He didn't understand how it all made her feel, like she was a table with a wobbly leg. She could prop herself up sometimes with a matchbook—a lot of times, really—but when the matchbook slipped, the whole table wobbled and everything on it threatened to crash to the floor.

He stroked her hair. "Hey," he said. "I really am sorry. I wasn't thinking."

"I know," Nina said. She closed her eyes for a moment and took a deep breath, relaxing into the feeling of Tim's fingers on her hair, stroking the length of it.

"Do you want to talk about it?" he asked, tentatively.

She did, she realized. But not with someone who didn't get it. She wanted to talk to Leslie. To Rafael. "Nah," she said. "I'm managing okay."

"I'm glad," he said. As she turned and looked at Tim's face, Nina wondered about the timing of death. About the when and the why of it. When her mother died, a few people told Nina that it was just her mother's time. She'd taken comfort in that then, like the rules of the game had been set long ago, and now her mother was just following them. But since then, she'd wondered. Was saying that just a coping mechanism, a way to make sense of a horrific event? Because if there isn't a reason for people to die, if there isn't a god who is calling people home or deciding it's their time, it's harder to understand, harder to accept.

"Your hair is so pretty," Tim said. He was still stroking it, but Nina wasn't paying attention to him. Her mind was off on its own odyssey, spinning.

If life is a series of random events, she was thinking, then her mother randomly had a car accident and died, her father randomly developed cancer, he randomly relapsed. Life is a crapshoot, a game of chance. And if you follow that logic, her father could've gotten sick ten years ago or ten years from now. Nina tossed the one-inch cubes of chicken into a pot with a quarter cup of oil and the already cooking onions and peppers. If that was the case, she figured, she should be grateful that her father didn't die when her mother did. Or when he was even younger. She should be grateful that she had all the time with him that she did. She should try to focus on that.

She stirred the vegetables in the pot.

And yet she couldn't focus only on that. She was not only grateful but angry. At life, at the way things turned out, and, illogically, at her father. *How dare you leave me before I've figured out my life*, she thought. *How dare you leave me before I'm ready to let you go.*

The vegetables sizzled.

Tim rubbed her shoulders.

And she took the food off the stove so they could eat.

22

A LITTLE WHILE LATER, NINA PEEKED INTO HER FA-
ther's bedroom.

"Tim's here, Dad," she said. "How about we have dinner in
your room?"

Nina opened the set of French doors between her father's
bedroom and his sitting room and set three places at the ma-
hogany table in the corner. He used to sit there to drink coffee
and read the *New York Times* and the *Wall Street Journal* every
morning. Now it was empty. The newspapers were on his bedside table and hadn't been opened.

Once the table was set, Tim came in carrying a tray filled
with food.

"Timmy!" her father said, a grin spreading across his face as
Nina helped him to a chair. "Will you go get the bottle of Macallan on the top shelf of the bar? This seems like just the right
time to drink it."

Tim retrieved the bottle of scotch.

"To having dinner with two of my favorite people," Joseph Gregory said, once Nina had handed him a glass.

"And to you, Uncle Joe," Tim said, raising his glass in a toast.

"Yes, Dad, to you," Nina said.

She had to concentrate on the sting of the scotch so she wouldn't cry.

After the Macallan and a few spoonfuls of soup, Nina's father winced.

"Is something wrong, Dad?" she asked.

"It's nothing, Sweetheart," he said. "Sitting up's not as comfortable as lying down."

Within a few more minutes, he couldn't take the pain anymore, and Nina insisted on giving him another lollipop as Tim helped him lie back down in the bed.

Then she looked at Tim.

"If you don't mind, Uncle Joe," Tim said. "I'm going to steal your daughter and bring her into the dining room for dessert."

"Oh, steal away," Nina's father said. She could detect a smile on his face, in spite of the pain.

When she and Tim dropped their dishes back in the kitchen, Nina said, "I don't know how much more of this I can take. Watching him like that—it's horrible. It hasn't been this bad before."

Tim put his spoon in the sink and then looked at her. Nina could see the concern in his eyes. Tim was quiet for a moment.

"We should get married," he said.

Nina stared at him. "Pardon?"

"I spoke to your dad about it. He and I were going to go this weekend to the safe-deposit box to get your mother's engagement ring. But . . . now it seems like too long to wait. We could get married tomorrow, or the day after. Your dad could be at our wedding. We could get his friend—that judge, what's his name?—to come and marry us in the apartment."

Nina's lungs felt constricted. That vine around her torso was back. She couldn't marry Tim tomorrow. "We haven't even been dating a year," she said.

"Long courtships are for people who haven't been best friends their whole lives," Tim said. "There's nothing more you can possibly learn about me at this point. There's nothing more I need to learn about you to know that we should spend our lives together. It just—it makes sense. We've always made sense. We should've been together for years by now."

But they hadn't been. After Nina and Tim had gotten together in January, she'd had a series of long talks with Leslie about it.

"Are you sure this isn't because your dad is sick again?" Leslie had asked. "I mean, I guess it's fine if it is, as long as that's not all that it's about."

Nina had thought about it. Some of it had to be, of course. All decisions were affected by the time in which they were made. Nothing existed in a vacuum. But it was more than that. She'd never wanted to risk their friendship before, but with her dad's diagnosis, it felt like . . . like time was running out. For everyone. And maybe the risk would be worth it.

"I THINK WE WERE AFRAID," Nina said to Tim, holding a dirty dish in her hand. "If we tried to date and it didn't work, it would change us."

"Well, it turned out there was nothing to be afraid of," Tim said. "And now we can make it official. You and me forever."

Nina worked hard to control her face, to smile, to nod, though inside she felt panicked. He was right. She loved being with him, spending time with him. She always had. He'd been the person she counted on ever since she was a kid.

Tim looked at her, his head cocked sideways. "You want a big wedding, don't you," he said. "The dress, the ballroom, the dancing—the publicity for the hotels. Me too—we should make a big splash with our wedding like your parents did. But we can do that after. Do something small now, for your dad. And do something bigger later, for everyone else."

He made so much sense. He always made so much sense. And though her brain agreed with him completely, her heart— her uncontrollable heart—didn't feel the same way. She heard Leslie in her mind; she knew what her friend would say.

"That makes sense," Nina told Tim. "But do we want to get married because it makes sense?"

Now Tim's face was starting to pale. "Do you not want to marry me?" he asked.

"No!" Nina said, putting down the dish and taking his hand. "I just . . . I guess I was hoping for a proposal that was more about us than about my dad."

"Of course it's about us," Tim said, kissing Nina on the top of her head. "I thought that was a given."

Nina wrapped her arms around Tim and heard his heart beat. *Say yes*, it was saying, over and over. *Say yes, say yes, say yes.* She was about to, but he spoke before she did.

"I think I bungled this," Tim said. "Let's forget we had this conversation, and I'm going to get the ring from your dad, and then I'll propose for real. A night out, the tasting menu at Per Se, a speech about how much you mean to me, a diamond hidden in your dessert. Okay?"

Nina laughed and nodded. "Okay," she said.

Tim smiled. He looked so relieved that Nina rose up on her tiptoes to kiss him.

23

TIM AND NINA HAD MADE PLANS WITH HIS FRIENDS from work that night, but Nina felt too drained to put up a good front.

"Would it be okay with you if I skipped?" she asked Tim. "I just . . . I can't."

He squeezed her shoulder. "Do you want me to skip, too?" he asked, concern on his face.

She shook her head. "No, it's fine. You go. Have my share of fun, too."

Tim laughed. "Are you sure?" he asked. "I can stay with you."

"It's okay," she told him. "I don't want you to miss out because of me."

Tim looked at her for a moment, as if he were trying to make sure she was telling him the truth. He must've decided she was, because he said, "All right. I'll talk to you tomorrow."

And then he kissed her and headed downtown.

The ride home to Tribeca seemed like too much for Nina, so she decided to sleep on Central Park West that night.

She straightened up the kitchen and then took out her phone to call Leslie, to try to make sense of the on-hold marriage proposal. But then she put her phone down. She didn't know what she would say. Didn't know her own feelings enough to explain them to anyone else. She contemplated calling Pris to make plans to go out later this week and celebrate Rafael's win, but she didn't do that either. Instead she sat on the couch with Carlos. She wanted to escape her own life a little, so she picked up her dad's copy of the *New Yorker* and was flipping through it while Carlos read something on a Kindle. After losing her place in an article for the third time, Nina put the magazine down and asked him if he wanted a drink.

Carlos asked for a beer, and she poured herself another glass of scotch. Not the Macallan, though. She felt like she'd need to ask her dad's permission for that. And then she realized, like a punch to the gut, that once he was gone, whatever was left in the bottle would be hers. She wouldn't have to ask anyone's permission to drink it. She closed her eyes for a moment. *Paper clips. Staples. Floor tiles.*

When she opened her eyes, Carlos was looking at her.

"You're in the middle of it now," he said, putting his beer down on the table. "I know it doesn't seem like your life will ever be okay again, but it will. I promise."

Nina swirled the scotch in her glass and watched the little cyclone she created rage and then dissipate. Were the answers there? In the shimmering amber?

"I know," Nina said, not believing it.

Then the two of them sat in companionable silence, Carlos reading again, and Nina lost in her own thoughts, until she decided to turn in for the night.

"He's usually better in the mornings," Carlos said, as she got up from the couch.

Nina nodded and headed down the hallway to her childhood bedroom, still decorated, so many years later, with the same pale-yellow chevron wallpaper Caro had chosen when Nina was eight. The same queen-sized four-poster bed she'd picked out when she turned ten. There was a picture on her dresser of her and Tim from about that time, too, both of them hanging upside down on a bar at the Dinosaur Playground in Riverside Park, their smiles looking like frowns, her father just inside the frame focused on the two kids, as if he was ready to spring into action the moment he saw either of them wobble. He wasn't around to take her to the Dinosaur Playground often, but when he was, she was the center of his world.

Nina looked at the picture. She thought about all of the moments in her life she'd shared with Tim. The big ones, the small ones. No matter how great something was or how awful, having Tim there made it better. It always had.

She should marry Tim.

24

LATER THAT NIGHT, NINA WOKE UP AT THREE A.M. IN
a panic. In her dream, she was playing hide-and-seek with her
father. She was two and thirty-two at the same time, and she
was running around the apartment and couldn't find him anywhere: under the table, behind the curtain, in the bathtub. She
started shouting for him to come out, panicked the way she was
when she was nine and they went to the Union Square Holiday
Market to buy presents for the people who worked in his office.
It was the first Christmas after her mother died—the holiday
itself would mark one year exactly without her mom—and
Nina hadn't wanted anything to do with it.

"I'll get you hot chocolate with whipped cream," he'd said.
"An apple cider donut. Both of them. Anything else you want."

"How about both of those and a candy cane that's bigger
than my arm?" she'd asked. Her friend Melinda had brought
one to school and everyone thought it was the coolest.

"Deal," he said. And so they went, bundled up against the
cold, Nina's scarf tucked tightly around her neck.

They were in a booth filled with finger puppets, and Nina got distracted by the one that looked like a giraffe and lost track of her father. Or maybe he'd lost track of her, one tiny head that had gotten swallowed up in a crowd of much taller ones.

When she realized he wasn't standing next to her, Nina's heart started racing. "Dad!" she'd yelled. "Dad!"

Ever since her mom had died, she didn't like it when she didn't know where her father was. He had even given her a copy of his meeting schedule to take with her to school, so she could always find him if she needed to. Checking it was the only way she could quell the panic that overtook her when she least expected it. At recess, in the middle of art class, in the car ride home from school with their au pair. But now? Now he had disappeared and nothing on the schedule would help her.

"Dad!" she'd shouted again, not sure what to do. "Find me!"

Just as she yelled that, her father pushed through the crowd. He lifted her up, and, even though nine was way too old for your father to pick you up like you were a baby, Nina felt so grateful to be in his arms.

"I'm so sorry," he said, when he put her back down. "I'm so, so sorry. I didn't realize you'd stopped walking."

"I didn't realize you'd kept walking," Nina said, blinking hard, so that the tears she felt forming in her eyes wouldn't get any farther than her eyelashes.

"It was my fault," he said, noticing her tears. "You didn't do anything wrong." Then he held her hand, and her tears stopped, and the two of them continued walking through the Holiday Market. They said thank you to the people who wished them a Merry Christmas and kept shopping until they'd bought something for everyone on her father's list.

Years later, when Nina thought about that day, she understood the blame he'd internalized when they'd become separated. He was a single father, and her well-being rested completely on his shoulders. Even with other people around helping him take care of her, he was still her only living parent.

WHEN NINA WAS STARTLED awake by her dream, her T-shirt and pajama pants were damp with sweat. Her heart raced just like it had that day she got lost by the finger puppets so many years ago. She'd heard about people who dreamed that a loved one had died and awoke to find it true. What about dreams where you couldn't find the person you loved? Did those mean anything? Nina reached for her glasses and started walking down the hall in the dark to check on her father. But the distance seemed too far. Soon she was running, her panic growing with each step.

When she got to her father's bedroom, she knew something was wrong. The panic snapped from synapse to synapse, filling her brain, her body. Her father wasn't breathing. His chest wasn't rising. It wasn't falling. He was still. So still.

"Dad!" she yelled, the way she had at the Holiday Market. "Dad!"

She ran to his bed, tears already falling. "Dad, no. No. You can't." Her hands were on his cheeks, then pushing on his chest, trying to get his heart to start again. "No! What if I need you to find me?"

But she knew. She knew, like she knew every contour of his face, that he'd never be able to find her again.

25

AFTER CARLOS WROTE DOWN A TIME OF DEATH THAT
Nina knew might have been off by minutes or hours, she wasn't
sure what to do. All she could think about was an article she'd
once read about a doctor from Massachusetts who did an experiment in which he tried to figure out definitively if human
beings had souls. He put a dying man on a table and measured
his weight constantly in the hours before he died. At the moment of death, the man lost three quarters of an ounce. The
doctor posited that the three quarters of an ounce was his soul
departing his body.

Tim had sent her the article when they were in college. *Comforting?* he'd written as the subject of the e-mail. Nina had done
a bit more research and discovered that the doctor, who had
conducted the experiment in 1911, had never been able to repli-
cate it exactly. She'd figured, at the time, that there was probably another explanation for the three quarters of an ounce.

But now, sitting in the room with her father who was no
longer breathing, she wondered. Was there such a thing as a

soul? Was his soul floating out of his body right now? Was it in the room? In the air? Was she breathing in the essence of her father's life at that very moment?

"I'm supposed to call the hospice center," Carlos said to her. "But no one has to come for him until you're ready. You tell me how long you want and that's when I'll tell them to come."

Nina looked at Carlos, her mind blank. What was the correct answer to that question? How long was appropriate? Nina looked over at her father. He was the one she would have asked.

She had the urge to brush his hair before anyone else saw him. Maybe give him a haircut. She'd never given anyone a haircut before. Not even herself. Most kids at some point took scissors to their hair, but she never had. Did you need special scissors to cut hair?

Carlos was looking at her, waiting for her to say something.

"I'm sorry," Nina said; her mind felt like it was in disarray, like someone had rifled through its compartments and left everything in the wrong place. "What did you ask?"

"Do you want to call someone?" Carlos asked. "It might be good for you to have someone else here with you now."

Nina nodded. But she didn't do anything. She didn't go back to her room to get her phone. The thought of explaining why she was calling, of saying the words out loud, paralyzed her.

"Your boyfriend maybe?" Carlos asked.

Nina nodded again.

"You should go get your phone," he added. "And call him."

This time Nina left the room. She dialed Tim as she walked back to her father's room. But his phone went right to voice mail. She hung up and switched to text. *My dad is*—she couldn't bring herself to drop her thumb on top of the *d*—*gone*, she finished, the phone blurring in front of her, her nose running. She wanted to add that she needed him. That she was alone. She'd never felt this alone in her life. That her mother's ring didn't matter. The romance didn't either. Or Per Se. They should get married right now.

But she said nothing. He said nothing.

Her phone was silent. Where the hell was he?

"He's not there," Nina told Carlos, trying to swallow back her tears but failing, panic fluttering against her ribs.

"Okay," Carlos said. "Here's what we'll do. I'm going to leave the room and make some phone calls. You can stay here with your father if you want, or you can go to your bedroom or sit on the couch or take a walk or call a good friend, whatever feels right. And I'll tell them we need a few hours."

Nina nodded. She took a deep breath. Carlos left the room. And Nina walked over to her father. She smoothed his hair into the left part that he preferred. She buttoned the top button of his pajamas that had come loose, exposing the sparse white hair on his chest. Tears filling her eyes, she leaned over and kissed the gray stubble on his cheek.

"You have no idea how much I'm going to miss you," she said quietly. And then she cried harder knowing he'd never know she'd said that.

26

NINA SAT WITH HER FATHER, HOLDING HIS HAND, which seemed to feel colder and colder as time passed—though she wasn't sure if that was actually happening or was just what her brain expected to happen. A line from *Laberinto de la soledad*, which she had studied in college and read many times since, kept running through her mind: *La soledad es el hecho más profundo de la condición humana. El hombre es el único ser que sabe que está solo.* It felt like it was on repeat, first in Spanish, and then in English, over and over: *Solitude is the profoundest fact of the human condition. Man is the only being who knows he is alone.* She just felt so alone.

After a while, she looked at the clock. 3:40 A.M. She knew Leslie kept her ringer off at night but dialed her anyway, just in case she happened to be awake. She wasn't. Nina hung up before she could hear Leslie's voice telling her to leave a message. She should call TJ, she realized, since he knew what was supposed to happen next—what her dad wanted to be buried in, who was supposed to get the Gregory Corporation's press release, what it was supposed to say, which picture should be attached.

Nina looked at the clock again. She could give TJ a few more hours. Let him at least get a good night's sleep before he had to deal with the death of his best friend for the past fifty years.

She pulled out her phone and instead sent an e-mail to Rafael and Jane with a subject line that said *My Dad.* The body text said: *Nothing's public yet, but I won't be at work today.* Hopefully she'd be able to finish out the campaign, get Rafael to election day. It was only seven weeks away. Maybe she could do that and take over her dad's role at the Gregory Corporation at the same time. Would it be that hard to juggle them both? She'd counted on more time. But she shouldn't have. She was smarter than that.

As she was trying to figure everything out, her phone rang. *Rafael O'Connor-Ruiz calling,* it said on the screen. She had never spoken to Rafael on the phone before. He had seen her e-mail and called her. The fact that he cared enough to do that made Nina's throat feel full.

"Hi," she said, trying to disguise her tears.

"Nina, Nina," he said.

"It's me," she said, wiping her nose with the bottom of her T-shirt.

"I don't sleep . . . I never sleep these days, but most people do, so I just wanted to make sure . . . is someone there with you?"

"Carlos," she answered. "My father's nurse. He's calling the hospice and I think the mortuary to come get—" But she couldn't finish the sentence. She tried, but it was impossible.

"Do you want me to come over? If you need someone, I can."

Nina thought about how nice it would be to have him there, to have someone she could lean on, someone whose opinions she could ask. But regardless of whatever connection they had, he was her boss, nothing more.

"That's such a nice offer," she said, "but you don't have to come." She paused for a moment, afraid this meant she'd have to hang up, afraid she'd be alone again. "Maybe we could stay on the phone, though."

"Whatever you want, Palabrecita," he said. "I know how awful it is to lose a parent. Do you want me to talk? Do you want to?"

Nina sat down at the table where she and Tim had eaten dinner. She couldn't bring herself to leave her father's body alone. She remembered the night she and Leslie drove from Connecticut to eastern Massachusetts when Leslie's mother had died. They'd joined Leslie's father and her three sisters as they sat in the funeral home, staying with Leslie's mother's body. It was a Jewish custom called shemira that Nina hadn't known about before. Leslie hadn't either—her family hadn't been particularly religious while she was growing up, but while her mother was sick, her parents read everything they could about Jewish customs surrounding death and dying. And Leslie's mom decided that she wanted her family to observe shemira, to sit with her from the time she died until the time she was buried the next day, keeping watch, not abandoning her before she was brought to her new home at the cemetery. There was something initially horrifying about sitting and talking near Leslie's mother's dead body—Nina had never seen her own mother after she'd died—but then somehow it became comforting. It had normalized death in a way.

"Have you ever spent the night in a funeral home?" Nina asked Rafael.

"Can't say I have," Rafael said. "Have you?"

"Mm-hm," Nina said. "When my college roommate Leslie's mom died. It's a Jewish tradition or maybe more a practice— not one that most people follow."

"How does it work?" Rafael asked. Nina imagined him relaxed against the pillows in his bed.

"Leslie's dad said you're really supposed to pray and read scripture, but we didn't. Instead we talked about Leslie's mom. Leslie and her dad and sisters told stories. I told one, too, about how grateful I was for her when Leslie and I moved in together our freshman year. My dad, unsurprisingly, didn't want to leave. And Leslie's mom took charge, shepherding him out of the room, convincing him to take her to Mory's so Leslie and I would have a chance to get to know each other and the people on our floor. It takes a strong personality to boss my father around, and I'd been amazed that she was able to do it after knowing him for only a few hours."

Nina leaned back in the chair she'd sat down in. It had been Tim's earlier that night. Forever ago, that was how it felt.

"Do you want to tell me a story about your dad?" Rafael asked. "Or I can tell you one."

"You can?" Nina asked. All of a sudden this felt incredibly important.

"I didn't know him, but I heard him speak once. And it actually changed my life."

"You're not serious," Nina said. She couldn't believe that in all of their talks, all of their work sessions, this had never come up. "Why didn't you ever mention that?"

"I'm completely serious," Rafael answered. "And I never said anything because I didn't want it to change your perception of me. I . . . I always wanted you to know that I valued your contribution to my campaign for who you are, not because of who your dad is."

"Was," Nina said, looking over at the body that looked now like a wax museum version of her father. No chest rising and falling, no eyelashes fluttering.

"Is," Rafael repeated. "Even if he's gone, he is your father. He doesn't stop being your father just because he's not here anymore."

Nina had always thought about her mom in the past tense after she'd died. And in some ways that made sense. Her mom was funny. Her mom was smart. Her mom was beautiful. Her mom loved to take Nina out for frozen yogurt with rainbow sprinkles, just the two of them. But what Rafael said made a lot of sense, too. Phoebe Gregory would always be her mom, no matter how long she'd been gone.

"Is," Nina echoed. "I like that."

She imagined Rafael smiling on the other side of the phone. "So my story," Rafael said. "About your dad."

"Yes," Nina said. "Your story."

"I was in high school," he started.

"Bronx Science," Nina supplied. She knew his official bio probably as well as he did.

"Right," Rafael said. "And I was part of Junior Achievement."

"What's that?" Nina asked.

"A kind of club where volunteers show kids the options that are out there. They were trying to get us to achieve great things in the future," he explained.

"I guess it worked," Nina said.

Rafael laughed. "Well, perhaps. But it was more about going into business, not so much politics. It was your dad who changed my mind. He came to speak to the group, and he talked about the fact that creating a business wasn't just about money—it became who you were, something to put your stamp on, a part of your legacy as a person. Something your children and your children's children would inherit. I'd never thought about it before, what I hoped to leave behind when I was gone. I decided then that I wanted to become an immigration lawyer, to help people like my dad and my grandma. And I thought about your dad's speech again before I decided to run for mayor. Basically it's because of him that we're having this phone call right now."

Nina hadn't known any of this. "You should've told me," she said.

Rafael was silent, and Nina could visualize him running his fingers through his hair. "I . . . that's not why I hired you," he said. "I want to make sure you know your dad didn't come into the equation at all. I hired you because I was impressed with your writing. And because you seemed easygoing and smart, like someone I could work with. And because—well, I liked talking to you. I still like talking to you."

"Me, too," she said, softly, trying not to read into his words, wondering if she should. "My dad told me—" Nina didn't get any further than that. She looked over at her dad, who would never tell her anything again and she started to cry. It was more than tears, she felt her breath coming in gasps, tried not to let Rafael hear.

"Hey," Rafael said. "You okay over there?"

"Not really," Nina sniffed, when she gained enough control over herself to speak. *Pencils*, she thought. *Paving stones. Street signs.* She looked at the clock. It was five a.m. They'd been on the phone for an hour and a half. *Sidewalks. Traffic cones. Manhole covers.*

"Are you sure you don't want me to come over?" he asked. "I'm only on Central Park North. Not far from you at all."

Nina wiped her eyes with her T-shirt again. "I'll be okay," she said. "I've been meaning to tell you," she added. "I came up with a kind of poem for my dad."

"Yeah?" Rafael asked quietly.

"Yeah," Nina answered. "A villanelle."

"Highly structured," Rafael said. "Well thought out. I can see that."

They were both silent for a moment. She heard fabric shifting on Rafael's end of the phone and wondered if he was lying back down in bed, rearranging his pillows or his blanket. Maybe he was on his couch.

"I think I have one for my mom, too," Nina told him. "I think she's a haiku. Her life was purposeful and elegant—and far, far too short."

"That's beautiful," Rafael said.

Nina looked out the window again, and the sky was now turning pink, streaked with orange. "The sun is starting to rise," she said. "I think I should probably make some calls now."

"Okay," Rafael said. "I'm here if you need me."

"Thanks for calling," Nina answered.

"Anytime, Palabrecita."

Hanging up with him felt like it compounded her loss. And it made Nina wish she'd agreed to him coming over. She felt centered now, after talking to Rafael.

She wondered if she would've felt the same way if she'd spoken to Tim.

27

AFTER SHE HUNG UP, NINA TRIED TIM AGAIN, BUT IT
still went straight to voice mail. Then she tried Leslie again,
who picked up on the first ring this time—she was up and
heading to the gym but turned her car around immediately.
"I'll be in New York City by dinnertime," she said. Nina texted
Pris after that, sure there was no way she was up yet, promising
more details about the wake and funeral when she had them.
And then Nina went to call TJ and Caro.

She dialed their landline. It was the first number she'd memorized after the one at her own house. It rang three times. Then
four. Then she heard Caro's voice.

"Nina?"

"It's me," Nina said. She wished she could put her father on
the phone. That he could say, *I died last night*, so she wouldn't
have to say it. He was the one who'd done it, after all.

You have to take responsibility for your actions, he'd always told
her. All Nina could think now was that her father was the one

who'd died; he should take responsibility for that. Nina could hear Caro's breath speed up. "Is your dad . . . ?" she asked.

"Gone," Nina said. She still couldn't say the word. *Dead.* The shape of it felt wrong in her mouth.

"Oh, darling," Caro said. "We'll be right over."

When Nina hung up with them, Carlos came back into the room. "How are you doing in here?" he asked.

Nina nodded. She didn't trust herself to talk about how she was feeling. She was worried that if she let herself cry again, it would take far too long to stop. When her mother died, it had felt like she'd cried for hours at a time, whole afternoons filled with tears, and she was unable to stanch the flow.

It was easier to talk about memories and poetry, speeches and ambitions. She wanted to call Rafael back. She felt it like an ache deep inside her. "TJ and Caro will be here soon," she told Carlos. "TJ knows everything my dad wants."

She looked over at her father again. His face was so relaxed. In real life it never looked like that.

NINA SAT THERE, lost in a rubber band of time, until she heard a commotion in the apartment. A door opening and shutting. Footsteps on the gallery floor. "Nina!" It was Caro, walking through the apartment.

She came into the room, followed by TJ, whose eyes were already red and swollen.

"Oh, Sweetheart," TJ said, as he embraced her.

In TJ's arms, Nina finally let herself stop battling against her tears. "I don't have any more family," Nina said to TJ, the lump in her throat making it hard to talk, the sobs making it hard to catch her breath. It was the one thing that she couldn't stop thinking about. Caro answered, taking Nina into her arms next, rubbing her back the way she did when Nina or Tim needed comforting as children.

"You have us," she said. "You'll always have us."

Which was true, but it wasn't the same. Not yet. Nina took a long, shuddering breath and pulled herself away from Caro. *I am an adult*, she said to herself. *I can handle this.* But even as she was telling herself that, she knew she couldn't.

"Have you spoken to Tim yet?" TJ asked.

Nina shook her head, wiped her tears. "His phone went to voice mail," she said.

"For us, too." He pulled out his phone and dialed again.

Nina looked at her father once more, her breath still unsteady, her emotions threatening to breach their dam again. She walked over and kissed him on the cheek one last time, feeling his stubble against her lips, and looked at Caro through a screen of tears. "You can take care of him now," she said. "With you both here . . . it's too real. I can't anymore." She wanted to stay caught in that moment of time, stretch it even more so she wouldn't have to deal with everything that came next. But time wasn't like that. You couldn't get lost in it forever. It marched onward, pulling you with it, a leash around your neck.

Nina left the room. She went into her bedroom, shut the door, and let herself cry into her pillow, muffling the animal sounds that came from somewhere deep in her heart. Or maybe it was her soul. That three quarters of an ounce that may or may not exist.

28

A WHILE LATER THERE WAS A KNOCK ON NINA'S BED-room door. She bit her lip to stop the sobs and ended up taking long gulping breaths instead. "Aunt Caro?" she asked.

"It's me," Tim answered, his voice choked with apology, with sorrow, with love. "I got home late and forgot to charge my phone last night. It ran out of battery. I'm sorry. I'm sorry I wasn't there for you."

Nina got off her bed and opened the door. Tim's eyes were red-rimmed, his face pale. He bent down to hug her, then lifted her with him when he straightened, so she was clinging to his neck, her feet a few inches off the floor.

"I'm so sorry, Nina," he said, as he leaned back over, so she was standing once more. "I'll never forgive myself. Of all nights."

"It's okay," she said, feeling the words against her sore throat. "I'm glad you're here now." And then she dissolved into tears again, and this time Tim cried with her.

29

WITH TJ AND CARO THERE TO TAKE CARE OF EVERY-
thing, Nina told Tim she wanted to go home. To her apartment.
Where the ghost of her father wasn't lurking around every corner. Where his shoes and medications and books and Thanksgiving turkey collection didn't feel like they were taking up all
the air.

"Will you come with me?" Nina asked.

"Of course," Tim said. "I told the office I was going to be
MIA for the next week. I'm here to help in whatever way I can."

"Thanks," Nina said. She laced her fingers through his. She
wanted to never let him go.

WHEN THE ELEVATOR OPENED into her loft, Nina took a deep
breath. Being here was better. Not great, but better.

"Did you eat yet today?" Tim asked Nina as he closed the
door behind them.

Nina shook her head. "I'm not hungry," she said.

"How about coffee?"

"How about we watch my dad's favorite movie while I deal with your mom's list?" she countered. Before they'd left, Caro had given Nina a list of the decisions that her father had left to her, and the phone numbers of the people who should hear from Nina directly before the press release went out.

"What do you want me to do?" Tim asked.

"Just . . . be here," Nina said.

Tim slipped an arm around her shoulder and squeezed. "That I can do," he said. "But you do have to eat something at some point today."

Nina looked up at him. She thought about all the meals she and Tim had eaten with her father. All the times the three of them snuck to the hot dog stand across the street from the Seaport hotel, even though they knew Caro wouldn't approve. With Tim, she would have that extra piece of her father. His memories as well as her own. *I should just tell him I want to marry him now*, Nina thought. But every time she opened her mouth to say the words, something stopped her.

"So, *Dune*?" Tim asked.

"Of course," Nina said. Her father's obsession with the movie had caused Tim and Nina to dress as Paul and Chani one Halloween in the late '90s. No one knew who they were, but they didn't care.

As Tim turned on the TV to order *Dune*, Nina dimmed the lights and grabbed a fleece blanket from her rocking chair. It was blue, with an embroidered *Y* in the corner, and was big enough to cover two people, if not three. Her father had picked it up at his last Yale reunion and given it to Nina. She held it to her nose, but it didn't smell anything like him. As the movie started, Tim and Nina sat together under the blanket, Nina's head leaning against Tim's chest, his arm around her back. He was keeping her from falling apart—holding her up, literally and figuratively.

"I love you so much," she said to him, as she unfolded the list of phone numbers.

"Me, too," he answered, resting his cheek on the top of her head. "Me, too."

Nina made phone call after phone call, telling practically everyone she'd ever met that her father had died. She accepted their condolences and swallowed everything she wanted to say when one of his longtime squash partners asked her if she was going to see a medium to speak to her father from beyond the grave and when their neighbors in East Hampton launched into a story about how their dog died a week ago last Thursday and how they thought it might be from the pesticide the gardeners put on the hydrangeas.

"Everyone's a lunatic," she said to Tim, who'd been half listening to her end of the conversations and half dealing with the e-mails on his phone.

"I'm not going to disagree," he said. "Well, except for us. We're the only nonlunatics out there."

Nina sighed. "I don't know," she said. "We might be lunatics, too. Do you know if you're a lunatic?"

Then Nina's eyes went to the television screen and she realized the poison capsule in Duke Leto's tooth was about to kill him. Nina flinched against Tim. This part had never bothered her before, but now she couldn't watch.

"Turn it off," she said. "Tim, please. Turn it off. Don't let it get to that part." She heard the panic in her voice but couldn't stop it.

Tim fumbled for the remote control and hit pause.

"He's Paul's dad," Tim said, realizing the problem.

Nina nodded. "I forgot that happened. Can we . . . can we put something else on?" she asked quietly.

"Of course," Tim said.

Nina laid her head back against his chest and he stroked her hair with one hand while flicking through the options on the screen with the other. "Here," he said. "How about this one?" He put on *Matilda*. "You used to like this."

"Better choice," Nina said, her voice small. "Thank you."

She took her glasses off and closed her eyes, listening to the familiar dialogue, feeling Tim's chest rise and fall against her.

ABOUT AN HOUR LATER, Nina woke up to the sound of a text message. She looked around and realized she and Tim had fallen asleep on the couch together. Somehow they'd both stretched out so they were lying like spoons, her body just in front of his, his arm draped across her stomach, the fleece blanket pulled up to their chins. She could feel his even breath on her neck.

Nina slowly reached in front of her to grab her glasses and phone from the coffee table, not wanting to wake Tim. She slipped on her glasses, flicked the phone to silent, and then looked at the text. There were two. Both from Rafael. They'd come one right after the other. The fact that there weren't any others meant the press release hadn't gone out yet.

Hey, Palabrecita, the text said. *Just wanted to see how you were doing. When my dad died, I was a real disaster. And that was with my brother and sister and mom there with me. Hope you have people to lean on.*

The office isn't the same without you here.

Nina took a quiet breath. In reading the text, she could hear Rafael's voice. She could see him, sitting at his desk, texting while drinking a cup of Jane's horrific coffee. Maybe he'd rolled up his sleeves and anyone who was watching could see the muscles in his forearm ripple every time he moved his thumb to type. Nina closed her eyes and let herself melt against Tim. She shouldn't be thinking about Rafael.

She reread his message.

Should she respond? What should she say? She didn't want to write anything that would've made her father say, *You're smarter than that.*

She'd planned to go back to work at some point before election day. Help Rafael win. But was that even fair, to take so much time off right before an election? And Nina knew her brain wasn't functioning properly. She'd be no help to him in the state she was in. Plus, there was the connection that they both knew was there, even if they'd never spoken it aloud. It wasn't smart to put herself in that situation. Even now, thinking about him made her cheeks feel warm.

She could quit. Focus on the Gregory Corporation. Focus on Tim. Live her life in a way that would carry forth her father's legacy—the one he cared so much about that he gave a speech to Rafael's Junior Achievement club about it. Her dad didn't approve of quitting in general, but this seemed like one of the extenuating circumstances that would make it okay.

Tim moved in his sleep and tightened his hand on Nina's stomach, pulling her closer to him. She took a deep breath.

Hey, she typed back to Rafael. *Thanks for checking in. I'm here with Tim. Good for leaning purposes. Listen, I've been thinking: Would it be better for you to hire someone else to write your speeches for the general? I'm not sure if I'll really be able to handle that on top of all of this. I don't know if I'll even be able to handle all of this, honestly. And you need someone who can give the election 100%.*

Her finger hovered over the send button, but she didn't press it.

She added: *I can send you some suggestions if you need.* And then she hit send. She felt an immediate pang of regret, a sense of loss that was an echo of the one she felt when she'd hung up with him that morning, but she knew she'd made the right decision. And maybe, in time, they could be friends. Without seeing each other nearly every day, whatever sparked between them might fizzle out and leave mutual respect and admiration behind.

Nina stared at her phone, waiting for a response. She wondered if he'd try to convince her to stay. Three dots appeared, then disappeared, then appeared, then disappeared again. Nina put her phone down on the coffee table, frustrated with herself for caring so much, frustrated that her heart was trying to talk her out of a decision she knew was the right one. She took off her glasses, then rolled over slowly, shifting so that she was facing Tim now, and scooted herself down. He rolled, too, so he was more on his back than his side. Nina closed her eyes and breathed deeply. She felt so safe in his arms. Before long, she'd fallen back asleep.

WHEN NINA WOKE UP AGAIN, Tim was awake but hadn't moved. His arm was still wrapped around her. Her head was still on his chest.

"Morning, sleepyhead," he said.

"Morning," she said back, pulling her hand out from under the blanket to rub her eyes. "What time is it?"

"It's not actually morning," he said, leaning forward to kiss her nose. "It's a little after noon."

When he moved, Nina felt his hip roll sideways and then there was a hardness against her thigh. Her eyebrows went up and Tim bit his lip. "Sorry," he said. "I woke up like that. It'll go away soon."

Nina reached down, trailing her fingers along his jeans, feeling him warm under denim.

"Well, it won't go away if you do that," Tim said.

Nina couldn't help it. She found erections fascinating. All of a sudden, men weren't completely in control of their bodies. This thing just happened. Sometimes when they wanted it to, sometimes when they didn't. And they couldn't make it stop. It wasn't like raising an arm or rising up on tiptoe. It was like something overtook them—awake or asleep, it didn't matter.

"Do you want it to go away?" Nina asked.

Tim shrugged. "It feels like the wrong day to have sex," he said.

Nina thought about that. Was it? Or would there be comfort in it? A statement to the world, to herself, that she was still alive. She was still here. She could experience pleasure in spite of pain.

"It might be," Nina agreed. But her fingers were still on his jeans. He got harder.

Then he looked at her, a question in his eyes. His hand moved to the hem of her shirt, asking permission. When she nodded he slipped it into her bra, running his fingers around her nipple.

Nina closed her eyes. She reveled in the moment of pleasure. And then she felt guilty that she was feeling pleasure on the day her father died. Tears began to drip from the outer corners of her eyes, gravity pulling them down her cheeks and into her hair.

"Are you okay?" Tim asked, his hand no longer under her shirt.

"No," Nina said, opening her eyes. "I'm not. But it's not your fault. It's not because . . ."

"It's okay," Tim said, his hand stroking her hair now. "You don't have to say anything. I knew it wasn't the day for this."

She wasn't quite sure if he was right, but, "I guess not," Nina said. She pulled herself closer to him, laying her head back down against his shoulder.

Then Tim's stomach growled. Nina could feel it rumble against her.

"You may not be hungry," he told her. "But clearly I need to eat something."

Nina knew she should, too. She straightened her T-shirt, re-adjusted her bra. "Want me to make us lunch?" she asked, wiping her eyes. She'd been making food for Tim since they were in elementary school, when she put peanut butter and sliced bananas on Ritz crackers and drizzled them with honey and called it Nina Nut Crunch.

"I think I can handle it," Tim said, shifting sideways so he could get off the couch.

Nina turned her head and kissed Tim's T-shirt. It was warm from his body heat—and hers.

"What was that for?" he asked.

"For being you," she said.

Tim bent to kiss the top of her head, and Nina watched him as he walked across the room, looking so comfortable in her kitchen, like he belonged there.

Then Nina's phone vibrated. She sat up on the couch, put on her glasses, and picked it up.

"The *New York Times* sent out an alert," she said. "About my dad."

There it was on her phone: *Breaking News: Hotelier Joseph Gregory, Dead at 69.*

And then a string of text messages and e-mails started coming in. From friends, acquaintances, colleagues. Everyone saying how sorry they were. Everyone asking what they could do to help. Pris offering to come over with a bottle of Brent's best wine—her drug of choice—and to help respond to all of the messages Nina must be getting now. One of Leslie's cousins offered a dime bag of marijuana. Nina politely declined both.

Then she scrolled down, looking for the one message she'd been waiting for a response to when she fell back asleep. Rafael. There he was.

I won't try to convince you to stay on if you don't feel like you can handle it right now. But if you change your mind, the door is always open. I never could have won the primary without you. Ciao for now, Palabrecita.

Nina felt another moment of regret when she realized she had no idea when she would see him next. But she was trying to make the right choice. It was too much. She had to cast Rafael from her mind and steel herself for the more serious things ahead. A wake. A funeral. A corporation to run. She looked over at Tim, making her lunch.

A wedding, too.

30

NINA AND TIM SPENT THE REST OF THE DAY TOGETHER.
After lunch they went back to Caro's list. *I'm a Gregory, I can do
this*, Nina thought, over and over, with every call, every choice
she made. But her last name didn't turn her into a superhero.
She was still human, still in so much pain. Her phone kept vibrating, and finally Nina turned it off completely. She couldn't
talk to one more person about her dad. She couldn't make one
more decision.

The downstairs buzzer rang. When Nina picked up the re-
ceiver, the doorman told her that Leslie was on her way up.

Then the elevator opened into Nina's living room, and Leslie
walked out, her arms already open for a hug. Nina accepted it.

Maybe it was because her mom died when she was so
young—or maybe it was just her personality—but Nina never
had tons of close friends. She'd always had Tim. For a while
she'd had Melinda, her best friend from lower school who
moved away. And there was Pris and the group of girls she hung
out with, who welcomed Nina as one of them in middle school,

but who Nina never felt all that close to, except Pris. And then Leslie, who Nina was lucky enough to have been matched with as a roommate her first year at Yale, and who had become Nina's closest friend, after Tim. And that was really it. That had always been Nina's support network, her team. Other people were on the outskirts, the B-team, but her dad, Leslie, Tim, his parents, and Pris, they were the A-team. The major league. Her people. Always.

"Oh!" Leslie said, once she put her bags down on the floor. "I forgot, I have something for you." She pulled a plastic bag out of her purse. Inside it were four drawings and an only-slightly-licked lollipop from Cole. "He wanted to make sure you'd like it before he sent it with me," Leslie said, handing her the lollipop. It made Nina laugh through her tears.

As Nina held the candy, she realized that she and her father had never settled up their debts. She owed him dozens of Twizzlers and Hershey's Kisses, he owed her just as many lollipops and Tootsie Rolls.

Nina put the candy in her mouth. In its sugary sweetness, she tasted her Monday nights with her father. She tasted comfort. She tasted home.

31

THE NEXT MORNING, NINA AND LESLIE GOT DRESSED
and headed over to The Gregory by the Sea. Nina was wearing
a black cashmere dress with a gray cardigan over it, black stock-
ings, and black heels. She'd gone to her jewelry box and pulled
out her grandmother's diamond earrings and a sapphire drop
her father had gotten her when she graduated from college. "It's
the same color as our eyes," he'd told her. "I checked in the
mirror at the store."

She'd laughed then, at the idea of her father holding a sapphire up to his eyes in the mirror, maybe asking to see other
stones to check their colors, too. The drop was the same color as
the stones in the bracelet he'd gotten her for her birthday. The
one she was wearing now, next to the diamond tennis bracelet
he'd had made for her mother—his last gift to each of them.

"Do I look okay?" Nina asked Leslie, as they got out of the
black car in front of the hotel. Gene, the driver she and her father liked best, had picked her up that morning with tears in
his eyes. He'd made sure there was sparkling water for her in

the back of the car. And butterscotch candies, too. Nina looked down and considered what her father would think of her appearance.

"You look as stunning as ever," Leslie said, as she put her feet on the asphalt. She was wearing a gray pantsuit with a black silk shirt and heels that were slightly lower than Nina's. It evened out their height.

As soon as they both stepped onto the sidewalk, into the cool fall sunshine, cameras started flashing. Nina wasn't sure what to do with her mouth. Usually when someone took her picture, she smiled. But now that seemed like the exact wrong expression. So she pressed her lips together, looked away from the camera, and hoped that nobody would read anything strange into it.

Tim was waiting for them in the lobby and took Nina's hand, squeezing it softly while they stood in the elevator. "I love you," he whispered, so only she could hear.

When they got to the top floor, TJ and Caro were already there. Tim and Leslie stopped to talk to his parents, but Nina crossed the room to stand by her father's casket.

"Would you like anything to drink, Miss Gregory?" Marty, the bartender, asked her. "Scotch?" he asked. "Neat?"

Nina didn't trust herself to speak, so she just nodded. It was really too early for scotch, but today was a day for exceptions.

As she drank, she looked out at the city, standing next to her father for what she knew would be the very last time. She wondered how many other people out there had lost their father this week. This year. This decade. There were 8.5 million people who lived in New York City. More than 1.6 million in Manhattan alone. Of those millions, how many of them had felt just like she did at one point in their lives? Bereft, afraid, unspeakably sad.

Rafael, she thought. Rafael lost his dad. Rafael once felt like she did.

And then, almost as if she'd summoned him, Nina felt a hand touch her elbow. She turned and Rafael was there, with Jane and Jorge and Mac and the whole rest of the office.

Nina hugged them all, taking an extra beat with Rafael, feeling his body against hers. She ended with Jane, who held on to her the longest. "I heard you're not coming back," she said, into Nina's ear.

The two women separated. "I just . . . I don't know which end is up, Jane," Nina said. "Rafael needs someone whose brain is working properly right now. Mine isn't. And I don't know when it will again."

"Well, you're all he's talked about since we got into work this morning. I told him we didn't have to be the first ones here, but he insisted." Jane left it there, but Nina could hear the question in her voice. Nina had no answer. She looked for Tim but couldn't find him in the small crowd that had shown up since they'd arrived.

Nina turned back to Jane. "I'm glad you came early," she said.

Nina talked to all of them, but the whole time she was aware of Rafael, aware of how he was looking at only her, sympathy in his eyes. After a while, the room started to fill up even more, and Jane announced that they had to get back to the office. They all hugged Nina again, and this time Rafael was last. "I told you I don't sleep," he said. "So if you ever need someone to talk to in the middle of the night, don't hesitate to call. I'm not your boss anymore."

Nina looked up at him. "We can be friends now," she said.

"We can be whatever we want to be," he answered before he turned to leave.

Nina could feel her cheeks turning pink and put her hands to her face to hide them. Though, of course, that brought more attention to her blush. Leslie walked over.

"That hottie who couldn't take his eyes off you, that was your boss, right?" she asked.

Nina felt her blush deepen. "I don't know what you're talking about," she said.

"You're not fooling me with that act. That was Rafael O'Connor-Ruiz, wasn't it?"

"Yes," Nina confirmed. "That was him."

Leslie looked at Nina with raised eyebrows. "And the two of you . . . ?"

"Nothing," Nina said. "Honestly. I'd tell you. It's nothing. I'm with Tim."

"Is this something we need to talk about?" Leslie asked. "Do you want to talk about it?"

"I don't know what I want," Nina said. Then she paused. "I want my dad, is what I want." And her bottom lip started trembling, as if it had a heart all its own.

Leslie pulled Nina to her. "I know," she said. "But you've got me."

Nina wiped her eyes and leaned her head against Leslie's, grateful, at least, for that.

"Come with me to the bathroom. We've got to fix your eyeliner."

Nina let Leslie lead her to the restroom, wondering how she'd get through the rest of the day without someone telling her what to do. Grief felt like it mixed up her brain and her heart, put them back in the wrong places. She wasn't sure how she'd set that right ever again.

32

LESLIE STAYED THAT NIGHT, TOO, IN THE GUEST ROOM that had the same bedding as the rooms in the Gregory hotels. When Nina was furnishing her apartment, her father went on a familiar tirade against guest rooms with uncomfortable bedding. Nina figured the easiest way to avoid an argument was to accept when he offered to outfit the whole room for her. So the sheets were Egyptian cotton. The blanket, merino wool. The pillows filled with goose feathers. All in shades of cream and gold.

The two women sat cross-legged on the bed, wearing pajama pants and T-shirts, looking almost the way they did fourteen years before, when they were trading essay outlines for Directed Studies, neither of them confident in her thoughts or the way she'd expressed them. But now Leslie dyed her hair to hide the handful of silver strands that kept appearing at her temples. And Nina rubbed cream around her eyes every night, trying to stop the progression of the crow's feet she saw forming when she smiled. They'd aged, they'd grown; Leslie had gotten married, given birth to a son. But when they were together, they became their college selves, Leslie brash and bold and unstoppable, Nina perceptive and observant and quietly commanding. Leslie's husband, Vijay, once said their personalities had rubbed off on each other over the years, tempering their extremes. But maybe they'd just gotten older.

"Are you thinking about tomorrow?" Leslie asked, when Nina had gone quiet.

"I'm thinking . . ." Nina said, "about kids. If I have kids, they won't know my dad. My mom either."

Leslie picked up one of the glasses of wine she'd poured for them. "Cole never met my mom," she said. "But he still knows her."

Nina lifted her wineglass and took a sip. She'd had more to drink today than she'd had in any twenty-four-hour period in her life. The low-grade buzz helped, though. It dulled everything and made her understand why people took Xanax. "I guess it's the same with my grandparents," Nina said, thinking more about it. "I know their stories—how the first painting my grandmother bought was a Lee Krasner. How my grandfather stole his teacher's grade book in seventh grade to try to hide a B in history."

"Exactly," Leslie said. "We put my mom's picture on Cole's dresser. And he knows that his name starts with a *C* to honor her. Whenever we go swimming we talk about how she loved to swim so much that Jodi and I were convinced she was a mermaid when we were kids. I almost cried in the middle of a Target a few months ago when Cole saw a mermaid doll and asked if we could buy it because Grandma Cheryl probably would have liked it."

Nina smiled at that. "He's a sweet kid."

"Thank goodness," Leslie said. "Imagine if I gave birth to an asshole?"

"Not possible," Nina told her.

"So what would you tell your future kids about your dad?" Leslie asked after another sip of wine. "What would you want them to know about him?"

Nina leaned back against one of the pillows, her head cradled by its softness. She thought about her imaginary children. In her mind now they always had Tim's auburn hair, her mother's freckles, and her father's blue eyes. Maybe she would make sweet potato pie with them, using the recipe her dad liked. Maybe they'd start their own turkey collection. And their own traditions in his honor.

"Remember that year you came home for Thanksgiving with me?" Nina asked.

Leslie nodded. "Our junior year. After my mom died. I didn't want to go back to Massachusetts."

"Mm-hm," Nina said.

"Your dad went all out for Thanksgiving that year." Leslie shifted so she and Nina were both resting against pillows, facing the painting on the other side of the room. It was something Nina had bought at a gallery on a whim when she and Tim had gone to an opening a couple of months ago. It looked like a Kandinsky, but with more attitude.

"He went all out for Thanksgiving every year after my mom died." Since Nina's mom had died on Christmas Day, for years afterward, she and her father couldn't look at trees or twinkling lights or listen to Christmas carols without falling apart. So Nina's dad decided that their big family holiday would be Thanksgiving. He made it a full-day affair, with an early-morning party to watch the Thanksgiving Day Parade out their window, and breakfast, lunch, and dinner for anyone who stopped by at any point in the day. He decorated the apartment with turkeys—first with the ones Nina had cut out using her hand to shape the turkeys' bodies in lower school and then later on with an absurd collection he'd pulled together from antiques shops. Once they'd heard about it, people started gifting him with turkeys; he eventually had so many that they took up an entire cabinet in the dining room.

"That first year," Nina continued, "he wrote a note to everyone who'd helped us, telling them how grateful we were for them. It went over so well that he kept doing it—a note each Thanksgiving for everyone in his orbit, thanking them for whatever it was that the person gave him—friendship, advice, help, a clean apartment, a recommendation for a new wine to try. If I'm being honest, I think it became part of the persona he cultivated, where everyone thought he was their best friend. I like to think it meant something anyway, though. That the messages were heartfelt, even if they had another purpose." She turned to Leslie. "Do I give him too much credit sometimes?"

Leslie shrugged. "Is the *why* more important than the *what*?"

Nina sighed. "That's what I've been trying to figure out for most of my adult life. . . . Maybe I'll start writing notes. I'll make Thanksgiving a big deal with my kids."

Leslie raised her wineglass and turned to Nina. "To your dad. To Thanksgiving." They looked at each other and clinked glasses, keeping their eyes locked until they took a sip. Years ago, Leslie's sister Jodi had told her that if you broke eye contact, it would mean a year of bad sex. Leslie had taken that superstition very seriously in college—at least until she met Vijay. But she and Nina had been doing it out of habit ever since.

Leslie must have been thinking about that, too, because she said, "I know this might not be the most appropriate time to ask this, but now that we're alone: What's going on with that former boss of yours? Because the tension between the two of you was thick enough that even I blushed when you were together."

Nina put her hand to her face, feeling her cheeks get hot again. "Oh God," she said. "Did everyone think that? Did Tim see?"

Leslie refilled Nina's wineglass. "I don't think so. And no one else knows you like I do, so they probably wouldn't have picked up on what I did. But—whoa!" Leslie fanned herself with her hand.

Nina cracked a brief smile. "Nothing untoward has happened, if that's what you're asking."

"But?" Leslie prompted.

"But he's . . . made it pretty clear he's interested. And I've . . . I've imagined a lot." Nina couldn't look at Leslie when she said it. It felt horrible to admit. A confession that even while she was dating someone she imagined her future with, her mind strayed. When Leslie didn't respond right away, Nina looked up and saw her friend looking down at her wineglass.

"Aren't you going to say something?" Nina asked.

"I don't want to say the wrong thing," Leslie said. "So I think I'm going to shut up for once. Maybe Vijay's right. You've been a good influence on me."

Nina groaned. "You never say the wrong thing. Sometimes it's not the thing I want to hear, but it's never wrong."

"I'll just say this, then." Leslie turned so she was facing Nina again. "When I was dating Vijay, there wasn't anyone else I was imagining anything with. There still isn't, twelve years later."

Nina tipped her glass of wine so she could get the final sip that was sitting at the bottom. Fortified with that last bit of alcohol, she decided to tell Leslie about Tim's aborted marriage proposal. But she found she couldn't do it. What she ended up with was: "I shouldn't be imagining anything with anyone either. It's just . . . it's not rational."

"Love isn't always rational," Leslie said, carefully. "You know you don't have to date Tim if you'd rather be with someone else."

Nina didn't say anything. She knew that. Of course she knew that.

Nina wondered, again, if her dating life would have been different if her mom were still alive. When Nina brought her high school and college boyfriends home to meet her father, he'd spent the next week talking about their flaws, why they weren't good enough for Nina—not smart enough, not successful enough, not driven enough, not wealthy enough. Her father had been concerned that part of why her college boyfriend, Max, was interested in Nina was her trust fund. And maybe it *was* part of it. She hadn't thought to worry about that before he'd said it.

And that was the thing. After her father brought up these concerns, Nina began to see what he saw. Her high school boyfriend wasn't as polite and respectful as she'd wished he would be. And Max did seem to start arguments with her father whenever they went out to dinner.

"Your grandfather would roll over in his grave if he knew you were dating someone so arrogant and ill-informed," her father had said after one particularly contentious dinner. "Can you imagine how badly he'd reflect on our family if you took him with you to the Met Gala?" Which Nina hadn't done, at her father's request, but she did take him to a family friend's wedding, which caused perhaps the third worst argument Nina and her father had ever had.

Joseph Gregory disliked Max so intensely that Nina didn't introduce the man she dated during business school to her father at all. But that felt wrong, too. And Nina realized then that no matter how exacting her father might be, she could never be with someone long term that he looked down on. And he'd practically given his blessing to Tim.

"Nina?" Leslie asked, softly.

"I think it's time for bed," Nina said, regretting the fact that she'd brought any of this up. "I'm drunk. And tired."

"I know," Leslie said, opening her arm for a hug.

Nina leaned in to her friend. "Thanks for staying the night again," she said.

"Stop it," Leslie said. "There's nowhere I'd rather be."

That night Nina fell into a fitful sleep, without Tim by her side. He'd wanted to give the two women time alone together, but that meant Nina was by herself in bed. She tossed and turned, saw images of her father and her mother merging into one. Stood alone on a barrier island, water lapping at her feet. The ocean became a sea of numbers, which she knew was a test she had to ace or her father would die. And then her father did die. She woke up at four in the morning, her pillow wet with tears and her head aching. That was what she got for going to bed drunk the night before her father's funeral.

She squinted at her phone and saw she had a new text message. Her stomach flipped and she slid on her glasses to see what it was: just a note from her cell phone carrier saying her bill was ready. And she felt deflated.

She'd been hoping it was Rafael.

She fell asleep wondering what her father would have thought of Rafael if the two men had met.

33

THE NEXT DAY, AFTER HER FATHER'S FUNERAL, AFTER TJ spoke about his legacy, his success, his power, after his grave was filled, after her heart felt like it was wrung out and squeezed dry, but somehow still full, Nina knelt down next to the freshly turned dirt and laid her hand on top of it. There was an early fall chill in the air. She hated the idea of leaving him there in the cold; it was his body, even if it was just a husk of who he'd been. Dampness seeped through her skirt where her knees were resting on the ground. There would be circles on the crepe when she stood. Still she stayed.

After a few moments, Nina felt a hand on her back. Then Tim was kneeling next to her.

"We're going to get through this," he said quietly.

"I know," she answered, just as softly.

And in her head, she knew it was true. But her heart was finding it hard to believe.

Tim's arm wrapped around her shoulder and squeezed.

Nina slid her arm around his back.

And the two of them knelt there together, each lost in their own mind for a moment.

"You ready?" Tim asked.

Nina nodded, and they stood, twined together like the hawthorn trees next to the Gregory plot, their arms wrapped so tightly around each other, it was hard to know who was holding up whom.

Maybe they both would've fallen long ago if they hadn't grown together that way.

34

"I HAD AN IDEA," TIM SAID THE NEXT NIGHT. NINA was going through the Gregory Corporation financials, trying to find the thing her father had wanted to talk to her about. But the numbers wouldn't stay in their columns. She couldn't concentrate.

Nina put down the spreadsheet.

"What's your idea?" she asked. Tim had been trying so hard all day, ordering breakfast from Nina's favorite brunch place, making a photo book of her and her dad online and ordering it to arrive the next day, going to the nearest Duane Reade and buying her every single butterscotch candy they had in stock. Things that would normally make her smile, but this time it wasn't working. Still, she loved Tim for trying; she loved him for knowing what she loved.

"Okay, it was actually Priscilla's idea," he said. "She called while you were in the shower and I picked up your phone. Anyway, she thinks the four of us should go to the Dining Room at the Met tonight. She remembered how much you loved it in high school."

She felt lucky to have them, Tim and Priscilla. But even so, she was in no shape for a night out. "I don't think so," she said. "It's a great idea, though."

Tim scratched his beard. Then he snapped his fingers. "The Temple of Dendur," he said. "Forget the Dining Room. They opened it to everyone in June, so it's not as special anymore anyway. But you love the Temple of Dendur."

Nina thought about the room that held the temple. The water, the windows out to the park, the ancient structure that always felt so solid, so stable. "There are always so many people on the weekends," she said. "I'm not fit for the public right now."

Tim smiled, triumphant. "Leave that to me."

A few hours later, they were in a car on the way to the Met. Tim had made a few phone calls, pulled some strings, called in a favor, and secured them a half hour of private time in the temple, along with Priscilla and Brent.

"So what did you say on the phone?" Nina asked, as the car drove up the West Side Highway, knowing that even for them, this was a crazy thing to do.

Tim shook his head. "I just said it was for you. You've got a lot of power in this town, Nina Gregory. Especially at the Met."

"Not true," Nina said. But she thought about his words. In New York City, money was power, and she did have a lot of it. Or at least she would soon. At one of the events she'd gone to with her father in the Met's rooftop garden, a woman had cornered her. "Just look around," the woman had said, swooping her arms around the party, her champagne sparkling along with her beaded dress. "Look who's here. We run this city."

Was that Nina now? Was she one of those people who would drink champagne on the roof of the Met, absorbed in her own importance?

"QUARTER FOR YOUR THOUGHTS?" Tim asked from his seat next to her in the car. They'd decided years ago that the penny hadn't ever been adjusted for inflation, so they'd made their own adjustments.

"Just thinking about power," Nina said.

"The measure of a man is what he does with power," Tim said. "A woman, too."

Nina looked at him for a beat. He wasn't usually someone who quoted Plato—quoted anyone but Mark Zuckerberg or Steve Jobs, actually. "So you've used yours to close the Temple of Dendur for us?"

"No," he said. "I've used yours. But I can't think of anything better to do with power than make the person you love smile."

He slid his hand into hers and held on tight. The car merged into the traffic to cross through the park on 79th Street, and she looked at the trees her father would have seen from his bedroom, might have been looking at just before he died.

35

A FEW DAYS LATER, THE BOARD OF DIRECTORS OF THE
Gregory Corporation were having a meeting. Nina knew she
should go. She should show her face. She should show them
how much she cared. How much she'd absorbed just by growing up as her father's daughter.

Nina got up. She stood in front of her closet staring at the
rows of grays and blues and blacks and browns and creams.
Pantsuits and skirt suits and sheath dresses and blouses.

"Do you need help choosing?" Tim asked, already dressed,
on his way to the kitchen.

"I have nothing to wear," she told him.

He laughed, but she didn't crack a smile. "Of course you do,"
he said. "Look at this closet. You have everything."

And Nina started to sob. "I don't," she said. "I don't have
everything. I don't have my dad."

Tim paled. "I didn't mean that. Nina, I didn't mean—" He
tried to hug her, but she pushed him away, fought her way out
of his grasp.

"Go away," she said. "Just go away."

He took a step back and she melted to the floor, her arms wrapping around her knees, curling herself into a ball.

"Go away," she said again.

And she sat there on the floor of her walk-in closet and cried.

She didn't make it to the board meeting that day.

36

LATER THAT WEEK, NINA WAS AT HER FATHER'S APART-
ment with Irena, packing up boxes of his clothes to donate to
Housing Works. Nina wasn't getting very far, though, because
she kept remembering the last place her father wore that tie, or
that tuxedo, or that striped button-down with paisley cuffs.
She hoped whoever bought that button-down would love it just
as much as her father had. He'd worn it to his birthday dinner
this past year.

Nina folded the shirt, first fastening every other button,
then pulling the sleeves toward the back and bending the shirt
in three, with the collar and buttons on top. She realized that
she folded shirts like her father. So much of the way she lived
her life was the way he did. He talked about his legacy, about
keeping the Gregory legacy alive, but Nina realized that as long
as she lived, so did he. He would be alive in her every time she
folded her laundry, made coffee, celebrated a holiday, took a ski
trip, went for a swim, ran a race. And so, so much more. He'd
always be there. Except that he wouldn't.

Nina put the folded shirt into a box, then went to his dresser to sort through his T-shirts and shorts. She thought about the ten years' worth of Gregory Corporation finances that she still hadn't managed to get through. The numbers swam whenever she looked at them. Even with a ruler, she couldn't keep the lines straight, couldn't keep the strings of profits and losses clear in her mind. But she had to. Soon. She would, she promised herself. She'd figure it out tomorrow.

TJ HAD SAID he needed to talk to Nina about her father's will, so she'd told him to come over after he finished work. When he got there, he looked exhausted, like he hadn't slept in days, his eyes bloodshot and puffy. He was running the corporation on his own, handling the board of directors until Nina got up to speed, until she took her rightful place as daughter and heir. She felt bad about how hard he was working, but she could barely string two sentences together. She kept walking into her kitchen and finding a stack of Post-it notes in the refrigerator or a carton of milk in the freezer, completely unsure of how they'd gotten there. She wasn't ready to do much of anything— certainly nothing having to do with her family's business.

"You doing okay?" he asked her.

Nina shrugged. She was still standing, still moving, still living. Though her relationship with Tim felt strained. It wasn't his fault. In the past week, the smallest word, the most innocuous sentence could set Nina off into a spiral of sobs or shut a conversation down completely. Her emotions surprised both of them. Her mind felt like a minefield and he was treading as cautiously as he could. He was treating her like she was fragile, unstable, about to explode at any moment. And even though she felt that way, she didn't want to be treated like that. So she'd started spending more time alone, with books, on the phone with Leslie. "As well as can be expected, I guess," she said. "I'm dressed. I ate today. I'm sorting through his race T-shirts without melting down completely." She shrugged again.

TJ nodded. She figured he probably felt the same way. He didn't say anything more, as if he were conserving his strength for something else altogether.

"Want to sit over there?" she asked, pointing toward the table and chairs on the other side of the great room. This, for some reason, felt like a conversation that needed a table.

"Sure," TJ said, walking over and putting the folder he'd had under his arm on the table. Then he rubbed his puffy eyes. "So," he said, "I have your father's will."

Nina nodded.

"I told you about the company," he said. "You always knew you'd be getting his majority stake in the Gregory Corporation."

Nina nodded again.

"Well," TJ said. "In addition to the company, it won't be a surprise that your father left you everything else: his stock portfolio, this apartment, your grandparents' house in East Hampton, the two cars out there, the Mercedes in the city, the boat, and . . . the house upstate."

Nina looked at him. "What house upstate?"

TJ looked down at his hands. He opened his mouth and closed it again.

Then it clicked. The house that her mother had been at when she'd died. The house her father had bought her as a wedding present. The house Nina hadn't seen since she was eight.

"My mother's house," she said, answering her own question. "I thought he sold that a long time ago."

"He couldn't," TJ said simply. "He hired a gardener to care for the property, someone to run the water so the pipes wouldn't freeze. He had it painted every few years, cleaned every once in a while. But he couldn't bring himself to sell it. And couldn't bring himself to visit it again either."

Nina was stunned. How had her father owned a house—her mother's house—for decades and not told her?

"These are the keys," TJ continued, handing her a key ring. It was a Tiffany ring with a heart on it. Priscilla'd had her apartment keys on a similar one when they were in high school. Nina wondered if her father had bought the key ring when he'd bought the house, if that was how he'd presented the gift to her mom.

"Thank you," Nina said, automatically, even as she wondered what other secrets her father might have kept.

"Jack, at the investment firm, will be able to walk you through all of the finances. He's been in touch with your father's lawyer, who will take care of whatever legal issues need to be handled. You should talk to Jack at some point soon. Not a rush, but not *not* a rush. Everything is part of your dad's estate for now, while the will is in probate. He made me the executor, so I can help, too, if you need something."

Nina nodded, still thinking about that house. Why didn't her dad tell her about it? He must've had a reason. Maybe he thought it would be too painful for her, especially when she was young. But still, that didn't explain now. That didn't explain the past twenty-four years.

"I mean that not just with the will," TJ said. "I know I'm not your dad, but I've known you since the day you were born, and I've loved you just as long. So if there's anything . . . I promised him . . ."

Nina saw the tears filling TJ's eyes and felt them in her own.

"Thank you," she said again, but this time it wasn't automatic. This time it came from her heart. She knew how much TJ had done for her father in the end, and how hard taking care of everything was for him. But that was how close TJ and her father's friendship had been—like Leslie and Nina, they'd been inseparable since their first year at Yale. Until now.

Nina and TJ hugged, and then TJ said he had to go take care of a few more things. Nina nodded. She would help soon, just like she'd promised her father. She just had to get her mind straightened out first. It had to be in working order before she started a new job, proved herself to a staff who thought of her as their old boss's daughter. Nina walked TJ to the door, then sat back at the dining table, looking at the keys. There was an address written on them in Caro's handwriting, taped to one side of the heart.

Nina pulled out her phone and typed the address into Google Maps, turning it to satellite mode. The house was small, white, two stories, with a wraparound porch and latticework that made it look like it was built out of gingerbread. Nina zoomed in on the door, which was painted a bright red. There were crocuses and hydrangeas in the front yard. She remembered that house. Her mother's house. Now her house.

Nina took a breath and called Tim.

"Hey," he said, after one ring. "You okay?" It was what he asked her every time they spoke now. Every time they saw each other. Nina felt like she was letting him down every time she said *Not really.*

"I just inherited my mom's house," she said, ignoring the question. "That I didn't even know my dad still owned. Can you take a drive with me tomorrow?"

"Of course," Tim said. "It'll be nice to get away. Go on a little adventure."

She appreciated his positivity, but this wasn't a weekend getaway. And she didn't think it was an adventure, either. Nina had no idea what she'd find in that house.

37

"I JUST DON'T UNDERSTAND," NINA KEPT SAYING AS she drove her father's Mercedes up the Hudson. Tim had wanted to call a car service, the way they usually did when they left Manhattan, but Nina hadn't wanted to let a driver in on this trip. It felt too personal. So Tim had relented. "My father didn't mention this house for more than two decades. Seriously. Who keeps a house hidden for more than two decades?"

Tim kept looking over at the speedometer. "Are you going too fast?" he asked.

Nina looked down. "I'm going exactly sixty-four miles per hour."

"That's above the speed limit," he said. "Be careful. You're not used to driving."

Tim had never bothered to get a driver's license—he'd lived in New York City all his life, except for four years at Stanford—and was never quite comfortable in the front seat of a car. Nina's father had insisted that she learn to drive, both automatic and stick, so she'd learned while she was at the house in the

Hamptons one summer, in a series of lessons with her father, who winced every time she popped the clutch on his classic TVR sports car.

But other than when she was out of the city, which hadn't been all that often that past summer, she rarely drove.

"I promise, we'll be fine," Nina said.

"We used to all come up here," Tim said after a moment. "Do you remember? I haven't thought about it in forever."

"Yeah, me neither," Nina answered, keeping her eyes on the road in front of her, "but we did. We went hiking, I think. You, me, my mom, your mom."

"I remember that, too. And one time we had a picnic somewhere there were sculptures."

"It must've been Storm King," Nina said. She wished she could remember more.

"It really is weird that no one talked about this house again after your mom died," Tim said. Nina could feel his eyes on her, watching her expression, checking to see if he'd said the wrong thing again.

Somehow the appearance of this house, her mother's house, made things worse. She felt like she was a water balloon—emotions filling her tight—and all it would take was one prick for them to gush out, soaking her and everyone around her.

The last time Nina ever saw her mother was Christmas morning. She and her parents were still in their pajamas, even though Maeve, the au pair, was fully dressed. Nina's mom was wearing red silk pajama pants with a matching top. That was the last thing she saw her mother dressed in—red silk pajamas. For years, Nina avoided the color red, even on pencils or notebooks. She still didn't have any red in her wardrobe.

That Christmas, she'd just opened her presents: matching

clothing for her and her American Girl doll, Molly—the one with glasses like Nina's. A set of Anne of Green Gables books, since she'd finished the Emily of New Moon trilogy and had loved it. An electric keyboard with a pair of headphones because she'd just started piano lessons. A ski sweater from her aunt Daphne, her mom's sister, sent all the way from Colorado. And a gold necklace with her name written on it in script, a heart over the letter *i*. Priscilla had gotten one that year, too—everyone had said how lucky she was to have two *i*s in her name, so she got to have two hearts.

Nina's father gave her mother a diamond tennis bracelet that she told him was too much, but which Nina could tell she really loved. And Nina gave her a Spanish novel. Her father had helped her pick it out and had said he was sure her mother hadn't read that one yet. Nina's mom had gotten a gift in the mail from her sister, too, a ski sweater that was almost the same as Nina's. They'd skied in Massachusetts and Vermont and for a week in Zermatt the year before. TJ, Caro, and Tim hadn't come on that trip, and Nina's parents had spent an entire day skiing the blue slopes with her instead of insisting she go to ski school. It was one of the best days of Nina's life.

"Are we going skiing this year?" Nina asked her mother when she opened the box with the sweater inside.

"Of course," her father answered. "Maybe Aspen next month."

Nina's mom looked at him. "We can't go to Colorado and ski Aspen." She was crumpling up wrapping paper, wadding it into a compact ball.

Nina stroked her new sweater. "What's wrong with Aspen?" she'd asked, following the path of the silver-threaded snow-flake across its blue woolen background.

"Nothing," her father said, and then went to open his gifts. Nina had made him a mosaic picture frame in art class and had put a picture of them inside, which he told her he'd put on his desk at work. And then he picked up another gift with his name on it and opened the card. When he read it, his eyes widened.

"What is it?" Nina's mother said. "Who's that one from?"

"Just someone at work," he responded. "Did one of the doormen bring this up? When did it get here?"

Nina nodded. "Harold gave it to me yesterday," she said, all of a sudden worried she'd done something wrong. "He told me someone dropped it off and said to give it to you. Since it was a Christmas present, I put it under the tree."

"Who's it from?" Nina's mother asked again, an edge in her voice now. "Joseph, can I see the card?"

Nina's head ping-ponged back and forth between them, trying to figure out what was happening.

"Nina," Maeve said, standing up from her seat on the couch. "Why don't you and I bring those Christmas cookies we made down to Harold? Let's see if we can find the super and the porters, too, and wish them all a Happy Christmas."

"But you didn't open your gifts yet," Nina said. "And Daddy didn't finish." All of a sudden Christmas felt wrong. Something was going on that she didn't understand.

"It's okay," Maeve answered. "I'll open them later. You can help, if you'd like. I bet Harold will be so glad to get your cookies."

"Okay," Nina said slowly, looking at her parents, still confused. But she knew when a sentence was an order even when it wasn't said that way.

• • •

WHEN NINA AND MAEVE came back from delivering cookies, Nina's mother had gone. "She went to the country," her father said.

"But why?" Nina asked. "We haven't had Christmas dinner yet. I'm still wearing pajamas. Why didn't we go with her?"

Sometimes her mom went to the country by herself for a day or two, when city life started to feel too chaotic, or when something unkind was said about her in the press.

"I'm a professor, not a fashion plate," she'd said once, in frustration, as the family drove up to the house together, after someone had written an in-depth article about her choice to wear ballet flats instead of heels to a cocktail party.

"You're both," her father had answered. "It comes with the territory."

"MOM NEEDED SOME SPACE," he told Nina that Christmas morning.

"But it's Christmas!" Nina said. "Did someone write something mean about her again? Is that what was in the card?"

Nina's father pulled her in for a hug. "Well," he said, "I guess you could say that."

AND THEN LATER THAT NIGHT they'd gotten word that her mother's car had slipped on the ice and crashed into a tree. The paramedics did all they could, but they hadn't been able to revive her. Nina had asked her father, over and over, but she'd never found out who that gift was from or why her mother left. And eventually, in the chaos of all that came next and the anguish of her grief, she'd forgotten about it. Now that she remembered, she wanted to pick up the phone and call her dad, ask him what really had happened the day her mother died. Why he'd never told her. She'd had all these chances over the years, millions of them, but hadn't thought about it. And now, now that it seemed so important, she didn't have any chances left.

Nina had the urge to press her foot down on the gas pedal, zoom forward, and fly, fly like nothing else mattered, like she could leave her whole life behind and start fresh, somewhere new. Her foot moved, the car sped up. Faster. It felt so good that it scared her.

But then she tapped on the brakes. She could handle this. She *would* handle this. She wasn't going anywhere.

38

WHEN THEY REACHED THE HOUSE, NINA BROUGHT THE car to a stop. A deluge of memories washed over her. She remembered much more than she'd thought she did: the rosebushes that she wasn't supposed to touch, the wild strawberry patch that grew berries so small they looked like doll food, the deep red and bright orange of the autumnal leaves. Wave upon wave of memories hit her, a tsunami of words and images.

"Shall we?" Tim asked, after they'd sat in the driveway for a while.

Nina turned the ignition off but didn't make a move to get out of the car. The urge to fly took over. To race out of there. But she suppressed it.

Instead, she gathered her courage like she did her memories, pulling them in close, and willed herself to open the door.

Their feet crunched on the stones of the driveway. The porch creaked, and so did the hinges of the door.

"We should oil that," Tim said.

Nina nodded. Then she saw the kitchen. The granite island

in the center, the framed advertisements for 1950s brands of soap and salt and soda lining the wall. She remembered herself dancing with her parents in that kitchen, wiggling around to "Twist and Shout," the whole family relaxed in a way they never felt in Manhattan.

Tim walked through the French doors into the living room, stopping in front of the fireplace. "We made s'mores here," he said.

"Did we?" Nina asked, but then she remembered marshmallows on wooden shish-kebab sticks, the smell of roasting sugar as they turned brown and gooey.

"Mm-hm," Tim said. "I think that was the same trip we made that gingerbread castle."

"That was here?" Nina asked. She remembered making the castle with him, but her memory had placed it in New York City. On Central Park West. In apartment 21-B.

"I'm pretty sure," he said.

Tim's memory of their childhood was always a little better than Nina's, maybe because he was two years older. "Wait, those chairs," Nina said, combing her memory of making the gingerbread castle with Tim. "Did we make it at that table?"

"I think so," he said. "I remember those chairs, too."

"Wow," Nina said. "I feel like my whole sense of our childhood is shifting. I can't believe I forgot all of this. I can't believe my mind moved those memories to Manhattan."

Tim shrugged. "Not talking about your mom. Not ever coming back to this place. It's easy to see how those memories would fade—or that your mind would alter them."

"I guess," Nina said, wondering what else her mind had changed, what other memories weren't quite true, suddenly not trusting her own history.

She walked into the kitchen and opened the refrigerator. Empty. Literally empty. The pantry too. No one had eaten a meal here in decades.

"We'll need some food," Nina said. "If we stay more than a few hours."

"Do you want to?" Tim asked. "Stay more than a few hours?" They'd packed clothes, just in case.

Nina looked around. She was pretty sure she remembered sitting on that couch while her mother read her *Caps for Sale*. "Yeah," she said. "How about we stay the night?"

"Works for me," Tim said. "I saw a grocery store in town. I can take a walk and get us some provisions while you explore your new old house a little more."

"I can come," Nina said, not sure she wanted to explore the house alone, but not wanting to admit it. She was tired of feeling so fragile, of letting anyone—even Tim—see that fragility. "We can drive, it'll be a lot quicker."

"We're Manhattanites," Tim said. "We walk places. Besides, I could use the exercise."

Maybe he was right; maybe exploring the house would be better without him. It would give her space to process her emotions. "Okay, go for it," she said. "I'll check out the second floor."

Once Tim left, Nina headed upstairs. She opened the first door on the right and saw her bedroom. As soon as she walked in, she remembered the white wallpaper with silver metallic polka dots and the lavender gauzy curtains. The furniture was all white wood, and so was the floor, with a lavender circular rug underneath her canopied bed. There were three books from her Baby-Sitters Little Sister series sitting on the dresser that she must've ended up rebuying in the city. There was even a pair of her elementary-school-sized snow boots in the corner of the room. It was a house stopped in time. Everything was covered in a light layer of dust. Nina wondered how long ago her father'd had the place cleaned. She continued down the hallway and found the bathroom, the guest room, the office, and—at the very end—her parents' room. She remembered the striped wallpaper, the brass bed frame. The television on the dresser was small and boxy, clearly from when George Bush was president. The first one.

Nina sat down on the bed. She didn't have a ton of memories of her mom, but sitting here, she remembered one she was pretty sure she could trust. It was summer, so her mom wasn't teaching, and Nina wasn't in school. They'd come up to the country for a long time, just the two of them. A few weeks, maybe a month. And her dad came up on the weekends, but not all of them.

"What would you think about taking a trip to Colorado?" her mother asked. "You know you have a new baby cousin out there."

"I do?" Nina said. She knew her mom had grown up in Colorado, that her aunt and uncle and grandpa lived there, but they hardly ever visited. Her dad didn't like it out there. He didn't get along with her mom's father or her younger sister very well. They thought that he'd changed her—turned her into someone who wanted to live in a world that made them uncomfortable. His gifts were never appreciated, which hurt him. It might have been why her father always wanted Nina to date men who traveled in the same circles she did. He didn't want her to repeat his mistakes, make her life more difficult than it had to be. Even if making money didn't matter to her the way it did to him, it was still there. It was still the world she knew.

"You know, Ballerina, you're not just a Gregory. You're a Lukas, too," her mother told her that summer. "That was my last name before I married your dad. Maybe we could make some plans to spend time in Colorado soon and you could get to know that part of the family better."

"Okay," Nina'd said. "And I can play with my cousin."

"Sounds good to me." Only it never happened. They didn't visit Colorado over the summer, and then her mom died that Christmas, and Nina had never met her cousin. Actually, after her mother's funeral, she'd only seen her aunt once more—and had never seen her grandfather again. When she'd asked her dad about it, he said, "They don't want to be a part of our world."

"But I want to be a part of theirs," Nina replied. Her aunt Daphne sounded just like her mom when she talked. They had the same laugh. And she always hugged Nina extra hard when they saw each other.

"No, you don't," he said. "I promise. They don't like us."

And that was what she'd grown up thinking. That her mother's family didn't like them. But was that true?

Nina wondered, now, if the time she and her mom spent at the country house that summer was an indication of something she hadn't realized then. Something that was wrong in her parents' marriage, that made her mother think more about her own family, about visiting them with her daughter and not her husband. Something that reached its apex on Christmas Day.

Nina walked to the closet, hoping to find something there. What, she didn't know. Perhaps a dress that would rekindle a memory. A bottle of her mother's perfume. A book she'd forgotten existed but had once loved.

With her heart beating hard, she opened the closet door. And there was something inside. But not what Nina hoped. A few pairs of jeans. Some sweaters. A pair of sneakers. Clothing she didn't remember at all. She was getting a small piece of her mom back, after all these years, but it wasn't enough, not nearly enough. Nina pulled out the jeans and held them up to her own legs. Her mother was shorter than she was, Nina discovered, by about an inch. She'd never wondered if she'd grown to be taller than her mother. In fact, she'd always assumed she hadn't. In her mind, her mother always seemed so tall. Nina was only a year younger, now, than her mother was when she'd worn these clothes. Nina wondered if her mother felt as confused as she did sometimes. As conflicted. She wished more than anything that she could ask her. *Mom*, she thought, *I wish you were here with me.*

Nina hung the jeans back up and opened the drawer in the night table she remembered was on her mother's side of the bed. Inside she found a drawing she had no recollection of making. It was a yard with grass and two bunnies. Nina had written *Hoppy Sunday!* on it. And she'd labeled all of the items in Spanish and English with arrows—*tree arbol*, her younger self had written, *bunny conejito, sky cielo, sun sol, lawn cesped, flowers flores*. She wondered now if it was a project her mother had given her, the Spanish professor helping her daughter learn, or if it was something Nina had created on her own to make her mother happy.

Either way the drawing made her smile. She wondered if Rafael had made similar drawings, or if it was different, growing up bilingual, two languages being an innate part of who you were instead of learning the building blocks of a second language one by one. Nina pulled her phone out of her back pocket and snapped a picture of the drawing.

Then she looked around the room some more. There was her parents' wedding picture standing on the dresser next to a picture of her mother holding an infant Nina. Both of them were asleep on a couch, Nina on her mother's chest, her hands gripping her mother's wavy, dark hair. Nina picked it up, trying to see herself in the tapering of her mother's fingers, or the tilt of her neck. She thought maybe the shape of their earlobes was the same.

It was mind-blowing to be here. This place she grew up in but didn't. This house she had known but forgotten. It was a place where memories lived. Where they'd been stored up waiting for her, but she never knew. And now that she did, now that she'd found them, the one person who'd been keeping them from her was the only person she wanted to share them with.

39

THERE WAS A KNOCK ON THE DOOR, AND NINA WENT downstairs to answer it. Tim was back, carrying two bags of food.

"You wouldn't believe what I found," he said as he walked into the kitchen and put them down on the island.

Nina began unpacking and smiled, realizing Tim had bought everything he usually bought for his own apartment. Roasted chicken, kalamata olives, cheddar cheese. At least dinner would be easy. "What did you find?" she asked.

He pulled an elaborate gingerbread kit out of the second bag of groceries. One that would look like a castle, with a drawbridge and parapets and four different turrets. "Just like the one we made a million years ago. The store was unpacking these when I got there—the first holiday shipment of the season."

"THIS IS LOOKING EVEN better than our castle did when we were kids," Tim said, later, as he held two gingerbread walls together so that Nina could pipe icing on the outside corner.

"I don't know, that was a pretty good one," Nina said, concentrating on keeping the icing straight and even. "If my memory serves." Though, of course, now she was wondering if it did.

"We had fun when we were kids, didn't we." Tim moved on to the balustrade, icing the bottom so it would stick to the top of the terrace before Nina added the piping. "We've always made a great team."

Nina thought about the epic sand sculptures they built on Georgica Beach with their dads' occasional directions, the surprise party they made when they found out that Richard, who took care of the house in East Hampton, was turning forty, roping in all the adults to celebrate and getting the cook they had that summer to make a cake in the shape of a football, since that was Richard's favorite sport. She remembered, too, how Tim joined her under the table during the first Christmas without her mom, when she couldn't face the adults anymore, with the sympathy in their eyes. Tim had crawled under the table with a plate of cookies. "Thought you might be hungry," was all he'd said. And they'd stayed there eating cookies until she was ready to come out again.

"We did. Nina and Tim, Friends Until the End—isn't that what our parents used to say?"

Tim paused in his icing to look at Nina.

"Okay, I'm too gooey," she said. "I have to wash my hands or I'm going to stick to the piping bag." Nina got up from the table, but Tim stopped her with his hand on her wrist.

"Wait," he said, his voice serious. She sat back down. "I want to say something. I've been trying to figure out how to say this the right way ever since the conversation we had in your dad's kitchen."

Nina's heart sped up. She knew what was coming next.

Unconsciously her eye went to her left ring finger. She licked off the tiny bit of frosting that was on her knuckle.

Tim cleared his throat. "I've been thinking about a lot recently, with your dad gone, with our lives changing. It's been hard, and I know I haven't always said the right thing or done the right thing, but Nina, I don't want to lose you. I keep thinking about what would happen if you died, how shattered I'd be. I know, it's morbid and awful, but I can't get the image out of my mind. And I keep thinking about being here with you now, being with you at your dad's funeral. I want to always be with you. The world seems more manageable when we travel through it together. This is what I should've said before, but it took me a while to figure out how to say it.

"I've never loved anyone else the way I love you. When I dated other women, I was always looking for what we have, the closeness, the comfort, the unconditional support. When I think about children, I think about having them with you. When I think about living out the rest of my life, I think about doing it with you by my side. That awe I felt when I first met you, when you were fifteen hours old and I cried when they made me leave you—I don't know if it's ever gone away." His eyes were wide, open, almost pleading. He got down on one knee and pulled a ring box out of his back pocket. "I couldn't get to your mom's ring," he said, "because of the will and everything. So . . . I bought you a new one. And maybe that's better. It's our story, not anyone else's."

"Oh, Tim," Nina said. She looked at him, the person she'd known and loved her entire life, and took the box from his hand, opening it up as she did. Inside was an exquisitely beautiful ring. A round diamond surrounded by sapphires, with smaller diamonds set into the platinum band that would encircle her finger.

The sapphires were the same color as the drop her father had gotten her, the same color as the bracelet, as her eyes. Of course she would say yes. Of course she would.

"Nina?" he asked, softly, as he stood. Then he reached over and brushed frosting off her cheek and she laughed, sliding the ring onto her finger. It fit perfectly.

"I'm a mess," she said. "But yes. Of course yes. And, Tim, this ring is gorgeous."

Tim kissed her, and she wrapped her arms around him. And she started to cry.

"It's gonna be okay," Tim said, wiping the tears from her cheeks with his fingers. His breath smelled like the gumdrop he'd just eaten. "We're going to make it okay."

"I know," she said, leaning her head against Tim's chest, feeling its solidity and warmth. Feeling his heart beat so strong and steady. He knew her. He was the man her father had always wanted her to be with—whom he'd given his permission to the day before he died. Maybe this was her dad's last gift to her.

40

THAT NIGHT, NINA HAD WANTED TO SLEEP IN HER
old bedroom, so they made up her double bed and climbed into
it, under the white eyelet canopy. Nina took the ring off and put
it next to her on the bedside table. She often slept in jewelry,
but that ring took up a solid third of her finger. It seemed too
big to sleep in, like she could hurt herself with it.

"Everything's going to be better from here," Tim said.

They'd decided to keep their engagement secret for a while,
even from his parents. It didn't seem like the right time to announce something joyful, so close to her dad's death.

Nina answered Tim with a kiss. Then they snuggled and
cuddled, running their fingers up and down each other's bodies, along the curves of their torsos. In other relationships Nina
had been in, physical attraction had been one of the main drivers of the relationship. She'd dated Alex the summer she lived
in D.C. after finishing her MBA. They would spend whole
weekends without putting on clothes. They couldn't keep their
hands off each other. In photos he would smile serenely while

secretly sliding his hand along her backside or, if they were sitting at a table, between her legs. The last night, before she headed back to New York, they'd gone to the Lincoln Memorial at two A.M. and had sex in the shadows of the monument, her sitting on his lap, a long skirt keeping them shielded from any passersby.

They'd both gone into that relationship knowing it would be a summer fling. He was joining the State Department, heading to Moscow in September. And she was fine with that. Sometimes the intensity of their attraction scared her. She found herself doing things she knew she shouldn't—calling in sick to work so she could spend the day with him, blowing off plans with college friends because all of a sudden his night was free. Alex never asked, never pressured her; she wanted to do these things to be with him, and that was what she found frightening. Tim never made her feel that way. He made her feel safe. In control.

Nina ran her fingers up his chest, under his T-shirt, through the tangle of hair there, feeling the smoothness of the skin around his nipples.

Tim followed suit, running his hand across the bare skin of her stomach, trailing his fingers under her silk cami, across her breasts.

This felt right. It felt like what was supposed to happen, how she was supposed to spend her life.

Then the pressure of his hand disappeared, and it was on the hem of her shirt, a question.

Nina answered by raising her arms so he could slide it over her head. After Tim took off her shirt, he removed his own, and she could feel the heat radiating from his body.

His hand played along the waistband of her lace underwear, dipping to touch the warm skin beneath it.

She reached for him under the covers, freeing him from the confines of his cotton boxers and then stroking her fingers along the length of him.

"Oh, Nina," he breathed, then slid his underwear down.

She did the same to hers.

And then he was inside her, moving slowly, purposefully. She joined in the rhythm of his rocking, and it felt like a slow dance, the two of them moving in time with each other to the music playing just for them.

Nina felt a pressure swelling inside her. "Right there," she whispered.

She was close, so close.

But then Tim's body stiffened, his mouth forming a perfect O as he groaned, and whatever was about to crest inside her faded away, receded like waves on the beach.

"Did you . . . ?" he asked.

She'd been getting there. Almost. Not quite.

She shook her head. "But it's okay," she said, relaxing against the pillow. "It still felt good. I don't always."

"I know," he said, reaching under the covers to find his underwear and slip it back on. "But I like it better when you do."

She laughed. "Me too," she said, patting the blanket in search of her own underwear, then thinking better of it. "I don't see any tissues in here. I'm going to go to the bathroom to clean up."

"Okay," Tim answered, laying his head down. "In case I'm asleep by the time you get back, I'll say I love you now. And sweet dreams."

"You, too," Nina said, and she kissed the tip of his nose before she got out of the bed.

After the insanity and sadness of the past weeks, there was something so nice about being here with Tim, as if crossing the city limits made the rest of the world disappear. But she knew eventually they'd have to go home, and she'd have to run the Gregory Corporation. Eventually the rest of her life would start. And maybe, once it did, she'd figure out how to tell Tim she wanted to orgasm, too. Every time.

41

IT WAS 3:22 A.M. AND NINA WAS STILL AWAKE. TIM'S arm was wrapped around her as if she were his security blanket. She knew she needed sleep, but her mind was awhirl. She stared at the lace canopy on the bed, trying to find shapes in the fabric the way she and her mother used to do with clouds on a summer day. When she closed her eyes, her thoughts kept spiraling through her mother's death and her father's death and marrying Tim, and not being able to tell her father, and all the new memories she'd unearthed by coming to this house. Memories she wasn't sure if she could trust but wanted to just the same.

Nina pulled her phone into bed with her and went to her photos to look at one of her father. He had been gone barely a week, and she was already afraid she'd forget what he looked like, the exact shape of his eyebrows, the depth of the widow's peak in his hairline. She brought him up on her screen, and immediately her eyes began to fill.

Nina wiped her tears and scrolled through more pictures.

And then she got to the photo she'd taken that afternoon of the drawing she'd made for her mom. The one that made her wonder if Rafael had ever made something similar. Rafael, who might be awake now. She thought about the conversation they'd had the night her father died, how he'd offered to listen if she ever needed someone in the middle of the night. Even though Tim was here, she felt like she needed someone. Someone else who could help her untangle all her thoughts. Rafael would be good at that. But then she remembered what he'd said to her at her father's wake: *We can be whatever we want to be.* She wouldn't call him.

The photo was blurry. Even though she wouldn't call Rafael, she might want to send him the picture, say hello. So Nina lifted Tim's arm off her stomach and slid quietly out of bed. She padded into her parents' bedroom and opened her mother's drawer. When she lifted the drawing to photograph it better, she discovered a sealed envelope underneath. Nina picked it up and flipped it over. It was addressed to her father in her mother's loopy handwriting.

Nina felt her heart race. Without giving it a second thought, she slid her finger underneath the envelope's flap and opened up the sheaf of handwritten pages inside.

December 25, 1992

The day her mother died.

Dear Joseph,

I don't know what to say. I don't know how it got this bad.

Nina stopped reading. She folded the letter back up and slipped it back into the envelope. She didn't want to know. This was private. Between her parents. For her father's eyes only.

But maybe it had the answers she'd been wondering about.

Maybe it talked about the mysterious Christmas present. Besides, her father was gone. Her mother was, too. Whose confidence was she really breaking?

Nina opened it again.

After the summer, after all we went through, all we talked about, you said you'd stop seeing her. I thought you'd do it, if not for me and Nina, then for your father and his legacy. But apparently you didn't.

I don't know if I'll be able to forgive you this time.

I don't know if I'll be able to trust you again.

And if we separate, if we divorce, if the truth about this woman comes out, do you know how that will affect Nina? What the press will do to all of us?

I think maybe she and I should go away. To Colorado, perhaps. I'll take a leave, and she can do the rest of the school year out there. We can say my sister needed me. Or we can figure out another cover story.

You screwed up, Joe. You really screwed up. I would say this all to your face, but I think I'd break down before I got through it, I think you might be able to convince me not to go through with it, but I need to, Joe, and I need you to know why.

There was more. There were pages more, but Nina stopped there. She couldn't keep going.

Her father had cheated on her mother.

He'd taken what was beautiful and destroyed it.

And now Nina knew.

Her father wasn't who she thought he was.

She couldn't trust her memories.

She couldn't trust him.

Could she trust anything at all?

42

NUMB, NINA CLIMBED BACK INTO BED, SLIPPED BE-
tween the sheets, and pulled Tim's arm back over her stomach.
Trying to draw comfort from his familiar solidity.

Her parents' love story was fake. The *People* magazine spread
framed in the lobby of the Gregory hotels was just a story they'd
created. Or maybe it was something that once was true but
wasn't for a long time. A glamour they allowed the world to
believe—wanted the world to believe.

She couldn't believe her parents had done that. Had lied.
Not just to the world, but to her.

Was her father too embarrassed to tell her the truth? Too
ashamed? She thought about the line in her mother's letter: *I
don't know if I can ever trust you again.* Could Nina trust anything her father had told her? And who was the woman? Was it
someone Nina knew? Had known? Someone who came to
Thanksgiving dinners? Ever? Still?

She pulled herself closer to Tim. He tightened his arm

around her in his sleep and she let her body shape itself around his. Tim opened his eyes halfway.

"Morning," he said to her.

"Not morning yet," she told him quietly. She wondered for a moment about telling him what she'd found, but she needed to make sense of it herself first. She wanted to shut off her brain, so she pressed her lips against his. Tim responded, kissing her back tentatively. But she wanted it to feel like it did with Alex: primal, animalistic. She wanted her body to control her mind, instead of the other way around.

She pulled the blanket down so she could see all of Tim, so he could see all of her.

"Nina?" Tim said, more awake now.

Nina needed to feel hands on her body, the pressure of someone's touch, even her own. She needed to focus on that. So she ran her fingers down the small slope of her breasts, across the muscles in her stomach, over the protrusion of her hip bones. Then she brought her fingers to her mouth and licked them before slipping them into her underwear, inside her.

She watched Tim's erection grow. Watched him take off his boxers.

His body was all sinew and muscle, strong and hard and taut. Nina rarely saw his body the way she did now. Usually he was just Tim. Now he was an object of desire.

"I want you," Nina said. There was an urgency in her voice. She could hear it. A desperation.

"Nina?" he asked again, his voice unsure. She'd never touched herself in front of him.

"Please," she said. "Touch me."

He ran his fingers down her stomach and she felt her body

respond, the sensation cutting her brain and her heart out of the loop, like she'd hoped it would.

She slid off her underwear, climbed on top of him, and enveloped him.

He thrust against her, moving faster and faster. "Like this?" he asked.

Nina tightened her legs and pulled herself closer.

"Yes," she said, abandoning herself to him. This was nothing like the sex they'd had earlier. Nothing like anything they'd done before. The pressure built between her legs and she called out as she came. It wasn't a sound she'd ever made in front of Tim. He shuddered inside her and bucked one last time.

They were both breathing hard.

Her mind had been wiped clean, her body exhausted. Now it was her turn to lay her head on the pillow. She pressed against Tim, skin to skin.

And finally, she could sleep.

43

WHEN NINA WOKE UP, TIM WAS GONE FROM THE BED. She found him, showered and dressed, in the kitchen.

"Coffee?" he asked as she walked into the room.

She finger-combed her hair into a messy ponytail. "Sure," she said. "Thanks."

She watched him pour her coffee.

"So last night," he said as he handed her the cup. "What was that?"

"What was what?" she asked, taking a sip.

"We've never had sex twice in one night," he said. "You've never . . ." His voice trailed off. He didn't have the right words.

The morning after, Nina was slightly ashamed that she'd let him see that side of her. That she'd touched herself in front of him.

Tim sat down at the island on one of the bar stools. "Don't get me wrong. It was great. But that's not you, Nina," he said. "That's not us. It just . . . I couldn't sleep after that."

"I . . ." Nina wasn't sure what to say next. That she almost never let herself lose control, even when she wanted to? That discovering that her parents weren't the perfect people she'd thought they were was somehow freeing? Or was that a cop-out? Was that a way to abdicate responsibility for her own desires? "Tim," she finally said, "I think this *is* me. Or at least part of me."

He stared at her, weighing his words, not saying any of them.

She stared back at him in silence, then looked over on the counter at the paper Tim had been reading when she walked in. Her father's face was looking up at her.

"What's that?" Nina asked, changing the conversation completely.

"I walked into town early this morning and picked up the *Times*," he said, letting her.

She looked at the picture differently now. Her father was a master manipulator. She'd known that, but what she hadn't realized was that it wasn't just the media and the public he manipulated, it was his friends, his family. It was her. Nina wondered what lies were going to be memorialized in this article and how angry they would make her feel. She picked up the paper.

But the anger she was expecting didn't come. Instead, it was sorrow.

She read the obituary, saw the photo timeline of her father's life; she was part of it, standing with her parents—one, the other, or both—throughout the years. At the end, it said: *Los tortolitos will finally rest once again in each other's arms.* And then the anger hit, fast and hard.

"You know, it's not true," Nina said to Tim, who was sitting next to her, their shoulders inches apart. Her voice was colder than she meant it to be.

"What do you mean?" he asked.

She walked upstairs and brought him back the letter she'd found. "I only read the first page," she told him. "Last night. Before I . . . before we . . ."

He took the pages from her hand, reading quickly. "Your father had an affair," he said. "Holy shit. I'm so sorry."

"I know," Nina shook her head.

"He was such a . . ." Tim said. "I'd never have guessed he would even think about—"

"Do you know who it might have been?" Nina asked.

Tim shook his head. "Do you want me to ask my parents?"

"No," Nina said. "Maybe I will, but . . . maybe they didn't even know."

"They must have." Tim reached out and brushed Nina's hair out of her face. "Your dad told my dad everything."

Nina shrugged, anger morphing into she didn't know what. Disappointment? Resignation? Distrust? "I don't even know what to think about him anymore. You know, when I was younger he said that my aunt Daphne didn't want to be a part of our world after my mom died, that she didn't like us. What if that was a lie, too?"

Tim rubbed his eyes before looking back at Nina. "I can't imagine he'd keep you from your family for no reason."

Nina thought about that. "Maybe he had a reason," she said. "Just not one I'd have agreed with."

Tim looked down, into his cup of coffee. "Your father was a good man, Nina. Don't let that get lost in all of this." Then he looked up and Nina was surprised to see tears in his eyes. "I loved him, too, you know."

"I know," she said, and leaned over to hug Tim. Love was complicated. It didn't disappear because someone did something horrible, something you didn't agree with. It lived there, with the disappointment, the disapproval. You had to figure out how to hold both of them in your heart, or you'd lose everyone, everything. Nina had been struggling with that her whole adult life. Now, it seemed, Tim was, too.

They spent the rest of the day going through the house, opening drawers and closets, finding a scarf that Nina threw around her neck, a stack of magazines from December 1992, and Nina's old umbrella, pink with red hearts, that years ago she'd assumed had gotten left behind at a restaurant or forgotten at a birthday party.

"I'm surprised no one cleaned this place out," Tim said, as they found a pile of board games in a cabinet. Trivial Pursuit, Monopoly, Scrabble.

"Me too," Nina answered. "This seems like it would've been a job for Super Caro."

Tim smiled. "I won't ask her unless you want me to, but I bet she knows more than we do."

Nina figured she probably did, but still wasn't sure she wanted to know. Her vision of her father had already changed last night. She wasn't sure how much more information she could handle at the moment.

She looked over at Tim and ran her thumb over the band of the engagement ring on her finger. She'd thought Tim had been her last gift from her father. But now she wondered. Did her father know anything about love at all?

44

WHEN THEY GOT BACK TO THE CITY, NINA DROPPED
Tim off at his place before heading over to her father's garage
to park the car.

"You sure you don't want me to come?" he asked.

"I'm sure," Nina said. She needed some time by herself to
process, to think.

Tim assessed her for a beat longer than he might have a few
weeks ago, then said, "Okay, sounds good. You'll wear the ring
around your neck?"

Nina nodded. "On a chain so it hangs next to my heart."

They'd decided that made the most sense for now. That way
there would be no questions until they were ready with answers.

"And we'll go over those financials together tomorrow? Two
MBAs are better than one?" He was trying to make her laugh.
Nina appreciated it.

"Sure," she said. "With the two of us looking together, I bet we can figure out what my dad meant. And if we don't, we can always call Irv."

They'd talked about it that morning, what her father might have wanted to say. It was something else that Tim suggested they ask his parents—TJ specifically—but Nina thought that if her father had wanted TJ to tell her whatever it was, he would've made that happen. Maybe it was something even TJ didn't know. They'd decided Irv, the Gregory Corporation's CFO, would be backup. But Nina felt the same way about him that she did about TJ—if her father had wanted Irv to tell her, he would've made that happen.

"Nina and Tim, friends until the end," Tim said, which made Nina smile.

As she drove back across town, she thought, almost as if it were a reflex: *I haven't spoken to my dad in a while*, and then realized afresh when she went to grab her phone that he was gone. That she'd never speak to him again. And that he'd lied to her. So profoundly. How could he leave, knowing that this secret existed, that if she discovered it, he wouldn't be there to help her through it? Was that why he'd told her she should be with Tim? Because she'd need someone to support her when the tectonic plates of her life shifted? When her father tumbled off his pedestal? How could he do this to her?

Nina couldn't stop the tears that came to her eyes then, hot and angry. They blurred her vision as she drove, and all of a sudden she thought about how her mother had died. An icy road, she knew. Up in the country. The car had gone out of control. She'd hit a tree. The car was totaled. And she was dead by the time the ambulance arrived.

But was it just ice? Or could it have been tears that made her veer off the road? Had her father's affair killed her mother? And if it had, would anyone ever know? That would be the worst headline Nina could ever think of. *Joseph Gregory's Affair Kills Wife. Leaves Young Daughter Motherless.*

A taxi honked behind Nina, and she took a moment to wipe her eyes before she stepped on the gas. There was no way she was going to let sorrow end her life. She would not let history repeat itself. Not now. Not ever.

45

IT FELT GOOD TO BE HOME. NINA HAD TAKEN OUT HER
contact lenses and filled up her bathtub with some fancy bubble
bath Leslie had sent over a few months before. An "I saw this
and thought of you" gift, which was Leslie's thing. She didn't
celebrate Christmas and sent beautiful cards on birthdays but
said that people got so many gifts then, it seemed silly to add to
the pile. Instead, she bought presents when she saw things she
thought her friends and family would like. It was actually
nice—gifts arriving when you least expected them.

Nina looked at her naked body in the bathroom mirror and
thought: *This body is now engaged to Tim.* It was a crazy thought.
Yesterday her body had been her own; now it felt like it was
partially his. It was amazing to think about how quickly a world
could shift. *Yesterday I had a parent, today I don't. Yesterday I was
working on a campaign, today I'm not. Yesterday Tim was just my
present, today he's my future.* It hurt her brain to think about it.

Nina climbed into the bathtub, letting herself disappear
under the bubbles. She hadn't brought a book into the tub with

her. Instead, she turned down the lights in the bathroom and tried to focus on relaxing. She relaxed her toes, her feet, her ankles. She relaxed her calves, her knees, her thighs. The only thing she found she couldn't relax was her mind, no matter how long she sat there counting her breaths, closing her eyes, imagining thoughts floating out of her head like balloons. She ran her fingers down her body, the way she had with Tim the night before, but instead of his naked body, Rafael appeared in her mind. Nina opened her eyes. Tried to float that thought out of her head like a balloon, too. That thought that never should have been there to begin with. This bath was the opposite of relaxing. So when she heard her phone ring in her bedroom, Nina took the excuse to get out of the tub.

She wrapped herself in a bathrobe and checked to see who the missed call was from. Leslie. Nina called her right back.

"Hey," Leslie said, after the first ring. "Cole made me promise I would call you today. He was reminding us last night about how the two of you made pizza dough out of beer last time you visited. He's asked me every day this week if I thought you needed another lollipop."

Nina laughed. "Tell him I'll come visit soon," she said. "We can make pizza again. And tell him he must've sent me a magical lollipop, because no matter how many times I lick it, it doesn't disappear."

"Ha," Leslie said. "I'd better not, or he'll want to buy all the lollipops in the store to see if he can find another magical one."

"Fair," Nina said. "No magical lollipop." She'd been remaking her bed as she talked to Leslie, and now she sat down on top of the blanket. "So, I did something yesterday. But it's a secret."

Nina heard a horn honk. Leslie must've been driving. "I'm gonna need more than that," Leslie said.

"I told Tim I'd marry him."

There was a pause on the other end of the line. A split-second pause. And then Leslie's voice came through. "Congratulations! How did he propose?"

Nina straightened the pillows on her bed. "With a beautiful ring and a gingerbread house like the one we built a long time ago," she said. "He told me that he thinks we belong together. And my dad gave him his blessing."

"Is that why you're marrying him? Because it's what your dad wanted?" Leslie's words were slow, careful.

"No," Nina said, feeling defensive, refusing to think about Leslie's question. She thought about forks and napkins for a moment to keep her temper in check. Calmer, she said, "I like my life with Tim. And I love him. I always have. It all makes sense."

"That's great, then," Leslie answered. Nina could hear the smile in her voice. "I'm glad you're happy, Neen. You deserve it."

Nina didn't feel happy, though. And she felt like she had to confess. "I'm not sure if I am, actually," she said. "At least not completely."

"Hm?" Leslie replied. Nina could tell her friend was trying to figure out what her role was in this conversation. Was she supposed to be supportive? Critical?

"I was," Nina explained. "When he first proposed, I was. But then I think I made a mistake last night. I touched myself in front of him. And took charge. In bed. And I thought maybe he liked it, but then it turned out he didn't. Or at least he said it wasn't 'us.' What if I want it to be, though? At least, sometimes."

"Well," Leslie said, "have you tried to talk to him about it? Tell him what you want? Couples do lots of things in bed. You know that game Sextris that Vijay showed me when we first started dating? The one that was like Tetris but with humans? We once spent a week trying every position that made the game pieces disappear."

Nina thought about how she wanted to phrase her response. "Do you remember that summer I dated Alex? In D.C.?"

"Of course," Leslie said. "The Summer of Freedom. I liked that guy."

"I wasn't Joseph Gregory's daughter that summer. No one in D.C. really cared who I was. And I let myself do whatever, because it didn't seem to matter so much—where I went, how I dressed, what I said. But then when I got a job back in New York, and I was with everyone who knew my dad, that part of me kind of went away. Or I didn't let it out. Tim has certainly never seen it."

Leslie honked her horn again. "So what changed?" Her turn blinker was on. Nina could hear it clicking rhythmically. "Last night, I mean."

Nina knew the answer to this one. She'd been thinking about it all day. "I found out that my dad had an affair," Nina said. "And I just . . . I don't know. I needed to disengage. I feel like I've been behaving a certain way for my whole life because it's what my dad expected of me, and it turns out he didn't follow the same rules. He held me to a higher standard than he did himself, or something. And now everything feels so complicated." She was thinking not just about Tim, but about Rafael, too, who'd popped into her mind in the bath. And before then, too. She got the feeling he wouldn't mind if she touched herself when she was with him. She stopped herself from thinking more about it.

Nina heard Leslie's car engine turn off and the doors unlock. She heard her friend take a deep breath. "Well, all relationships are complicated. I'm sure Tim could get used to you wanting to fuck more creatively, if that's all this is. But I feel like there's a lot more to unpack here."

Nina massaged her forehead. "I don't know, Les," she said. "I just feel like the whole world is changing and I don't like it."

They kept talking, and while nothing was worked out, nothing changed, it made Nina feel better knowing Leslie was there, listening, on the other end of the phone.

46

A FEW NIGHTS LATER, NINA WAS PLACING THE WATER glasses on the table when the elevator door opened into her living room, revealing Tim.

Tim had gotten busy with work the last few days, so she'd spent her time looking at balance sheets on her own, calling the heads of the different departments, catching herself up on the business, starting with the most recent year's results and working backward. She did call Irv, but just to get a rundown of the business from his perspective. She knew a lot just from growing up around the hotels, living with her dad, having conversations with Caro and TJ, all those classes at business school. But there was more to learn—more than she'd let herself believe. Now she was learning it. She was doing it for her father, while at the same time wondering if she'd ever really known him at all. She wasn't sure if she'd found the thing he'd wanted to talk about, but she was discovering a lot about the company that made her question him even more. The marketing seemed like it was from a different decade. The decisions didn't quite make sense.

Was he really the brilliant businessman everyone made him out to be? And what about TJ? Where was he in all of this?

"Hey," Tim said. "That smells delicious." Nina smiled. For the last few hours she'd been cooking. Chicken sautéed with apples, onions, garlic, and thyme. She'd paired it with an autumn salad and a freshly baked loaf of bread.

There really was something rewarding about putting a meal together. About following a recipe, measuring ingredients, chopping and dicing, and then ending up with exactly what you'd planned. Nina never made up recipes as she went, adding this, switching out that. For her, the joy was in the rules and the result of following those rules to the letter. Today, though, she'd thrown some hot pepper flakes into the bread. She'd added some pomegranate seeds to the autumn salad. And was embarrassed by how satisfying it felt to see them there, nestled in with all the other ingredients.

Tim helped Nina bring the dishes of food to the table, then served her before he served himself.

"Thanks," Nina said.

"Thank *you*," he said. "For making me such a fantastic dinner. Though you've never put pomegranate seeds in salad before. New recipe?"

"Old recipe," Nina said, "with new flair."

Tim looked surprised but didn't say anything more.

Nina picked up a forkful of salad, her mind still on the conversation she'd had with the head of marketing. Jeff had told her he'd been hoping to increase their social media presence and their ad buys in a handful of key markets, but his request had been denied. She wasn't going to suggest any changes to TJ yet but wanted to know what each department would want, if they could have anything. Some of the items seemed easy to provide.

But she knew that nothing in business was ever as simple as it seemed at first glance. Changing the soap in the bathrooms, for example, meant negotiating a whole new partnership, perhaps new costs. Research into that company to make sure they weren't using child labor to make their soap into the shape of hearts or donating to lobbyists who were working to deregulate waste management. And even as she was trying to think about that, in the back of her mind she kept seeing her father, cheating on her mother. Indirectly causing her death. She couldn't get it out of her head.

"So how was your day?" Tim asked.

Nina shrugged. "Busy. Interesting. Vaguely destabilizing."

"Destabilizing how?" Tim asked, getting up and taking a bottle of Cabernet out of Nina's wine rack.

"I guess . . . I don't know," Nina said, trying to get her feelings to cohere into sentences. "I realized today that there are business decisions my dad made that I might've made differently. And when things like that happened in the past, especially when it had to do with the company, I'd just assumed he was right and I was looking at things the wrong way. But I think . . . I think there are some things he could have done better. And I'm not sure why he didn't see that. I would have expected him to." Nina took a sip of the wine Tim had poured her.

"Nobody's perfect," Tim said. "But your dad was great. He took what his father started and made it even more successful. Do you know how many people in your father's position would've just coasted on what already existed—or even worse, run it into the ground? You see it all the time."

Nina took another sip, letting the flavor settle on her tongue. "That might be true," she said. "But it's about more than his business success. It's what we found out up in the country, too.

And now I feel like—I was anchoring myself, my life, to a rock that wasn't as solid as I thought it was."

That was really what had been bothering her most. Her father wasn't the man she'd thought he was. She had created a version of him that, in this moment, felt imaginary. Like the Great and Powerful Oz. Or the Emperor without any clothes. And not only had the "real" Joseph Gregory, the one who was so much more flawed than she ever knew, been hidden from her, but now she'd never have the chance to know him.

"Well, you can anchor yourself to me," Tim said, smiling. "I'm the most solid rock around."

Nina had to force herself to smile back. That wasn't what she'd meant at all.

LATER THAT NIGHT, Nina and Tim were in bed. Nina had just put her phone away, but not before seeing that Rafael had texted to ask how she was doing, to see if she wanted to get together for coffee. She put him off but couldn't bring herself to say no. She didn't want to think about what the reason was, especially not when Tim was here in her bed. Not when they were supposed to spend the rest of their lives together. Not when she was afraid to let herself go around him, to tell him what she wanted. Not when their relationship felt like it was changing, had been changing, in a way she didn't quite understand.

47

THE NEXT MORNING, THE DOORMAN CALLED UP FROM downstairs. It was TJ Calder, there to see her. Nina was worried he was coming by because of the conversations she'd been having with all of the department heads. She hadn't spoken to him yet. She felt too weird about the fact that she would basically be his boss. It would be like telling her father what to do. Incomprehensible. Impossible.

"Nina, Sweetheart," he said when the elevator door opened. He looked better than he had the last time she'd seen him. His eyes weren't swollen, his face didn't seem as hollow. "How are you?"

"I'll be okay," she said. It was how she'd decided to answer that question. It was the truth, and also didn't invite more discussion.

TJ sat down at the island in the middle of Nina's kitchen. "I brought muffins," he said, placing a bag on the counter in front of him. "Apple cranberry's your favorite, right?"

"It is," she said. And then she found herself getting choked up. TJ knew that about her. He'd remembered. It was like having a second dad. A bonus, a backup. Maybe he could retire. And then she wouldn't have to be his boss. After she married Tim, she could just be his daughter. Maybe she should talk to Tim about that. She opened the bag of muffins and brought some napkins over from the pantry.

TJ took a lemon–poppy-seed muffin and rested it on a napkin in front of him. "I've been trying to stave them off, but the board of directors would really like to meet with you. I came in person because your dad would want me to impress upon you how important this is."

Nina thought about the last time she'd planned to meet with the board. Her meltdown. She was afraid to put herself in front of them until she was more sure of herself, more sure of the business. "Can't I take another week?" Nina asked. She was unwrapping her muffin, not looking at TJ. She needed to figure out what she wanted to do. And that meant with TJ, too.

"This week would be better. There's a lot of talk about what's going to happen to the company now that your father's gone. It would be helpful if you held a meeting. I'll be there with you. I can limit it to fifteen minutes. Twenty tops."

Nina massaged her temples. "Okay," she said. "I'll try for Friday." Even though she knew she wasn't likely to be ready by then.

"That sounds good," TJ said. "You remember Ned? He's been grumbling about having an investment banker evaluate strategic options."

She knew what that meant. The board was thinking about trying to convince her to sell her majority stake in the company.

Nina felt herself physically recoil. It was a gut instinct. Intuitive. "I'm not selling," she said immediately. "That's my family's company. That's my name. No one else can have it."

Then she heard TJ sigh. "I know," he said. "But are you ready to run it?"

"I will be soon," Nina said. "Maybe you and I can sit down tomorrow and talk about your vision for the company. The next three years. Five." Maybe he would tell her that he wanted to retire, now that her father was gone. Then she wouldn't have to bring it up.

TJ sighed. "I know you're capable of running it, Nina. And I know your father expected you to, but I'm going to ask you something he never would: Do you want to?"

She was supposed to. That was what she knew. It was her responsibility. A job she was born to do. The future she'd always known she would have. And she'd accepted it. She expected it. It was part of who she was.

"Just think about it," TJ said, getting up to give Nina a hug. "I have to go to the office."

She hugged him back and insisted he take the rest of his muffin with him, wrapping it up in tinfoil. "I'll see you tomorrow?" she said.

"Call Rita," he told her. "She'll find time in my schedule."

"Oh wait," Nina said. "Before you go. I was flipping through the financials my father gave me. From 2008 to 2011 there's a $60,000 fee paid to a consulting firm each month. Manxome Consulting? Do you have their reports? I'm curious to see what they said about the business. They don't seem to have a website."

An expression Nina couldn't name crossed TJ's face. "I'm not sure where they are," he said. "I'll look into it and let you know if I can locate them."

"Thanks, Uncle TJ," she answered.

"Of course." He tightened the scarf around his neck before heading to the door.

After she saw him out, Nina went back to the balance sheets. She wondered if her dad had chosen the firm because they'd named themselves after "Jabberwocky."

Whether or not running the Gregory Corporation was something she wanted to do, it was something she was going to do, and at least for now, that was enough.

48

THREE WEEKS HAD PASSED SINCE HER FATHER HAD died and even though on one hand it had felt like no time, on the other hand it was getting harder for Nina to remember the exact timbre of his voice and the specific feel of his hands on hers. Her emotions weren't quite as raw, quite as ready to erupt at the strangest moments. And her brain was starting to function again at its usual speed. She felt like she could reenter the world.

Nina picked up the newspaper from her breakfast table. There was an article on Rafael. He was planning to march in the Village Halloween parade at the end of the month, about a week before Election Day. She wondered how everyone at the campaign was doing. Whether she should stop by and say hello. To Jane, who'd been texting every few days to see how Nina was. To Jorge, who maybe would do his touchdown dance if she asked. To Rafael, who had texted her a few more times, offering to talk, to meet up. She had responded enough to be polite but still hadn't made any concrete plans. Instead she ran along the Hudson River, with breaks to admire the bravery of the people taking trapeze lessons on Pier 40. She spent hours wondering what the hell her father was thinking when he cheated on her mother, spent a few more debating with Tim as to whether or not they should ask his parents what they knew about the affair. And now Tim was asking her when she thought it might be the right time to tell everyone else about their engagement.

"The old Nina would be so excited," he'd said the other night. That was how he started a lot of comments now. "The old Nina wouldn't have put pimentos in this sandwich." "The old Nina wouldn't have gone and gotten her ear cartilage pierced in the middle of the day." Which Nina had done. Two days after she'd spoken with TJ and realized that her dad was definitely not the star businessman she'd always assumed he was. The day she'd put off her meeting with the board.

It turned out TJ had been making most of the decisions, doing his best to keep the business in the black while her father networked and hobnobbed and was the figurehead of the corporation. He was the publicity driver, but TJ had done the real work. And he'd done it in a way that Nina didn't always agree with.

She'd felt like she was living in a house of mirrors, where up was down and left was right. Then, for some reason, she remembered back to when she was sixteen and wanted to get the cartilage at the top of her ear pierced, and her father had told her no. That it looked low-class. She didn't agree. She'd made a list of girls at school who'd gotten their cartilage pierced. But he'd still said no. So now, seventeen years later, she'd done it herself. And her fiancé hated it just as much as her father would have.

As Nina took a bite of her English muffin, she wondered if

maybe she could volunteer at the campaign. Just a few hours a week to help out. It might make her life feel more grounded, less like she'd walked into a movie about herself, where the best friend became the fiancé and the main character was left rudderless, floating in a sea of half-truths and outright lies.

Then her phone rang—it was campaign headquarters.

"Hello?" Nina said, wondering who she'd find on the other end.

"Nina? It's Christian." Other than coming to her with a few introduction requests, Nina and Christian hadn't had a ton to do with each other while she was working for Rafael.

"Is everything okay?" she asked.

Christian made a noncommittal sound on the other end of the phone. "Well," he said, "we were hoping that Marc Johnson's donors would come on board after the primary, but they haven't. At least, not in the way we'd hoped."

"Oh," Nina said, "I'm sorry to hear that," while her brain spun, wondering who had donated and who hadn't, whether her calls might make any difference. "Do you want me to try to convince some people?"

Christian cleared his throat. "Your father used to host fundraisers at The Gregory Hotel," he said. "A thousand dollars or more a head."

Nina was nodding. "Right," she said. "He would raise a few hundred thousand dollars for the candidate."

Christian cleared his throat again. And Nina realized: "You want to ask me if we can do that for Rafael?"

"Perhaps next week?" Christian answered. "I wouldn't ask except . . ."

"Except you need it. Rafael needs it. I understand. Let me make some phone calls. I'll see what I can pull together." She wondered if Rafael had authorized this ask. He must have. Maybe that was why he'd been wanting to meet her for coffee.

There was a sigh on the other end of the phone. "Thank you," Christian said. "So much."

Nina said good-bye and then called Caro. After explaining what they wanted, Nina said, "What do you think, Aunt Caro? Is this possible?"

Nina heard Caro's mouse clicking. "The ballroom at the Park is free Tuesday night. I know it's not a lot of time, but . . ."

"But we'll make it work," Nina said. "That's fantastic. Do you know how Dad used to do these? How he would choose who to invite?"

Caro was quiet for a second. "Darling," she said, "I planned those fund-raisers with my team. I gave him the list—went through his Rolodex and added the people I thought were most likely to donate to the particular candidate. He just invited them."

"Oh," Nina said. "Right. Of course. Well, I'll invite every-one this time." Something else she'd given her father credit for that he hadn't deserved. "And I can make my own list. You don't have to do that for me, Aunt Caro."

She could imagine Caro nodding on the other end of the phone. "How many are you thinking?" Caro asked.

Nina knew the room held three hundred comfortably if you put tables on the dance floor. Two hundred forty if you didn't. "I'll aim for three hundred," she said. "Do I need to run this by anyone?"

Caro laughed. "You," she said. "And me. So we're all clear."

"All right, perfect," Nina said. "We should probably sit down together and go over exactly what else you've been doing, just so I know what's going on."

"Let's do that after the fund-raiser's over," Caro said. "In the meantime, I'll whip something together. You'll put me in touch with the right person to coordinate with at the campaign?"

"I will," Nina said. "Thanks, Aunt Caro."

"My pleasure, darling."

After they hung up, Nina called Christian back and gave him the date and Caro's phone number. He wasn't the kind of guy who did touchdown dances, like Jorge, but Nina could tell he was relieved. And grateful.

It felt so good, being part of this again. But it felt wrong to be part of it without talking to Rafael. She opened up a text message. *Hey,* she thumbed into the box. *Looking forward to the fund-raiser.*

He wrote back right away.

Thank you so much, Nina. You have no idea how much this will help.

She smiled, picturing his smile. *How's the campaign going otherwise?* she typed.

Not the same without you. This new speechwriter is good, but you were better.

Nina smiled again. *You just knew me better,* she wrote.

You know it was more than that.

She did, of course she did. *Maybe,* she typed.

Then she saw the three dots appear. Rafael was writing something. Then not. Then writing again. She stared at her phone for at least two minutes, waiting for him to figure out what he wanted to say and how he was going to say it. Finally words appeared on her screen. Not nearly as many as she'd expected, considering how long he'd been typing.

Any chance I can convince you to review the speech Danny wrote?

She smiled once more. Rafael's words often seemed to have that effect on her. Probably because she could read around and in between them. See the shape of what he meant to say. She was pretty sure this time it was: *I want to see you. And I don't want to wait until Tuesday night.* After how complicated everything was feeling with Tim, the simplicity of this felt refreshing. Rafael missed her. He wanted to see her.

I think I could manage that, she responded, ignoring the part of her brain that was asking what this meant, why she thought this was a good idea. She didn't. She knew it wasn't. But she didn't care. She liked how being around Rafael made her feel, and she wanted to feel that way again. Especially now.

Rafael's reply took so long to come that Nina put her phone down and refilled the electric kettle she used to heat water for her French press. The best way to make coffee, she'd decided years ago.

As the kettle started to boil, her phone pinged.

Great, it said, *I'll e-mail you the speech. Can you come by tomorrow night to review it?*

Tim was going to some work drinks thing the next night. Nina had said maybe she'd come but hadn't committed. She hadn't been out that much in public since her dad died. She'd canceled the dinner plans she'd made, changed her RSVP to no for a few fund-raisers and gallery openings. It felt weird, everyone living their lives, going on just as they had been, when her life was so different. She felt like she was on another planet, and it took so much effort to engage in small talk.

Sure, she wrote back to Rafael. *See you at HQ tomorrow around 6.*

THE SPEECH CAME OVER a few minutes later, attached to an e-mail from Rafael.

She got to work, and while she did, she breathed, she relaxed, absorbed completely in the world in front of her, in the words, in making them better. This was something she knew how to do. Something that felt easy.

When TJ called later, Nina ignored it. Maybe this was what she should be doing right now, not trying to figure out what message her father had left for her in the Gregory Corporation financials. That could come later.

49

THAT NIGHT, NINA'S DOOR OPENED AT CLOSE TO MID-
night. She was asleep, but not deeply, and woke when she heard
the elevator ping in her living room. She sat up in bed.

"Who's there?" she called out. "Tim, is that you?"

"Hey," Tim said, walking in.

"Baseball game's over?" she asked. She knew he'd been out
with some guys from work watching the Yankees take on the
Twins.

"Yeah, we won," he said.

"That's good," she answered, lying back down on her pillow.
"You didn't say you were coming over."

Nina watched as Tim took off his blazer, button-down, and
jeans, leaving on his boxers and his undershirt. "I just . . . I
missed you," he said. "I wanted to sleep next to you tonight."

He disappeared into the bathroom to brush his teeth.

When he got into bed, Nina was fighting to keep her eyes
open. "Did something happen?" she asked.

Tim kissed her cheek. "I wanted to remind myself how much I love you."

Nina wondered what he meant by that but was too tired to ask. "Okay," she said. "I love you, too."

She turned toward him and tucked her head under his chin, and they lay together, T-shirt to T-shirt, arms overlapping until they both fell asleep.

THE NEXT MORNING, Nina asked Tim what she'd been wondering the night before. "Why did you have to remember you loved me?" she asked as she handed him an omelet. She'd made it just the way he liked it—sautéed onions, cheddar cheese, not at all runny.

"Is that what I said?" Tim answered, carefully cutting his omelet with the side of his fork. "I was drunk. I just missed you." He took a bite. "This is delicious."

Nina let it go, but the thing about Tim was that he didn't lie when he was drunk; he didn't mess up his words. He'd said what he'd meant. Something had happened last night.

Nina wondered if this was the first time Tim was hiding the truth from her, or if it had happened before and this was just the first time she'd noticed. She really hoped not. But she wasn't sure about anything anymore.

50

LATER THAT DAY, AROUND LUNCHTIME, NINA CALLED Leslie.

"So Tim," she said, when Leslie picked up. "Something's off."

"What do you mean?" Leslie said. "I'm in the deli, grabbing a salad, so if you hear weird noises in the background, that's why. What happened?"

Nina looked out the window of her apartment, watching people walk down Jay Street, some alone, some in groups, some in pairs. "He came over last night, late, to remind himself that he loves me. That's what he said. He shrugged it off this morning, but I can't help but think he shouldn't have to remind himself, you know? And why won't he tell me what made him need reminding? It's just . . . it's weird. Something weird is going on."

Leslie was quiet for a moment. "Well, that does sound a little strange, but not too horrible. Is that all that's worrying you?"

It wasn't. Nina knew it wasn't. "I just . . . I feel like he expects me to be the Nina he's known his whole life, but I don't even know if she was real. I was making decisions based on

how my father would see me. I don't even know what I would
have done differently, if I hadn't been trained to think that way.
Would I have chosen a different school? A different profession?
Would I have moved to Boston with you or stayed in D.C.? Or
joined the Peace Corps? Or learned to play jazz piano? I don't
know who I would have been. I want to figure all of that out . . .
and I think Tim just wants me to be the same. The person who
reflects her father's choices in all of hers, that's who Tim thinks
I am."

A pile of plates clattered in the deli. "Is this still about the
night you wanted to have sex and he made you feel bad about it?"

"It's that he's so predictable." Nina paced around her living
room. "And he wants me to be. And I don't feel predictable
right now. Can I marry him if I feel this way?"

"Well," Leslie said, serious now. "Things have changed in
your world. A lot. There's so much that's up in the air. Maybe
this just isn't the time to agree to anything so momentous. Isn't
that a rule that people quote? You're not supposed to make any
major changes for at least six months after a loved one dies."

Nina sighed. "Maybe it'll all be fine. But . . . I'd told him we
shouldn't tell anyone we're engaged because it felt strange making that kind of announcement so soon after my dad died. And
now more time has passed and I still don't want to say anything
to anyone."

Nina heard the register at the deli chime. "Well," Leslie said,
"that doesn't seem like the best sign."

"My heart is so messed up these days. My brain, too. They're
just . . . they're confused."

"Then maybe give yourself some more time," Leslie said.
"You'll know when it's time to know."

Nina flopped down on her couch and closed her eyes. "How Zen of you," she said.

Leslie laughed again. "Yeah, not my usual behavior. Look, I've gotta go, but I'll call you later."

"Okay," Nina said. "Hugs to everyone."

"You got it."

Leslie clicked off, and Nina stayed lying on her couch. She wanted to feel so filled with love for Tim that she didn't question it. That it bubbled over and made every aspect of her life happier.

And she wanted to be that for him, too.

But she was worried. She was worried it wasn't the case for either of them. And if it wasn't, did that mean that there was even more wrong with their relationship than just Nina trying to put herself back together after her father died? She wanted to feel as sure about marrying Tim as she did about the fact that she and Leslie would always be there for each other whenever they needed to be.

But she wasn't.

51

THAT NIGHT, NINA HEADED OVER TO CAMPAIGN HEAD-
quarters at nine thirty. Rafael had changed the time on her,
asking her to wait until the new speechwriter went home so he
wouldn't feel like Rafael didn't like his work. Nina thought it
was kind of Rafael. But it also meant that a lot of the office
would be gone by the time Nina got there. She'd have to schedule another visit if she wanted to see the whole team.

Nina's key card didn't work anymore, so she texted Rafael to
let her in. He was wearing a T-shirt that said: *Hedgehogs: Why
don't they just share the hedge?* Nina laughed when she saw it.
Rafael flashed a megawatt smile at her.

"Funny, right?" he asked.

"Funny," she confirmed. She'd forgotten just how handsome
he was. Just how good it made her feel to walk next to him.

They sat down in the conference room off the elevator lobby,
and even though in some ways it seemed like nothing had
changed in the last three weeks, everything had. Nina wasn't a
staffer anymore. Now she and Rafael were equals. Now they

were friends. She opened up her laptop and showed him her notes.

"Here's what I was thinking," she said. "We take away this part about the benefits of magnet schools that reads as a bit generic, and instead we replace it with your own experiences at Bronx Science. And maybe we contrast your experience with your cousin Kevin's, about how you ended up in law school, and he ended up in prison."

Rafael scratched the stubble on his chin. "You think we're okay focusing on the Irish side of my family? I know that being the first Latino mayor is something Mac wants to message. We've been sticking to the refugee script, Operation Peter Pan, the bootstraps, the Spanish."

Nina looked at him. The notion struck her that underneath his T-shirt, he was naked. Which of course he was. Everyone was naked under their clothing. But once the thought was in her mind, Nina got stuck on it.

"Do you really think Kevin is a good idea?" Rafael continued.

Nina hadn't realized seeing him again would be this hard, this distracting. "Well," she said, forcing herself to refocus. "What do you want to message? How do you want to be known?" She knew bringing up his cousin Kevin was a risk. Perhaps one she wouldn't have suggested if she were still working for the campaign. Maybe one that wouldn't have occurred to her if she hadn't remembered the day her mother told her that she was half Lukas, too. "If you want to be known as the first Latino mayor and nothing else, we can scrap Kevin. But if you don't . . . you're in the general now. It's your chance to show the voters who you are."

Rafael looked at her. "This is why we need you back," he said.

Nina laughed.

"No, I'm serious," he said. "No one has asked me that. They've just told me how they think I'll best win elections. What part of me it makes sense to showcase to gain votes. You make me think, Nina."

Nina looked at him seriously. "I did that, too, though. I focused your speeches on what Mac wanted. We crafted your political persona out of pieces of who you were, stressing some aspects of your biography and ignoring others."

"So why aren't you anymore?" Rafael asked her, resting his chin in his hand, his eyes focused on only her.

Their intensity made her shiver. "I've been thinking about that since my dad died," Nina said, bringing her thoughts together as the words exited her mouth, "and . . . I don't know if that's the best way to live a life. It might be the best way to win an election or create a . . . I don't know . . . an urban legend. But is it the best way to live?"

Rafael got up from his spot across the table from her and sat down in the seat next to Nina. "What happened?" he asked. He was so close now. Close enough to touch. She wouldn't touch him, though.

Nina looked back at the document in front of her. "We should finish this speech," she said.

Rafael studied her. Nina felt like she was under a microscope. "Let's do two versions," he finally said. "One using both sides of my heritage, and one just the Cuban side. I'll think about how I want to be known tonight and I'll decide tomorrow."

Nina nodded. It wasn't a snap decision, what you would share with the world and what you wouldn't, how you wanted people to see you.

52

BY ELEVEN THEY HAD TWO WORKING DRAFTS. NOTH-
ing perfect, but getting there. And Nina had gotten used to
sitting next to him, could ignore the heat they seemed to
create.

"Are you hungry?" Rafael asked after they'd hammered out
a paragraph about bilingual education and the benefits it would
give to all New York City students.

Nina realized she was ravenous. She nodded. "Want to order
something in?" she asked.

"How about a quick burger next door?" Rafael countered.
"The kitchen's open for another hour."

Nina rolled her neck. "I'm afraid if we leave, we might not
make it back," she said.

Rafael ran his hand through the hair above his ear. His tell.

"What?" Nina asked.

Rafael smiled. "You always know," he said. Then: "I was
going to suggest that maybe you could come back tomorrow
night."

She'd canceled on the book club Priscilla had tried to convince her to rejoin, so there was nothing in her calendar. Probably Tim would want to have dinner, but maybe they could eat early and she could help Rafael after.

"Sure," Nina said.

She sent Rafael the drafts and powered down her computer, and then they headed to the bar next door. She'd been there with Jane and Jorge over the past few months. Sometimes with her interns, whom she still felt badly about leaving without any real notice.

"How are Jasmine and Rob?" Nina asked Rafael as they sat down.

"Getting along well with Danny," he answered. "So that's good. I think they liked you better, too, though."

Nina smiled, then studiously hid behind the menu. When the waiter came, they ordered burgers and fries and a couple of beers. But those beers somehow turned into half a yard of beer for each of them. A gift from the owner, the waiter said when he dropped them off.

"Wow," Nina said, looking at the length of the cup.

"It's dramatic," Rafael said, waving his thanks over to the owner. "That guy always tells me to bring my next girlfriend here for a pint. I think he's hoping I'll post pictures or something. Free advertising for his bar."

"Mayoral Candidate Rafael O'Connor-Ruiz Enjoys Beer at Local Haunt," Nina said, before she realized what she was doing.

"You writing Page Six headlines now?" he asked.

Nina blushed. "My father and I always did that," she said. "It's so dorky."

"It's not," Rafael replied, taking a swig of the beer. "It's kind of adorable."

Nina followed with a sip of her own. "Adorkable?" she asked.

Rafael laughed. "So you do that in English, too," he said. "Were the headlines a game?"

"Yeah, but I think it was actually his way of getting me to think about consequences," Nina told Rafael, running her fingers along the base of the glass. "He'd ask me what the best and worst headlines were that someone could come up with. He wanted me to think about the worst spin a reporter could put on a situation."

"Wow," Rafael said.

"I know." Nina took another sip of beer. "Sometimes being his daughter was a little intense. I'm realizing it more and more these days."

Nina had the urge to tell Rafael about the house in the Hudson Valley, what she'd learned while she was there, how talking to employees at the Gregory Corporation had unearthed surprises, and how it all had changed her opinion of her father. But she didn't say anything. Even though she had a feeling Rafael would understand. Talking about all of these raw emotions made her feel vulnerable. And she didn't want to go there. Not when she was trying so hard not to watch Rafael's lips as they touched the rim of his glass.

"I think a lot of fathers are a little intense," he said after he swallowed. "I know mine was."

"How so?" Nina asked, wondering if Rafael's father monitored his behavior in the same way hers did.

But their burgers arrived just then, and Rafael didn't answer. So Nina opened up the ketchup, trying to get some onto her plate. It was stuck in the bottle.

"May I?" Rafael asked.

Nina handed the ketchup bottle over, and Rafael recapped

it, shaking it three times. Then he uncapped it and gave it to Nina. "Try it now," he said.

Nina turned the bottle upside down and the ketchup flowed smoothly onto her plate.

"It's a non-Newtonian fluid," Rafael said.

Nina looked at him. "Is this a Bronx Science thing?" she asked.

He laughed. "Actually, I did learn it in high school physics. Non-Newtonian fluids sometimes act like solids and sometimes act like liquids, depending on how much force is exerted on them. When you shake up ketchup, you exert enough force that the spherical particles turn into ellipses and basically become a thousand times thinner than they were pre-shaking."

Nina blinked at him for a moment.

"I guess it was my turn to be dorky," he said, looking a little embarrassed.

"Dorky people are my favorite kind," Nina answered, realizing too late that she probably shouldn't have said that.

Rafael didn't look embarrassed anymore. "Mine, too," he said, looking at her as if she were a book in another language he needed to translate.

Nina handed the bottle of ketchup back to him, so he could pour some onto his plate.

And then a camera flash went off.

Nina and Rafael both looked toward the bar, where the flash went off again.

"Rafael! Nina!" the photographer said, trying to catch their attention. But Rafael and Nina had looked back at each other.

"Madre de Dios," Rafael muttered under his breath. "This guy has been popping up everywhere. He took my picture as I was walking out of the gym last week."

Nina thought about what the owner had said to Rafael, urging him to bring a girlfriend. And then she thought about how long it takes to drink a free half yard of beer. "You were set up," Nina said. "The bartender. The beer. That guy's paying him off to get photos of you."

Rafael looked at the photographer and then at the man behind the bar. "I have an idea," he said, grabbing their jackets from the hook behind him and getting off the bar stool. He reached out his hand. "Come with me?"

Nina took Rafael's hand and slid off the stool. She felt the calluses on the tips of his fingers. As the photographer kept snapping pictures, the two of them ran into the kitchen. Their waiter hurried after them saying, "Sir! Ma'am!"

Rafael settled up the bill, paying in cash, and then said, "Just so you know, I won't be coming back here. I don't appreciate this sort of thing."

The waiter looked at the floor, which made Nina suspect maybe he was in on it. But she didn't want to make this any worse.

Rafael kept going. "I'm assuming we can get out the back entrance into the alley?"

The waiter nodded. "Yessir."

"Great," Rafael said. "That's where we're going. Where does it let us out?"

"Tenth and Fiftieth," one of the line cooks answered from behind Nina. "Espero que ganas, vato."

"Gracias," Rafael said, walking over to shake the man's hand.

Nina followed. "Cual puerta debemos usar?" she asked him, wondering which door he'd tell them to use.

He looked surprised that she spoke in Spanish but replied

her question, pointing to the door next to the freezer. "Ese," he said.

"Gracias," she responded.

"Come on," Rafael said, handing Nina her jacket.

The two of them walked out the door into the alley behind the restaurant, and then Rafael started jogging. Nina had no trouble keeping up with him, and they ran down the darkened city streets until they reached the Hudson River Greenway, overlooking the river. They sat on a bench that was illuminated by a streetlight, its glow making a halo around them in the crisp autumn night. They were both slightly out of breath.

"Well," Rafael said. "That was a nice escape."

"I can't believe we did that," Nina said. "Now the story's going to be even crazier than if we'd just sat there. Mac and Jane are going to kill us."

"Candidate and Former Speechwriter Hide from Press in Kitchen?" Rafael asked.

Nina smiled at the fact that he was playing her father's headline game. But then she got serious again. "Maybe . . . *Joseph Gregory's Daughter Enjoys Night Out Three Weeks after Father's Death.*"

Rafael touched the gray silk blouse that was skimming Nina's forearm but moved his hand away before she could feel the warmth of his fingers on her skin. The hair on her arms stood at attention.

"They won't say that," he said. "Maybe *Mayoral Candidate Romances Former Staffer.*"

Nina looked at him, her heart beating faster. "Are you romancing me?" she asked.

"What do you think, Palabrecita?" he said, actually squeezing her forearm this time, perhaps emboldened by the fact that she hadn't moved it away when he brushed his fingers across her shirt.

His touch made her shiver. "I think if you wanted to romance me, burgers and beer and a physics lesson and an escape to the Hudson River Greenway—"

"Isn't enough," Rafael finished, seeming disappointed. "I know you're used to more than that."

"No," Nina said. "If you were trying to romance me, this would be just the way to do it."

Rafael put his hand on top of hers and interlaced their fingers. Nina knew she should take her hand away, should say something about Tim, but she didn't want to. His hand was so warm. She imagined it caressing her cheek. *Don't*, she told herself. But her self-control was weakening.

"You know," Rafael said, "my whole life I've felt like a chameleon. I can be whoever people want me to be. Talk about my family in Ireland, or my family in Cuba. Pepper my conversations with Spanish, switch into it completely, or pretend those words aren't in my mind at all. I can be the kid who grew up in Queens sharing a bedroom with my sister and brother, or the one who got taken out to the fanciest restaurants in New York City when I was a summer associate at Sullivan and Cromwell."

Nina tried to concentrate on what he was saying, but her attention was split between his words and the feel of his hand on hers.

"My sister . . . she said she's always felt wrong. Too Cuban to be Irish, and too Irish to be Cuban. Never the right amount of anything. But me . . . I feel like I can present the right front, the right face, say the right thing, and people see what they want to see in me. I've been thinking about what we were talking about in the office, before the burgers. I want to use the speech about my cousin Kevin. I don't want to be a chameleon anymore. I want to be myself, my whole self, not just who people expect me to be. It might cost me some votes, but I hope the authenticity will gain me some others."

Nina thought about that. People expected she would act a certain way, too. Mac always thought so. They expected her to be their idea of what it meant to be a Gregory, what it meant to grow up in a world of excess. And as well as she knew Tim, for as long as she'd known Tim, he expected that, too.

"You know," Nina said. "I'm a Lukas, too."

"A what?" Rafael asked, his hand still around hers.

"A Lukas," she said. "My mother's maiden name. She grew up in Colorado, and her family was from Greece originally, generations ago. That's really all I know. Not even the island they're from."

"You're Greek!" Rafael said.

"Can I claim it, if I know nothing about it?" Nina asked. She'd been wondering about that for the last week.

"It's part of your DNA," Rafael said. "It's part of your blood. But it takes work to make it part of who you are, I think."

Nina nodded. "It also takes work not to hide who you are," she said. "I'm glad you're going to use the speech about Kevin."

Rafael looked at her. Their hands were still touching and now their eyes locked. "I feel like I can be myself around you," he told her. "All of me. I never feel that way. Not even with my ex-wife."

"I feel like I can be myself around you, too," Nina said. She was whispering. The pieces of her that felt new, the questions she had—Rafael didn't seem like he had expectations of who she would be. More like he wanted to learn who she was, deep inside.

"Is that a new earring?" he said, reaching out to touch the pierced cartilage on her left ear.

"Yeah," she said, her stomach flipping at his touch. "I'd always wanted one. My dad told me not to, but I did it. A few days ago."

"Well, it looks good," Rafael said, seeming to weigh exploring what she'd said about her father, then deciding not to.

Everything had gotten so quiet, it seemed like the city had paused, waiting for them to make a confession, to open their hearts to each other after so long.

"I realized that being alone with you might be dangerous that time we rode in the car together to the Norwood Club," Nina said, knowing she shouldn't say it, but doing so anyway. "And then I was sure of it when we talked the night my dad died." Her voice caught in her throat. Tears threatened to spill and she didn't fight them, because she wasn't afraid to feel vulnerable any longer. He'd told her his truth; she could tell him hers.

Rafael wrapped his arm around her, and Nina leaned into him, wiping her tears on his coat. "Dangerous how?" he asked.

She felt his strength through the wool. "Dangerous because you make me feel out of control."

"Is that a good thing?" His voice vibrated against her back.

"I think it might be," she said. Once she uttered those words, a million thoughts went rushing through her mind. *What about Tim?* was the first one. The one that rang like church bells in her head. And then: *Where do we go from here?*

Rafael tightened his arm around her and pulled her close. Nina leaned her head against his shoulder.

"Can we do this again?" Rafael asked, running his fingers along her arm.

"Sit on a bench?" Nina asked. She felt the weight of Tim's

engagement ring around her neck, pressing against her heart under her blouse.

Rafael laughed. "Well, sure," he said. "But I meant go out. Preferably somewhere with no photographers."

When Nina didn't answer, he continued, "Did you . . . did you feel that rush when we were in the same room? The adrenaline and cortisol that races through your body when you're with someone you have a crush on?"

"Is that what it is? Adrenaline and cortisol?"

Rafael nodded; Nina could feel his chin move against her head. "Yup," he said. "It means my biology likes your biology."

Nina closed her eyes as she admitted, softly, "Yes, I felt it."

Rafael turned his head sideways and kissed her temple.

Her pulse was racing. She wanted to feel his mouth against hers. She wanted to give in, to catch his lip between her teeth, to feel his naked skin beneath her fingers.

He hugged her closer to him, and her engagement ring pressed into them both.

Nina took a deep breath. She had to stop this. "Rafael," she whispered. "We can't . . . I can't . . ."

Rafael pulled away from her, six inches of air now between them where there used to be heat.

"What's wrong?" he asked.

"I'm still with Tim," she said. "I'm sorry. It doesn't change how I feel when I'm with you, but . . ."

"You can't," he finished, pulling farther away. It was like someone had dialed up the air conditioning, thrown a switch on the freezer. "I'd hoped . . . I'd hoped that your response when I said I was romancing you, when you put your head on my shoulder . . . I'd hoped it meant you were free to—"

She cut Rafael off, not wanting to feel the guilt, to have to examine her actions.

"I'm sorry," she said again. "I should've been clear. I didn't mean to . . . I should've . . ." She trailed off, not sure where to go. And then she looked at him, focused in on his dark brown eyes with their flecks of gold. "It's true," she said. "Everything I told you. It's all true. I just . . . everything feels so tangled right now."

He looked at her for a silent moment and then sighed.

"I'm still helping you with your speech tomorrow night, right?" she asked quietly. "And we're still doing the fund-raiser on Tuesday?"

Rafael took a deep breath and let it out. "Right," he said.

And then Nina's phone vibrated. She looked down. As if he had read her mind, it was Tim calling. There were texts, too. Ten or twelve of them that she hadn't seen. *Call me*, they all said. *Call me now.*

"I'm sorry," Nina said to Rafael. She was worried that something bad had happened to TJ or to Caro—or to Tim himself. "I need to pick this up."

"Are you okay?" Nina said when she answered the phone.

"What in the hell is going on?" Tim replied. "Twitter just told me that you're cheating on me. With your ex-boss, in fact. Please tell me Twitter is wrong."

Nina looked over at Rafael.

Was she going to lie to Tim? Or finally be honest about her feelings for someone else?

"It's wrong," she said. "I'll be right over."

In her heart, all she could think was: *Joseph Gregory's Daughter Follows in Her Father's Footsteps.*

53

ALL THROUGH THE TAXI RIDE TO TIM'S APARTMENT, Nina kept trying to figure out what to say to him, how to say it. She'd told Rafael that a picture of them was posted on Twitter, and she was really sorry, but she had to go. They'd talk tomorrow, she'd said. She'd told him that in spite of the crazy photographer and the way it ended, this was the best night she'd had in a long while. And then she'd hailed a cab and asked the driver to take the quickest route to East 10th Street.

I wasn't cheating, she would say. Which was true. They didn't kiss. They'd kept their clothes on.

It was just a business dinner. Which was also true. It was. They'd been in the office and went to get a burger. It wasn't a big deal. As a working woman, as the head of the Gregory Corporation, she'd have business dinners all the time. Tim would understand that. He'd have to understand that.

But she knew it wasn't just a business dinner. She knew it was more. And she knew she wanted to do it again. She wanted to sit with Rafael. And talk with him. Lean her head against his shoulder. Touch her skin to his. The way she felt when she was with Rafael was so different from how she felt with Tim. The spark, the zing. The freedom.

Nina pulled up the web browser on her phone and Googled her name and Rafael's together. The first thing that popped up was a photograph of the two of them, holding hands and running toward the kitchen at the Dublin Pub. She was looking at him, and he was glancing at her over his shoulder. There were grins on both of their faces.

She clicked on the photograph, and a headline came up: *The Princess and the Politician: How Long Have They Been Together?* Then underneath that photo was a smaller one of the hug that Samira had tweeted the night of the primary. Rafael's eyes were closed, his cheek against Nina's hair. And her arms were so tight around Rafael's back that her fingers made dimples in his suit jacket. God, was that what they'd looked like? No wonder Tim was so upset. But honestly, why couldn't the media have just left them alone? Why did anyone care?

Nina went back to the Google search list and clicked on another news outlet. The same original photo was there, the one of them racing into the kitchen, but then next to it was a picture from that ages-ago spread of Nina's parents in *People*. This headline said: *Rafael O'Connor-Ruiz Looks at Nina Just Like Joseph Gregory Looked at Phoebe*. Nina inspected the photo, the expression on Rafael's face, on her dad's. And it was true. The awed, amused, adoring look was there for the world to see. Jesus.

Nina's phone chimed. It was Rafael.

Jane just sent me the links, he wrote. *It's more than Twitter. We're all over the Internet. I'm really sorry.*

Nina stared at her phone. She didn't know how to respond. This was why her father had created the headline game. This was the worst-case scenario. She opened up the last conversation she had with him. *I could use some help here, Dad*, she thought. *You, too, Mom.*

She scrolled through their last weeks of texts, looking for inspiration. How would he have fixed this? What would he have said to create the least amount of damage? She wished she could ask him what to do. And at the same time, she was almost glad he wasn't here to see his daughter disappoint him so publicly.

Nina pulled a tissue from her purse and tried to blot the tears threatening to overflow her lower lashes. She took a deep breath. *Rocks*, she thought. *Pigeons. Turtles. Grapefruits.*

NINA HAD GOTTEN HER EMOTIONS under control by the time the cab pulled up to Tim's building. The external could be fixed with a press release from the campaign and an announcement of her and Tim's engagement. If that was what she wanted. But the internal. The feelings she had when she was with Rafael. That was so much harder to figure out.

Nina took the elevator up to Tim's floor. She could've opened his apartment door with her key but felt like she shouldn't. He'd seemed so upset. So she knocked.

Tim opened the door. "You don't let yourself in anymore?" he asked.

Nina sighed. Already she'd done the wrong thing. "I didn't want to surprise you," she said.

"You mean like how you surprised me by making bedroom eyes at that politician?"

"I wasn't—" Nina knew getting defensive wouldn't help, but it was hard not to when Tim was on the attack. This wasn't a side of him she saw often, but she knew it existed. She'd seen it directed at other people before, but never at her. She took a deep breath. "May I come in?" she asked.

Tim stepped aside. She walked in and sat down on the couch. Tim sat on the love seat, across from her. His body was rigid.

"I really don't know what to make of this. I know you said you weren't cheating on me, but it sure as hell looks like you were. That hug picture from primary night. The way you looked at him. What's going on, Nina? Do you know what your father would've said about this? About these headlines?"

Nina took a deep breath. She knew. Of course she knew. And she also knew that Tim didn't believe her. She could tell. He'd chosen the press over her. And he knew just what to say to cut her deeply. He'd hurt her on purpose. It took a lot to get Nina to show her anger. An anonymously quoted source, some-one who worked for the Gregory Corporation, once described her father as a "slow burn"; he wasn't easy to anger, but once he did, watch out. Nina thought that wasn't quite right. He was like her. The anger was there, but it was controlled. It took a lot for her and her father to let their emotions show. The feelings had to seem justified, the repercussions worth the expression. Nina clenched her fists to keep herself in check.

"I'm going to say it again," she told Tim. "The media's wrong."

"But that hug picture—" he protested.

"Was just a hug," Nina said. "On primary night. We were all happy. He hugged me. The end."

"But his face—"

"I can't control his face," Nina said. "And the fact that you're blaming me for his expression is inane. Do you hear yourself?"

Tim had the grace to look embarrassed. "What about to-night, then?"

This was the harder part to explain. "Tonight . . . he asked me for help with a speech. I told you that. So I went over. Mostly because I wanted to feel like myself for a little while. And after we worked for a few hours, we were hungry, so we went to get a burger next door at the Dublin Pub. A business dinner. Like people have when they work together. I assume that photographer had told the restaurants near the office that he'd pay for tips, if Rafael ever came in alone with a woman, and he did, and the photographer came. And so we ran into the kitchen."

Tim looked visibly calmer now. "So it really was innocent? Nothing happened between the two of you?"

Nina wished she had a glass of water. Or wine. Or anything, really. Something to sip, to give her time to think while she swallowed.

"Nothing physical happened," Nina said, not wanting to lie to Tim, answering what she'd wished he asked.

Tim blanched. "What does that mean?"

"I'm sorry," Nina said. "After that, we were running, and holding hands, and talking on a bench along the river. And I didn't kiss him, we didn't do anything—but, Tim, I wanted to." She bit her lip to keep it from trembling. In admitting this, she felt like a failure. Like she wasn't strong enough. Like she was a kid again and her father was telling her not to cry in front of the guests, but she couldn't stop the flow of tears. And she knew telling the truth like this would hurt Tim, which she never wanted to do. But after finding out so many of her father's se-crets, she didn't want to keep any of her own. Not any longer.

"But you didn't," Tim said. He was cooling down. "You're just colleagues."

Was Tim telling himself a story? Purposefully misunderstanding her?

"Did you hear me?" Nina asked, hating to repeat it. "I just told you I wanted to kiss someone else."

Tim rubbed his hands along the thighs of his jeans. "It's okay. I want to kiss other women, too, sometimes. But I don't. I'm not really worried about you wanting to kiss someone else as long as you don't actually do it."

Nina looked at him now. His hair slightly out of place, as if he'd been raking his hands through it. His beard neatly trimmed.

"Wait, you want to kiss other women?" Nina asked. "Legitimate people you know, or celebrities? Like, how you've had a crush on Anna Paquin since she played Polexia Aphrodisia in *Almost Famous*?"

Tim sat up a little straighter. "Are we being completely honest?" he asked.

"Of course," Nina said. Why would he even need to ask if they were being honest? She thought about last night, when he came over and said he needed to remember that he loved her. Did something happen then that he'd kept secret? Was he afraid of his feelings for someone else, too?

"You know Casey from my office? The one with really long hair who heads up the team of web designers?" Tim said, slowly, as if the confession was costing him something, but it was something he was willing to pay to make things right with Nina. "I wouldn't mind kissing her."

Nina was quiet.

"I haven't," Tim said quickly. "But you said to be honest, and if we're being honest, I wouldn't mind. That's why it's okay if you want to kiss Rafael. It's normal. Just . . . you know, there's a difference between wanting and doing."

Nina took a deep breath. Was it normal? She swallowed hard. She knew that what she was going to say next had the ability to explode their world. "Maybe we should do it," she said. "Maybe both of us should, if that's what we want."

Tim stood up and sat down next to Nina. "Wait, no," he said, grabbing her hand. "That's not what I meant. I don't want to date Casey. I don't want a future with Casey. I want a future with you. Everything's going to be better soon. Once we get married. And you're on the board of the Gregory Corporation. And we have kids. And I can be CEO after my dad retires. Everything will be perfect."

Nina's brain screeched to a halt. She blinked at Tim. "You want to run the Gregory Corporation?" she asked him.

"Don't you want me to?" he asked back.

Nina looked at him. How had they never talked about this? How had she not known that this was his vision for the future?

"I . . . I don't know," she said. "I haven't thought about it."

"What do you mean you haven't thought about it?" Tim looked perplexed. "Remember when we played 'business' when we were kids, when everyone else was playing house? I was always the CEO. You were always the chairman of the board. And we carried those briefcases my mom got us and used your dad's old crossword puzzles as our balance sheets."

They had done that. They had pretended. But they were kids. They'd also thought they could climb a rainbow if they put suction cups on the bottom of their sneakers. "That was a game, Tim," she said. "I didn't think it was real."

Tim looked at her. She looked at Tim. It seemed like they didn't know how to speak to each other anymore. She didn't know how to fix what was happening between them. The ring Tim bought her felt heavy on its chain around her neck.

"I . . . I don't know what to say," Tim said. "I don't understand how we got so far off track."

"Me neither." Nina looked around Tim's apartment, as familiar to her as her own. There were photographs of both of them everywhere. A small painting she'd had commissioned for him for his birthday, of the pier where they'd first kissed. Neither of them said anything for a while. Finally Tim spoke.

"Do you . . . want to stay over tonight?" he asked. "And maybe we can talk more in the morning?"

The easy thing to do was to stay. But Nina thought about that letter in her parents' nightstand. She thought about her conversations with Leslie. What it felt like to be next to Rafael. She thought about the parts of herself that she still wanted to explore and develop and discover. It was too much. Everything was too much.

"I think it might be better if I sleep at my place tonight," Nina said. "I just . . . I'm so mixed up right now."

"Are you sure?" he asked.

"I think . . . I think I need to be alone tonight," she said.

"Okay." His hands were in his lap, and he lifted one as if he were going to touch Nina again, but then didn't. "I love you," he told her. "More than anyone else in the world. I really love you."

Nina took a deep breath. "I love you, too," she said. "That's never been the problem."

Tim stood up and held out his hand. "We'll talk tomorrow?" he said.

Nina took it. "Of course," she answered.

As Nina walked out the door, she turned back to Tim. "Last night," she said. "Before you came over. Was Casey out watching baseball with you and the guys?"

Tim quietly closed the door without answering.

54

EVEN THOUGH IT WAS A LONG WALK, NINA DECIDED
not to jump in a cab or take the subway. She needed to clear her
head, to think, to move. Despite the fact that it was late, the
city was alive with people and noise, and she took comfort in
being a part of it. In New York City you were never alone in any
situation—by the laws of probability there had to be at least
hundreds, if not thousands, of people who were going through
the same thing at the same time. Nina found it consoling.

As she walked, she pulled out her phone; it had blown up
with calls and voice mails and texts from Leslie and Jane and
Pris and Rafael. Nina scrolled through them.

Is this real? (Leslie)

Holy shit. We have to talk strategy. Call me ASAP. (Jane)

*What's going on over there? Brent just showed me a picture of you
and Rafael on Twitter.* (Pris)

Don't read the comments! (Leslie again)

Are you okay? Will you please call me when you can? (Rafael)

Nina called Rafael. He picked up on the first ring.

"I'm so sorry," he said. No greeting, just that. "I shouldn't have grabbed your hand. We should've just sat there and had our picture taken. I made it worse. I wasn't thinking."

Rafael's voice was heavy with apology. Nina could hear it through the phone. "It's okay," she said. "It's not your fault."

"It is," Rafael insisted. "I should've been thinking about the end result of those photographs. I'm just . . . I'm not used to it yet. Was Tim very upset? Jane just practically crucified me."

Nina thought about the media, the paparazzi really—there was a difference. Her father used them to his benefit, to the Gregory Corporation's benefit. He knew how to play them, what to say to whom, how to achieve the desired outcome. He'd trained her to think that way, but she hadn't been thinking. Not where Rafael was concerned.

There was a bench in a small park across the street. Nina sat down on it.

"It's funny. He was livid at first, and then he wasn't," Nina said. "He told me he wanted to kiss this woman Casey at his office. That it was normal to want to kiss other people, no matter who you were with, as long as you didn't do it. I . . . I don't know what to make of it all."

Rafael was quiet. In the silence, Nina realized she'd just told Rafael she wanted to kiss him. Before the conversation had a chance to veer off in that direction, she asked, "What do you think?"

She could picture him running his hand through his hair on the other end of the phone. "I don't think you want my advice, Palabrecita," he said.

A late-night pigeon cooed somewhere behind her. "I think I probably know what it would be," she said, thinking once more about what it felt like to have Rafael's arms around her on the bench, the electric feeling she got when she was near him. What did he say it was? Adrenaline and cortisol.

"I'm just going to say one thing," he said, "which is that since I met you, I haven't wanted to kiss anyone but you."

Nina took a deep breath. She thought about kissing Rafael and goose bumps rose on her arms. She stopped herself from thinking about it.

"What did you tell Jane?" she asked.

Rafael sighed. "I told her we're just friends, of course. That you were helping me out. That the media was reading into things that weren't there."

Nina thought about her night with Rafael. She thought about how their conversation felt easy and comfortable. How her body thrilled when she looked at him, when their hands touched, when his lips were on her temple. She thought about the photograph of the two of them. The way he looked at her. The media was right.

"Good answer," she said.

"Nina—" he started.

Nina could tell she didn't want to hear what was going to come after that, so she jumped in, cutting him off. "What did Jane say?" she asked.

Rafael shifted focus. "She said that if that's the case, we could ignore it completely, but that if we do, it might distract from the campaign."

"She's not wrong," Nina said. "We should probably just issue a statement. And then not say anything more."

"Yeah," Rafael said.

She looked up at the lights of the city that twinkled like stars, all those people Rafael wanted to lead—wanted to help— tucked into their apartments, their lamps glowing strong and steady. "If anything were to . . ." She swallowed, not sure if she should finish that sentence. But then she did. "If anything were to happen between us, it shouldn't happen until after the election anyway," she said, knowing that she was giving him the idea that something could happen. "Even if we see each other as friends now, the media will see me as a staffer."

"I never saw you that way," he said. "To me, you were always an equal."

Nina sighed. The truth was more complicated for her. "It doesn't change what we were, though. And that's all they'll hear."

"You're right," he agreed. "So . . . friends for another month? And then we can see?"

"And then we can see," she echoed.

She had to figure out what she wanted. She and Tim could probably get past this—they had enough history, enough of a foundation that it could be fixed. It would take work. It wouldn't be easy. It was doable, though. But was that what she wanted her life to look like?

She had a month. Then she'd see.

55

THE NEXT MORNING, NINA CALLED CARO FIRST THING, approving the menu for the fund-raiser and explaining how the media had blown everything out of proportion. Caro had seemed to believe her, but Nina could sense that there was something else Tim's mom wanted to say. Something she might have said if Nina weren't dating her son.

Then Nina started reviewing how much money the Gregory restaurants spent on vegetables each day, which seemed astronomical. She wanted to know how many of those vegetables were used, and how many went to waste. And what the profit margin was on each of the dishes. She wished someone would locate those Manxome Consulting reports. As she went through the spreadsheets slowly and methodically, she stuck Post-it notes with questions everywhere. She even climbed into the lofted storage space in her apartment to pull down some of her business school textbooks, glad she'd decided not to send them out to the East Hampton house, where anything she and her father didn't really need went to retire.

Then Jane called.

"Hi there," Nina said, when she picked up the phone.

"I'm surprised you didn't call me the moment you woke up," was Jane's reply.

Nina took off her glasses and rubbed her eyes. "Rafael said that you were going to issue a statement, and there wouldn't be any more trouble," Nina responded. "I figured you didn't need me bothering you. It was just a business dinner. And the hug—we were happy."

Jane was silent for a moment. "Am I going to look like an asshole tomorrow or next week or next month if I put out a statement that says that nothing is happening between the two of you? Is a photograph going to appear, or a voice mail or text exchange that someone hacked, making me look like an idiot?"

Nina thought back to the night before, to what she'd said, to what he'd said, to what their texts read. "We haven't as much as kissed each other," Nina answered. She was pivoting. "You know I'm with Tim."

"So if I'm quoted as saying, 'Rafael O'Connor-Ruiz and Nina Gregory have a purely professional relationship,' would I be lying?" Jane pressed.

"Well," Nina said. "I might use the word *friends*, instead."

"Shit," Jane responded. "Are you fucking kidding me? We've put in too many hours for too many days for this . . . if you screw everything up because you couldn't keep your goddamn hands off the candidate . . . Don't do this to me, Nina. I swear to God, if he loses this election because the two of you—"

"We're not," Nina said. "Jane. Relax. I'd never do anything to mess up the campaign. You know me. Rafael and I are friends now. Just friends."

"You'd better be telling me the truth," Jane said.

"I am," Nina said. "I am."

Jane hung up, and then a text came through from Rafael.

Sorry about that, it said. *If it makes you feel any better, she said worse to me.*

Nina didn't usually use emojis with anyone other than Tim, but she sent back the one with very big eyes and pink cheeks.

You said it, he replied.

Nina paced around her apartment. Jane wasn't right. She hadn't screwed up Rafael's campaign. Or had she? She'd already screwed up her relationship with Tim. And she was afraid she was going to screw up the Gregory Corporation—if her father hadn't done that already. Why not screw up a campaign, too?

Her loft felt tiny. There wasn't enough air, enough space to breathe.

She picked up the phone and called Priscilla.

"Lunch at Ippudo?" she asked when Pris picked up the phone. "In, like, two hours?"

"Would love to," Priscilla answered, "especially because I want to know the story behind that photograph of you and Rafael, but I've got a spin class in an hour and a half and I scored the best bike. Want to come?"

Nina was not a fan of spin class. All the effort and you stayed in the same spot the whole time. But she needed to get out of the apartment. "Sure," she said. "The cycle studio near your place?"

"Always," Pris said. "I'll sign you up."

"Thanks," Nina replied, hanging up the phone.

She put on some running gear that seemed spin class appropriate, and then dialed Leah, who was in charge of the Gregory restaurants, saying she was trying to get to know the company a little better and would love to ask some questions. Leah's voice seemed to take on an extra-professional tone when Nina asked her first question.

"We fill the Dumpster about twice a week, and most of that is food waste," she said.

"And the Dumpster is how big?" Nina asked.

"I think it's four cubic yards," Leah answered. "It's mostly food people leave on their plates. And rolls. We throw away so many rolls. Once we put the basket on the table, they're done."

Smaller portions, Nina thought, *personal rolls instead of a basket, so the customer could say no.* But someone must've thought of this before and rejected it.

"What about the food that goes bad before it's eaten? How much of that is there?" Nina asked.

"Not a ton, but some. We're pretty good at predicting how much we'll need, but it's not a hard science."

Donations, Nina thought. *Tax write-offs maybe.*

"Thanks," she said. "I might call back later."

Nina flipped again to the pages with the Manxome Consulting line items. She couldn't find a listing for them anywhere on the Internet. Maybe she'd ask her father's lawyer to look the company up in the Corporation and Business Entity Database. Or maybe she'd ask Rafael. He should have access, too. She really wanted to see what they had to say. Not reinvent the wheel if she didn't have to.

Nina jumped in a cab to head across town.

56

AFTER THE SPIN CLASS, NINA AND PRIS SAT DOWN IN the cycle studio's juice bar, Pris with carrot juice and Nina with a mango smoothie.

"I didn't realize how close you and Rafael were when you asked me to throw that fund-raiser for his campaign," Pris said, as she tightened her ponytail.

"We weren't," Nina said. "And we're not all that close now, really. The photo made us look closer than we are." She was lying to Pris, but she'd learned years ago from her father that if you were selling one story to the press, you didn't tell the real story to anyone who didn't need to know it. Pris didn't need to know. Leslie had always been an exception, since she was so far removed from New York society. Pris, though, was at the center of it.

"But Tuesday's fund-raiser in your dad's—I mean, your—hotel? Brent and I can come, by the way."

"Oh good! I'm so glad," Nina said. There had been lots of RSVPs already. About seventy-five couples had said yes so far.

Nina wondered how much of it was a morbid curiosity to see how Joseph Gregory's daughter handled the company's first corporate event without him. "And I'm doing that because Christian asked—and because my dad probably would have." She shrugged.

"Yeah." Pris took another sip of her juice and winced slightly. "I always feel so good ordering carrot juice, but then when I go to drink it, I remember that it doesn't really taste that good at all."

For the first time that day, Nina laughed. That sentence right there illustrated why she'd stayed friends with Pris for so many years. Pris wasn't the kind of person who would pretend to like carrot juice if she didn't, and there are so many people in the world who would.

"Want to split this smoothie?" Nina asked.

Priscilla looked around. "If you don't tell my trainer," she whispered with a wink.

Nina laughed again and slid her smoothie over so it was halfway between her and Pris. "Secret's safe with me," she said.

Pris dipped her straw into the smoothie and took a sip. "Oh God, that's so much better," she said after she swallowed. "Did you pierce your ear?"

Nina lifted her hand to touch her piercing. "I did," she said. "Tim hates it."

Pris inspected Nina from a few different angles. "I don't," she said. "I like it. It makes you seem multilayered. More than you appear at first glance."

Nina found herself laughing once more. Pris always had that effect on her. "Are you saying that I'm boring?"

"No," Priscilla said. "Not that you *are* boring, just that sometimes you might *appear* boring."

Nina stopped laughing. "What do you mean?" she asked.

"To be honest, your clothes are always nice but kind of bland."

"My clothes?" Nina looked down. She was wearing black capri leggings and a gray tank top. Pris's top was turquoise.

"You just . . . you seem to dress to blend in instead of to stand out. You always have," Pris said, taking another sip of the smoothie.

Did she? Nina thought about it. Most of her clothing was black, gray, navy, brown, cream. Elegant but sensible. Respectable. Why did she dress that way?

"Maybe I should change that, then," Nina said. "You have time to go shopping?"

57

THEY WENT BACK TO PRIS AND BRENT'S NEW APART-
ment to shower.

"Brent wants to start trying," Pris said as they walked by the
door leading to the wing waiting for the children the two of
them planned to have one day.

Nina smiled at her friend. "That's exciting," she said. "You
two are going to have the cutest, blondest baby on the Upper
East Side."

Pris laughed. "I haven't said anything to anyone else yet. Not
even Hayley."

Nina reached out and squeezed Pris's hand. "I won't say a
word. I'm glad you told me—it's nice to have something happy
to think about."

Pris squeezed Nina's hand back, then led her to the guest
bedroom, which had an en suite bathroom. "I'll grab you some
clothes," she said.

While Nina showered, she thought about the babies she'd
been imagining she'd have with Tim. The ones she'd expected

would be friends with Pris and Brent's kids. She'd assumed they'd spend time together out in East Hampton, maybe ski together on family vacations. If they had girls, they'd send them to Brearley, and the boys would go to Collegiate. As much as Nina thought she was different from her father and her friends, she was the same, too. If she and Tim broke up, she'd lose that whole life. She'd lose those kids. And TJ and Caro as second parents. And all of the traditions they'd built up over the years. The intimacy, too, of knowing someone as well as she and Tim knew each other.

"Clothes are on the bed!" Priscilla called from the guest room. "And since we're getting you a new, more exciting wardrobe, I left you a fun outfit. Just giving you fair warning."

Nina got out of the shower and found a comb and an assortment of hair products in the vanity. She chose a volumizer and then blew her hair dry upside down. She looked different already.

As she was putting on a pair of artfully ripped gray jeans, a white tank top, and an off-the-shoulder yellow sweater, Pris came into the room. "Here," she said, "try some navy mascara."

Nina wanded her eyelashes and then blinked into the mirror. "I like this," she said.

"Keep it," Pris told her. "It looks better on you."

THE TWO WOMEN HEADED down Madison Avenue and then stopped in front of Reiss.

"First stop?" Priscilla asked.

"First stop," Nina answered. Then she walked inside and pulled out a simple gray dress.

"Not that!" Pris said. "Okay, you go to the dressing room. I'm picking. And you have to try it all on!"

Nina found herself wearing intricate patterns and bold color blocks. The minute the clothes were on her body, Pris rendered a verdict: definitely yes, definitely no, or needs further consideration. Looking at the woman in the mirror, with her wild hair and ear piercing and blue eyelashes, Nina felt like she did when she was out with Rafael: free.

They went from store to store, and except for a red slim-fitting pantsuit that Nina refused to try—and Priscilla knew better than to push—the afternoon was what Pris declared "a smashing success."

Nina had bought so much that she'd called a car to bring it all home. Patterned wrap dresses and form-fitting cigarette pants. Flouncy skirts and tiny belts. She loved all of them.

Pris had even insisted that she buy a royal blue purse that Nina switched her wallet and phone into immediately and carried for the rest of the day, jamming her old black Birkin in a shopping bag. Her father had gotten it for her, and she'd never felt completely comfortable carrying it anyway. She had no problem spending money when she loved something, but that bag seemed like the sort of thing her father bought so that when his daughter walked around with it, it would telegraph his success to the world.

"This is the new me," Nina had said, when she slung the blue bag over her shoulder, tossing a fringed scarf she'd also just bought around her neck.

"Love the new you," Priscilla said, giving her a kiss on the cheek.

Nina loved the new her, too. In these clothes, she felt confident and powerful. Like someone worth noticing. Like someone who would make bold choices, whatever they were.

She knew, though, from the moment she saw herself in the

mirror, that Tim wouldn't agree. And then she felt bad for thinking that. Maybe she wasn't being fair. They needed to talk. She needed to tell him how she'd been feeling, what she wanted, give him the chance to know her in the way she hadn't been, tell him how important it was to her that things change. If she could surprise Tim, maybe he could surprise her, too. Maybe he'd understand.

58

THAT NIGHT, SHE MET TIM FOR A DRINK IN ONE OF
her new dresses. Magenta satin, cinched at the waist, 1950s style.
It made her look like she had more of a shape than she actually
did, giving her curves where her body dealt in straight lines.

Her hair was still wild, and she'd reapplied the blue mascara. It was going to be fun. A date. Just the two of them, outside either of their apartments, getting a drink and spending
time together. Tim said he was okay with Nina going back to
campaign headquarters that night at eight, as long as other
people were going to be there, too. She understood, and appreciated that he was comfortable with her going at all.

Before then, she wanted to focus completely on her time with
Tim. Do her best to remember all of the reasons she'd liked dating him, why she'd agreed to marry him. To make sure that it
was Tim she wanted, not just the life she'd lead with Tim. And
most important, give him a chance to understand her. No matter
how Rafael made her feel, Tim had been Nina's forever. Her
past, her present, her future—and she couldn't throw that away.

Help me figure this out, Mom, she thought. She'd been wondering all day what her mother would do in her situation. Or, even more to the point, what her mother would want *her* to do.

Nina was sitting at the bar when Tim walked in.

"Well, that's bright," he said, before kissing her hello.

She slid off the bar stool. "It's new," she said, doing a little twirl. She wasn't usually a twirling sort of person, but this dress begged for it. And she was determined not to let his criticism deflate her mood.

"There's a lot that's new these days, isn't there," Tim said. He wasn't being snide or critical, just observing. And it gave Nina the kind of opening she'd hoped for.

"Listen," Nina said, getting back on the stool, "I know you like it when things are the same—it's actually something I love about you, how stable you are, how dependable—but now, for me . . . it's . . . Just because I did something one way once doesn't mean I want to do it that way forever. There are things that I'm just discovering and . . . I'm not feeling very predictable right now. I need you to be okay with that."

She'd been trying to figure out the right words to say, and those were definitely not them. But maybe he'd get her meaning anyway. She hoped he would.

Tim cleared his throat and ordered a vodka tonic before he responded. "I can try to be more open," he said. "If you need me to be."

Nina let out a breath. "Thank you," she said.

She wasn't sure where to go after that. Neither, it seemed, was Tim.

"So, how was your day?" he asked.

"I went shopping with Pris," she said. "And found out that the Gregory Corporation is wasting a ton of bread."

"All restaurants waste bread," he answered. "I'm sure our dads have looked into that and minimized it as much as they could."

Nina shrugged. "I'm not really sure if they did," she said.

"Of course they did," he said, dismissing her words with the wave of a hand. "If there's one thing our fathers did well, it was run that business. They made it so much more profitable than it had been when your grandfather died."

Nina looked at Tim as he took a big swallow of his vodka tonic. She knew what their fathers had done. She'd grown up hearing about it, too. The second hotel. The restaurants, the bars, the clubs on the roof, the redesigned event spaces that brought in millions each year alone. But that didn't mean it was perfect, that there wasn't an even better way to do things, or a different direction to go in.

She thought about what he'd said the night before, how he wanted to be the CEO after his father retired. If this was how he was going to respond to her, how he was going to think about her ideas, that couldn't happen.

"I've been thinking," Nina said. "About what you said last night."

"Which part?" Tim asked, taking another gulp of his drink. She could tell how hard this conversation was for him. How much he wanted things to work but didn't know how to make that happen. He wasn't happy. She wasn't happy. And she knew that what she was about to say wasn't going to help the situation. But it had to be said.

Nina swirled the wine in her glass, watching the light reflect off the deep burgundy, turning it gold and navy and amber. "When your dad retires, I really think it would be better to hire someone outside the family." She wasn't looking at him. "Things are less complicated that way."

He didn't say anything. Nina shifted her eyes up.

There was a look on Tim's face like she'd just punched him in the stomach. "What's going on?" he said. "Is this your way of telling me you think I'm not up for the job? I could do it, Nina. I could do it well. I can't believe I have to even say this. I thought you believed in me."

Nina felt tears rushing to her eyes. She'd always hated when Tim looked that way, and hated it even more that she was the one who brought that expression to his face. "It's not that," she said. "I do believe in you. I think you'd do a great job. I just don't think it's a good idea, us working together. Me being your boss."

"But our fathers—"

"Aren't us," Nina said. "They were friends."

"Best friends," Tim said.

"Best friends," Nina amended.

"But aren't we?" Tim asked.

Nina drained the glass of wine in front of her and placed it carefully on the bar. "I don't think we are anymore," she said, biting her lip. "I think we changed that, when we kissed each other, when we slept together. When you date your best friend, he's not your best friend anymore. He's your boyfriend. It's different."

"Your fiancé," Tim said, mumbling the words. Then: "I'm your fiancé," he said, loudly.

Nina pulled the ring out from where it had been hanging on its chain under her new magenta dress. She rolled it around in her fingers. The word *fiancé* made her uncomfortable. In all honesty, from the day after she'd told Tim she'd marry him, things hadn't felt right. And they'd felt more and more wrong as time went on.

The old Nina wouldn't have done anything about it. But she was her new self now. Or at least on the way to becoming her new self.

"Maybe you shouldn't be," she said, quietly.

She hadn't gone into the night with this plan. It hadn't been what she thought would happen at all, but it felt like the right thing to say. It felt true.

"Tim, I love you. I will always love you, but I don't think I should marry you. At least not now. I don't know who I am anymore. You keep talking about the old Nina, but I'm turning into a new one. You want me to stay the same, and I don't want to do that. As much as I love you, I can't compromise myself for you."

"What does that mean?" Tim's voice cut through the din of the bar straight into her heart. "What are you compromising? My father's been picking up your slack while you go shopping for dresses and get your goddamn ear pierced like a teenager. What are you compromising?"

The bartender came over. "Is everything okay over here?" he asked.

"We're fine," Tim shot back.

But the bartender didn't move until Nina echoed his words. "We're fine," she said. "It's okay."

He nodded and headed to the other end of the bar, but Nina could feel his eyes still on them.

"So what are you compromising?" Tim said, not as loud this time, but just as intense.

"I'm compromising the idea of being with someone who wouldn't criticize me for that," she said, matching his intensity. "My father just died. The last family member I had. I'm sorry if your dad has to run the business he's getting paid to run, while

I grieve my father. I'm sorry if you don't like—what is it you don't like, new dresses? Earrings? Pimentos and pomegranate seeds?"

"It's not that," Tim said.

"Then what?" Nina said. "What is it?"

Tim rubbed his face with his hand. "You know how you feel like you didn't know your father? How you're all off balance now because the man you thought he was wasn't the man he actually was inside? That's how I feel about you." His voice broke. He was crying. "I thought I knew you. And it turns out I don't. And it kills me that you never trusted me enough, or loved me enough, or whatever it was, to share yourself with me until now."

Nina felt tears overflowing her eyes, too. In finding her freedom, she had hurt the person she had once loved more than anything. "But I didn't know who I could be," she said. "It wasn't that I didn't trust you. I just didn't really know me. Not until now. And now that I'm starting to . . ."

"Now that you're starting to, you don't love me anymore."

"No!" Nina said, reaching out and grabbing his hand. "That's not true. I do love you. But I'm just not sure if I'm in love with you. Or, honestly, if you're in love with me."

Tim didn't say anything. His hand was limp in hers.

"Maybe," she ventured. "Maybe we can go back to being friends for a while? Until we figure things out?"

Tim pulled his hand away and wrapped it around his now-empty glass of vodka. He wasn't looking at her. He was staring at the glass.

"What if I don't want to?" Tim said, so quietly that she could barely hear him. "Nina, I've known ever since college that I wanted to be with you. Us together was always my plan. But I wasn't ready then. I didn't want to start something unless I knew it could end in forever. It's rare to get more than one chance to make a relationship work. And we were both focused on our own paths. We weren't in the right place. And so I waited and dated other people, and I watched you date other people, always wondering if something would work, if we'd miss our chance—"

"I think we might have," Nina said softly.

"Maybe we can still make it work," Tim said, leaning toward Nina. "I'll try harder. And maybe you can try harder. And we can figure it all out. We can live the life our parents always dreamed for us."

Nina shook her head sadly. He wasn't even listening. "I don't think it'll make a difference." She was slipping the necklace over her head. "No matter how hard we try, I don't think it'll work. You're right. I'm not who you thought I was. I'm not who *I* thought I was. And I want to live my own life, not one that was dreamed for me by someone else."

"Nina," Tim said. He looked heartbroken. She felt heartbroken, too. But for the first time in a month, the low-level panic, one she couldn't put a name to, subsided. This felt right. "We're partners. We're a team. We always have been."

"Maybe we were, but . . . I'm sorry." Nina held the ring in her hand, the beautiful ring he'd picked out just for her, with sapphires the color of her eyes. "You're someone I love and care about and want to spend time with until we're as old and gray as we'll ever get. You've been in my life forever and I always want you there. But—"

"Then why can't we fix this?" Tim still looked broken.

"I don't think I can agree to marry anyone right now," Nina said. The ring had slipped between her fingers and was dangling from her hand, swaying slightly on its chain. "At least not until I figure out who I am."

"Is this because you found out your parents' marriage wasn't as wonderful as you thought it was?"

"No," Nina said. "This is about us, about me. Not about them."

"Is it?" he asked, quietly.

Nina thought about it. It wasn't, but also it was. This conversation was the culmination of everything that had happened over the past month—or maybe even longer. "It's both," she said.

He took a deep breath. "You're still holding that fund-raiser on Tuesday, right?" he asked.

Nina nodded.

"Let's decide after that. And there's no need to rush a decision about whether we should work together or not. I really believe, with all my heart, that we're meant to be a team. In everything. I'm not ready to give up on us. Let's try. For a few days. Let's really try. And then we can see."

And because she loved him. Because he was her oldest friend, Nina said yes. And she called Rafael to say she wasn't going to be able to make it that night after all.

59

NINA AND TIM SPENT THE WHOLE WEEKEND TOGETHER—
a visit to MoMA, dinner at the Modern, a ride on the
Carousel—but even though it would've looked to anyone on
the outside like they were having a great time, Nina felt awk-
ward, like everything was strained, like one wrong word would
deflate the whole weekend. The only way she made it through
was by concentrating on the fund-raiser. In her spare moments,
she worked with Christian, with Caro, with Jane, making sure
that everything was perfect. On Monday, she spent an hour
with the bartender at Los Tortolitos creating a specialty cocktail. And she promised TJ that after the fund-raiser, she'd be
there full time, ready to take over the company.

She also called her father's lawyer and left a message with
his secretary, asking if he wouldn't mind looking up whether
Manxome Consulting was still an active corporation.

AND THEN TUESDAY NIGHT came. They had 250 RSVPs,
and Christian was glowing when he showed up at the hotel.

Nina had arrived early, too, and Caro kept shooing her out of the way. "You're hosting this," she said, "not staffing it," when she found Nina rearranging the leaves in one of the centerpieces.

Mia walked in with a couple of other people who worked advance for the campaign, and Nina stopped to say hello.

"That's a beautiful dress," Mia said.

Nina had put on a Badgley Mischka maxidress with an elegant floral design that looked as if it had been hand-painted on the fabric. It was one of her recent Pris purchases and made Nina feel like a living, breathing piece of art.

"Thank you," Nina said.

Soon after, Tim appeared in a perfectly tailored three-piece suit, and the two of them circulated, saying hello to friends and acquaintances and encouraging them to try the specialty cocktail and the chef's newest hors d'oeuvres creations.

"We're so good at this," Tim said to her as their paths crossed in the ballroom, a glass of scotch in his hand. "And you look gorgeous."

"Thank you," Nina said with a smile. Maybe this was what Tim wanted her to see. What their life could be like, would be like. As she was greeting people, though, Nina had the same feeling she did at the Saturday brunches—like she was playing a role, the part of the heiress. Though she was no longer the heiress, she realized, she was the chair of the Gregory Corporation. The realization bowled her over, and she knew she had to leave the room or she'd start to cry. She went to take a breather in the green room they'd set up down the hall.

But when she walked in, Rafael was there, practicing his speech in the mirror.

"Oh!" she said. "I'm so sorry." It was the first time they'd seen each other since their conversation on the bench last week, and her heart raced. Cortisol and adrenaline.

He looked over at her and smiled. "No need to apologize," he said.

She wondered if his heartbeat was speeding up, too. The vibrations of his voice echoed deep inside her, as if it were set at the same frequency as her muscles and bones. God, she needed to leave this room, too. Nowhere was safe.

"Is it time for me to go on yet?" he asked.

Nina shook her head. She couldn't take her eyes off him. Clearing her throat, she said, "About another fifteen minutes. And—I'm sorry again I wasn't able to come by on Thursday. But it's probably for the best."

"Probably," he echoed. His eyes traced her bare neck and shoulders, before catching her gaze.

All she wanted to do was touch him. "I should head back," she told him. "But I'll see you in there. There's a decent crowd."

Rafael nodded. "Thank you again," he said. "For doing this."

"Of course," she answered softly.

As Nina walked back toward the ballroom, she ran into Caro in the hallway. "The campaign staff has been looking for you," she said. "Is everything okay?"

Nina felt heat rise to her cheeks and put her hands on her face. "I was just talking to Rafael," she said. "Giving him a fifteen-minute warning."

"Darling," Caro said, her eyes on Nina's cheeks, clearly noticing her blush, "be careful. You know, I have a Twitter account, too."

Nina's blush deepened. "I should go find Jane," she said.

60

AFTER SPEECHES WERE GIVEN—BOTH NINA'S AND
Rafael's—and dessert had been served, Nina took a moment to
sit down with Pris and Hayley.

"We're really the grown-ups now," Hayley was musing as
she rolled the stem of her wineglass between her fingers.

"What do you mean?" Pris asked.

"I mean we're doing what our parents used to do. All of us. I
didn't realize until I saw you up there"—she looked at Nina—
"but we've taken over. It's our turn now."

Nina looked around at the room. Hayley wasn't wrong.
Some of her father's friends had come, but it was mostly people
her age—hers and Tim's.

"We *have* grown up," Nina said, leaning back in her chair.

Pris opened her mouth to respond but then focused on something behind Nina—her eyebrows raised. Nina turned around
and immediately stood. Tim and Rafael were walking out the
door of the ballroom together. She followed as quickly as she

could in her heels. Rafael's bodyman was already there by the time she made it to the door frame, just out of view.

"—man to man," Tim was saying, in the hallway. "She's with me."

"Pardon?" Rafael said, with a quiet intensity. Nina wanted to stop them, but she was frozen, riveted.

"I saw how you look at her," Tim said. "I know we don't know each other, but if you're going to travel in these circles, other men's women are off-limits."

If you're going to travel in these circles? Other men's women? This didn't even sound like Tim. She was embarrassed. Of him. For him.

Everyone in the corner of the ballroom closest to the door had stopped talking and was trying to see what was happening.

Nina cleared her throat. "What's going on here?" she asked, stepping forward. Tim turned, surprised to find her standing there. She could see from his eyes, how they weren't quite focused, that he'd had one drink too many. And likely a conversation with Eric Lancer. He'd been a bad influence on Tim since lower school. *If you're going to travel in these circles* was absolutely something he would say.

"He keeps looking at you," Tim said, gesturing to Rafael. "I told him to stop. He can't look at you like that."

Nina looked at Rafael. "I'm sorry," she said.

"Why are you apologizing to *him*?" Tim asked. "He should be apologizing to *you*. And to me."

He turned back to Rafael just as Caro appeared at Nina's elbow. "Timothy," she said. "Come with me. Now."

As she led him down the hallway, Nina turned around and walked back into the ballroom. The guests were silently watching her. She plastered a smile on her face. "Well, that was quite a show!" she said. "When you tell your friends about it, please don't forget to mention what a lovely dress I was wearing."

A few people laughed, and then a few more, and then conversation started up again. Rafael turned to Nina. "I wasn't expecting that tonight," he said.

"Me neither," Nina replied. "I really am sorry."

"You don't have to apologize for him," Rafael told her. Then he leaned a little closer and whispered, "And he's not wrong. I can't take my eyes off you." Nina blushed again, and Rafael smiled. "I'd still love the rest of your thoughts on my new stump speech," he said.

"I . . . I don't know," Nina said.

Rafael nodded. "It's okay. I understand. Thank you again . . . for tonight, I mean."

After he left the ballroom, Nina did, too. She needed to find Tim. And Caro. After asking a few people on the staff, she located them both in the bridal suite, where Tim was sitting silently with a cup of coffee in front of him.

"He won't talk to me," Caro said when Nina walked in. "I don't know what's going on with him, or you, or you and Rafael, but whatever it is, Nina, this isn't acceptable. This is not how we do things around here. Not in this family."

Nina felt tears spring to her eyes. Now that she didn't have to pretend anymore, the weight of the whole night, the whole weekend, the whole last month, crushed down on her. "I know," she whispered.

"Can I leave you to figure this out?" Caro sighed.

Nina nodded, and the two women embraced. "I love you both," Caro said.

"I love you, too," Nina answered.

Tim didn't respond, and Caro walked out the door.

Nina looked at Tim.

Tim looked at Nina.

"What the hell were you doing?" Nina said, on the verge of losing her temper, her fists clenched, her voice shaking. Her first fund-raiser without her father. Her fund-raiser for Rafael. "Did you really think that was going to make things better? Seriously, Tim. You screwed up the whole night."

Nina braced herself for a fight, but Tim's face crumpled. He started to cry drunken tears, wiping his nose with the back of his hand. "I'm sorry," he said. "I'm so sorry. I fucked up. I'm sorry."

And as angry as she was, Nina's heart broke for him. For the pain she knew he must be in to act the way he had. She walked to him and opened her arms. He fell against her and then she cried, too, for all she would lose when their relationship ended. Because she knew now it had to.

61

THE NEXT MORNING, AFTER TIM HAD TAKEN SOME
Advil and a shower and drunk a cup and a half of coffee, Nina
walked into her kitchen and sat down next to him. She'd contemplated asking him to sleep at his place last night, but she
had been worried about him. He needed someone. He needed
her. So they slept in the same bed one last time.

But now the night was over. And everything was clearer in
the harsh light of day. She opened her hand and the engagement ring he'd given her was inside. He looked up at her.

"I really am sorry about last night," he said. His voice was
ragged.

"It's not just last night," Nina said. "I wanted us to work. I
really did. But we don't anymore."

Nina knew she was losing the children she'd imagined having
with him. She was losing the life she'd expected. And she was
probably losing Caro, too. *Be careful*, Caro had said last night.

Tim took the ring from Nina's hand.

"I don't have the energy for this now, Nina."

She looked at him. His eyes were tired, his face pale.

"I don't have the energy to keep pretending," she said. "I can't be your fiancée anymore."

He took a deep breath in, like he'd been slapped, and then slid the ring on the tip of his pinky. It stopped at his first knuckle.

"If you can't be my fiancée," he said. "Then . . . I can't . . . I don't want to be the friend watching from the sidelines, Nina. I think it would kill me to see you with someone else."

Nina ran her fingers along the rim of her coffee mug. She couldn't look at him.

"If we say good-bye now," Tim continued, "you shouldn't call me for a while. If I'm not your fiancé, I can't be your friend. Not for a long time."

Nina couldn't imagine her life without Tim in it. She wanted to argue. She wanted to explain why that was ridiculous. Spiteful even. That they were better as friends. And that he'd miss her, too. But she loved him, she truly did. And if she couldn't give him the first thing he wanted, at least she could give him the second. She took a deep breath and let it out. "Okay," she said. "If that's what you want."

Tim seemed surprised she didn't fight it. He almost wavered; Nina could see it in his expression. But then: "It is," he said, reaching into his pocket and putting her apartment keys on the table. "I'd like my keys back, too."

Nina walked across the apartment to where her bag was sitting and unhooked his keys from her key ring. "I guess this is bye for a while, then," she said, as she handed him the keys, tears blurring her vision.

Tim stood up.

"I guess so," he answered.

They hugged stiffly, Nina afraid to let herself hold him the way she wanted to, realizing she no longer had the right to. Now he was just supposed to be someone she used to know.

Nina couldn't watch as he walked out her front door.

62

A LITTLE WHILE LATER, NINA LEFT HER APARTMENT in her running clothes feeling stunned. There was a pit of guilt in her stomach that made her stop and lean against a street post, sure she would throw up. She didn't; the guilt just ate at her. And the uncertainty. She'd made a decision her father would never have agreed with. She'd given up the man he'd imagined her marrying for more than thirty years. She'd lost her best friend.

A truck was parked in front of her with a mirror at eye level. Nina peered at herself. She hadn't gotten all of her eye makeup off from the night before. Her eyes were swollen from crying. And her hair was stringy now, ratty in its ponytail. Nina fumbled in her runner's backpack for a tissue and another hair tie. Even if she felt like shit, she didn't need to look like shit. A braid might fix things a little.

She couldn't find an elastic. But she did find her tiny Swiss Army knife, a gift from Caro for her twenty-first birthday. "Just in case you ever feel threatened," Caro had said. Nina had never used it, but now she took out the scissor tool. Right there on the street, Nina decided it was time to cut her hair. She didn't want to see her old self in the mirror anymore.

Chin length, she decided as she let her hair out of its ponytail. She'd made it through just a couple locks when she realized this was insane. Down the street was a hair salon.

"Can I help you?" the woman behind the front counter asked, taking in Nina's day-old makeup and puffy eyes. "I was just opening up the shop," she said. "We don't take customers for another half hour."

"I . . . I was hoping for a haircut," Nina said.

The woman eyed her partially cut hair.

"Sometimes when something terrible happens, a new haircut is a good first step," the woman said. "I think I can squeeze you in before my first appointment."

She led Nina to a chair and threw a cape around her shoulders. "I'm Hannah, by the way. Hannah Lee."

"I'm Nina," Nina answered, leaving off her last name.

Hannah cut quickly and efficiently. As they finished up, she shook out Nina's hair with her fingers, letting it fall back into place.

"It's a great length on you," she said. "Really brings out your cheekbones."

Nina looked at herself in the mirror. She was someone else now. Her transformation was complete. Short hair, pierced ear, no Tim.

"Thank you," she said.

"Hey," Hannah answered. "Women have to stick together, yeah?"

"Yeah," Nina agreed. "We do." She thought about Leslie and Priscilla, about Caro. And she thought about her aunt. Why hadn't she stuck around? Why hadn't she been there for Nina after her mother died? Nina was going to find her. Talk to her and figure out why she'd disappeared. "How much do I owe you?" she asked Hannah.

"That'd usually be about sixty-five, but I'll give it to you for fifty," she said.

Nina nodded and handed over her credit card. "Thank you," she said, as she took the credit card receipt and left Hannah a $200 tip, equaling out what it usually cost to get her hair done. "I really needed this."

When Hannah took the receipt back her eyes opened wider. She looked at the name on Nina's credit card and Nina saw her make the connection. But Hannah didn't say anything. All she did was hand Nina back her card and a small square wrapped in foil. "This is my favorite eye makeup remover, if you want to give it a try," she said.

Nina thanked her again and, while Hannah went to the back of the shop, Nina walked over to the mirror by the door and wiped off her eye makeup. War paint, Caro had always called makeup. "Give me a minute," she'd say on family vacations, "I need to put on my war paint."

Nina winced. Would she really lose Caro now? Forever? She looked in the mirror again and wished she had mascara with her. Eyeliner. Lipstick. She needed war paint. Especially if she was heading into battle on her own.

63

AS NINA STARTED WALKING HOME, HER PHONE PINGED. She wondered if it was Tim, saying maybe they could be friends after all. It was Jane.

We need to talk about last night. Can you come to HQ ASAP? Take the service elevator just in case photogs are out front.

Nina looked at the time. Eight forty-five. She wasn't looking forward to a conversation about last night with Jane. But it had to happen.

I'll be there in an hour, she wrote. She'd go home and get ready first. Put on her war paint.

WHEN NINA GOT TO campaign headquarters, she went around the back, like Jane had suggested, and texted so someone could come down and unlock the door.

While she was waiting, she started a text to Leslie and another to Pris, explaining what had happened with Tim, but before she'd gotten the words right, the door opened in front of her, and Rafael was standing just inside the entrance.

"I wasn't expecting you," Nina said. She ducked inside, and Rafael studied her for a moment before they started walking. "New hair?" he asked, as they moved through the loading dock, toward the freight elevator.

"Mm-hm," she said.

Rafael paused. "It looks great."

His responses were so different from Tim's.

"I'm sorry if I provoked your boyfriend last night," he said. "I really didn't mean to."

"My ex-boyfriend," Nina answered quietly.

Rafael looked at her as he pushed the elevator button, sympathy on his face. "I'm sorry," he said.

"Really?" she asked.

Rafael laughed as the elevator dinged. "Well, no," he said. "But that's what you're supposed to say when someone tells you they've broken up with their boyfriend. And I know it's a hard thing to go through, no matter what caused it." His face turned serious again. "Was it because of me?"

Nina shook her head. "Not really," she said. "That was maybe part of it, but there was a lot more."

"There always is," Rafael said.

The freight elevator opened, and the inside was covered in padding. It went all the way around, obscuring the buttons and covering the camera in the corner.

"I felt like I was in a gift box on the way down," Rafael said, holding the side of the elevator door with one hand, letting Nina go in before him. "One marked *Fragile*."

Nina walked in and leaned against the padding. It was nice to relax for a moment.

"I feel like a china figurine," she said, closing her eyes.

"You look like you could be one, in that dress," Rafael said. His voice was right next to Nina, and she felt his weight pressing down on the padding to her left.

She opened her eyes and turned her head.

When she did, she found that her face was so close to Rafael's she could feel his breath on her lips. It seemed like there was a magnetic force between his mouth and hers. And just like magnets, without even realizing it was happening, Rafael's head tilted forward and hers did, too, and then they were kissing. He tasted like cinnamon gum—spicy and sweet at the same time. Rafael ran his top teeth along her bottom lip, and she shivered. Then, as if by mutual agreement, they broke apart and looked at one another.

"I didn't mean . . ." Rafael said, grabbing her hand. "It's not why I came down. I didn't know you'd broken up with Tim. I just . . ."

"I know," Nina said, her heart beating faster, her body awash in him.

The elevator opened on the twelfth floor, and Jane was standing in front of them. Her smile fled quickly when she saw their hands intertwined. "Stop that right now and follow me," she hissed, staring pointedly at their fingers.

Rafael and Nina separated and then followed Jane into the conference room off the elevator lobby. Nina felt chastened. She heard her father's voice in her mind: *You're smarter than that.* And she was. But sometimes it wasn't about intelligence. Not when the heart got involved. Her father never seemed to understand that. Or maybe he did. All too well.

"Not a word," Jane said when she shut the door behind them. Then she grabbed a napkin from the stack that sat on a table pushed up against the wall. "You," she said to Rafael, "have her lipstick on your lips. Wipe. Now."

"And you." She turned to Nina. "What in the hell happened to your brain? First you tell Rafael that you think he should change campaign strategies without talking about it with me or Mac, and now you cheat on your boyfriend and lie to me—you both lie to me—about what's going on here. No wonder there was a fiasco last night. I know you lost your dad and that's not easy, but what the hell, Nina?"

The old Nina would have apologized. Would have retreated. But the new Nina did not. "First of all," Nina said. "Tim and I aren't dating anymore. So I didn't cheat on anyone. And second of all, what Rafael and I told you was true at the time we told it to you. We were just friends. The fiasco last night, as you call it, was Tim getting too drunk and too jealous for anyone's good. And as far as the campaign strategy, I don't work here anymore. I can talk to Rafael about whatever ideas I want."

Jane looked at Nina openmouthed. Rafael had an amused smile on his face. "Watch out, Jane," he said. "Nina's on fire."

Nina felt a rush of adrenaline after speaking up that way. She smiled back at Rafael.

"You both are killing me," Jane said. "I was going to talk to you about how we should handle the photographs that are being leaked from last night, but it seems to me like we might need some other kind of strategy now. There's still goddamn lipstick on your face, Rafael."

"Sorry," Nina said. "Chanel stays on pretty well."

"Chanel!" Jane threw her hands up in the air. "Jesus Christ. Both of you stay here while I get soap and Mac. We need to figure this out."

She left the room and Rafael started laughing. "Am I really wearing Chanel lipstick?"

Nina looked at him carefully. "Barely," she said.

He slid his arm around Nina's shoulders and she leaned into him. "You know Jane's right," she said. "We shouldn't start anything now. What we talked about last week is still true. We should wait until the election is over before we pull any attention from your policies, before we mess around with your voter margins."

"I know," Rafael said. "But we hadn't kissed then. I don't know if I'll be able to think about anything else now."

Nina looked up at him, feeling that magnetic pull not only in her lips but in her heart. "Of course you will," she said.

"Don't think so," Rafael answered, and then she was in Rafael's arms and he was kissing her, his lips warm and soft. He slid his hands down the back of her dress and ran them over her hips. She laced her fingers together across his shoulders and pulled him closer.

They broke apart for a moment. "Rafael—" Nina started. But then his mouth was on her neck, kissing the hollow of her collarbone.

Nina leaned her head back, exposing more of her neck for him to kiss. "We have to stop," she murmured, not wanting to. "Jane's going to be back."

"Mmm," was Rafael's response.

"I'm serious," Nina said, even as she slipped her hands in the back pockets of Rafael's pants, so she could pull him toward her.

"Me too," Rafael said again. And then his lips were on hers and their bodies were pressed together so tightly that she could feel the buttons on his shirt pushing into her skin.

Nina took a deep breath and stepped back. She closed her eyes and breathed slowly, deliberately, trying to tamp down the desire she felt, the need to be close to Rafael. *French fries. Milkshakes. Interoffice envelopes.* Her old tricks still worked, but barely.

"This is torture," Rafael said.

"There's more lipstick on your mouth now," she said, grabbing another napkin to wipe it off.

And that was how Mac and Jane found them when they walked into the room. Nina wiping Rafael's lips with a napkin.

They were not happy.

64

AFTER A DRESSING-DOWN FROM MAC, AFTER PROMISING she wouldn't give any more speech input, and after swearing that whatever was going on between them would be private, out of the spotlight so that they wouldn't make headlines so help them God, Nina and Rafael were alone again in the conference room.

"So what do we do now?" Nina asked, wanting to touch his hand, to move closer, to press herself against him.

"Well," Rafael said, looking at Nina so intently it felt like he was trying to memorize every square inch of her face. "I have a few interviews to do today. I'd love to see you after that, but I'm afraid dinner at a local restaurant is out. I'd suggest cooking at my place—or at yours—but Mac would kill us both if someone snapped a picture of us walking into either one of our apartments alone together at night."

Nina thought of her mother's house. Her house. Hardly anyone knew it existed. "What are your thoughts on the Hudson Valley?" she asked.

"Nice apple picking this time of year?" Rafael answered.

"I've got a house there," Nina said. "That's basically a secret. If we make our way there separately, no one will know. It's only about an hour and a half from here."

Rafael handed her his cell phone. "Key in the address," he said. "My last interview should be done by eight tonight. Then there's a drink with a donor . . . and final prep for tomorrow's meeting with the union reps . . . so how about . . . I'll meet you up there around eleven thirty?"

"I'll book a driver now," Nina said.

Rafael gave her one last kiss as he took his phone back. "Until soon," he said, heading for the door.

Nina tossed him a napkin. "Wipe your mouth!" she said.

AS SHE WAITED in the conference room alone, Nina realized she felt truly alive for the first time since her father had died.

65

BEING WITH RAFAEL MADE NINA FEEL STRONGER.
Smarter. Like she could tackle whatever needed tackling. So
she headed over to the Gregory Corporation headquarters.
They were on the twenty-ninth floor of a glass high-rise building in Midtown.

After taking the elevator upstairs and telling the reception-
ist she wanted to see TJ, who, as far as Nina knew, still thought
she was dating his son, Nina sat down on an overstuffed taupe
couch. She picked up a Gregory Hotels pamphlet and flipped
through it, surprised to find a photograph of herself at ten years
old standing next to the sign for Nina's Nest, her hands on her
hips and a smile on her face. She remembered when that was
taken. She was wearing red sparkly shoes like Dorothy's from
The Wizard of Oz. She'd loved those shoes so much that her
father had bought her a second pair when they got too small.
The caption said: *Even Nina Gregory knows how great birthdays
can be at our hotel restaurants.*

Her dad used to bring her to Nina's Nest all the time,

making sure to take her picture next to the sign, watching as Nina grew taller than the letters that spelled her name. He used one for a publicity campaign when the hotel had been open for sixteen years. The tagline said: *Sixteen Never Looked So Sweet!*

"But I'm eighteen in that picture," Nina had said, on a phone call home from college, after people had started sending her shots they'd taken of the billboards with Nina's photograph on them. "It's the hotel that turned sixteen. Why did I need to be in it?"

"Because you're prettier than I am," her father had joked, not picking up on her annoyance.

She wondered if he was the one who had chosen to include the picture of her ten-year-old self in the pamphlet. And if that was before or after the billboard incident. The surprises seemed endless.

"NINA," TJ SAID as he walked across the lobby. "So glad to see you. I hadn't realized you were coming by today."

"Sorry I didn't give you any warning," she said, getting up and following him through the glass doors that he unlocked with a wave of his key card. "I'd said I'd start at the company after the fund-raiser had ended, and this afternoon seemed like a good time to start sorting things out."

They'd reached the executive hallway. Nina looked to her left and saw the door to Caro's office, but she wasn't inside. They kept walking to the corner of the building, where TJ's executive suite was, next to Nina's father's old office.

"You can head in there, if you'd like." He nodded down the hallway toward her father's door. "We haven't touched it. We've been waiting for you."

Nina walked the twenty feet alone. She had a distinct impression that everyone was staring at her—the people in the offices on the other side of the hallway and the people in the cubicles out front. She nodded at Melissa, her father's former administrative assistant, and then walked into his office and closed the door.

She looked around. There was a picture of her and Tim on her father's desk from the day Nina was born. Tim's red hair was in corkscrew curls and he had a bundled Nina in his lap. The look of awe on his face was unmistakable. Nina's heart clenched. She could make out Caro's hand in the photo, reaching in to avert any potential disaster. No matter how hard Caro tried this time, disaster struck. Even with evening plans to see Rafael on her mind, Nina still felt the hole that Tim left behind.

She kept looking at the shelves. There was a picture from her business school graduation. The mosaic picture frame she'd made for her father the Christmas her mom died was there, too. The picture inside showed Nina and her dad sitting next to each other on the couch, their heads bent over a book of children's crossword puzzles. Her mom had taken it one Sunday—up in the country, Nina now realized, recognizing the print of the couch. Not in 21-B.

Nina opened her father's desk drawer and found the usual office supplies. Pens, pencils, Post-it notes, paper clips. She opened the drawer a bit farther and found a coupon she'd made him one Father's Day, good for a Yankee game of his choosing. Even though Nina had tried, she could never really get into baseball. Her father loved it, though, so she went with him once in a while. Though sometimes he just took TJ and Tim and left Nina and Caro to spend the day together. Once Caro had signed them up for a self-defense class, where Nina learned what to do if anyone ever tried to kidnap her. Poke them in the eyes. Knee them in the groin, if it was a man. Scream as loud as she could. Another time they'd climbed the rock wall in Chelsea Piers. "Women have to be tough," Caro had told her. Nina hadn't understood what she'd meant then. But she'd been figuring it out.

Her cell phone's vibration pulled Nina back into reality. It was her father's lawyer. "Miss Gregory?" he said, when she picked up the phone.

"Nina, please," she responded.

"Nina," he repeated. "I'm sorry I didn't get a chance to call you sooner. But that company you asked my secretary about—Manxome Consulting."

"Oh!" Nina said. "Yes. I'd love to get in touch with them. Did you find contact information?"

He cleared his throat. "Nina," he said again. "That was your father's company. I set it up for him years ago."

Understanding struck her almost immediately.

Nina swallowed hard. "Thank you," she said. "I'm—I'm sorry, but I've got to go."

"Wait," the lawyer said.

"I'll call you back," Nina told him, her heart pounding hard in her chest. "I'm sorry."

She'd taken forensic accounting. She knew what it meant when the chairman of the board created a company and billed his own corporation for services. He was increasing their compensation package illegally. This was embezzlement.

She picked up her father's phone and pressed the button that said *Melissa*. "Can you get me Irv?" she asked.

The phone rang out, and the CFO picked up. "Do you have access to the canceled checks from payments we made six or ten years ago?" Nina asked after she said hello.

"I do," Irv told her.

"And each check needs to be signed by two members of the executive team?"

"The big ones, yeah," he told her.

Nina looked down; her knee was bouncing. She tried to still it. "Could you tell me who signed the checks to Manxome Consulting? They worked for us from 2008 to 2011."

Irv had been in the business long enough to know he shouldn't ask questions, just answer them. "Of course," he said. "Let me just type in a few . . . here we go. I'm scrolling. Your father and TJ Calder signed all of those checks."

"Thank you," Nina said. "I appreciate the help."

"Any time," Irv responded before he hung up the phone.

Nina sat, dumbfounded. She thought for a moment she might be sick. Her world was turning upside down again. She was like Alice, through the looking glass. Her father and TJ had embezzled from the Gregory Corporation. There wasn't any other explanation. Literally none.

She wished that she could call her father and ask what the hell was going on. Why he'd risked the hotel's reputation, his freedom, their family name. The one he had built and grown and was so proud of.

How much more could come at her? How much more could she handle? She pressed the button marked *Melissa* again.

"Yes, Miss Gregory?" Melissa answered.

"Can you ask TJ Calder to come here, please? Tell him I need to speak with him?"

She had no idea what she was going to say, no idea what she was going to do. But without her father here, TJ was the only person left to talk to.

66

THE LOOK ON TJ'S FACE WHEN NINA TOLD HIM SHE'D
found out who owned Manxome Consulting was almost exactly the same as the look on Tim's when she'd told him she
didn't think he should be the CEO of the Gregory Corporation.

"Uncle TJ," Nina said, trying to keep her anger in check,
"help me understand. What were you two thinking?"

TJ stood up and began to pace in front of the bank of windows, his body alternately blocking buildings and light, causing
a slight disco effect in the office. "It was 2008," he said. "The
market was bad. Bookings were down. Your father had just in-
vested a ton of money in the renovations of both gyms and the
aquatics centers and he had a cash flow problem. His stock
portfolio had dipped so far down that he didn't want to sell,
and if he sold any of his stake in the corporation, he'd lose his
majority share. He'd asked for an increase in his compensation
package, but the board voted against it. Rightly so, honestly."

Nina had never known about this. "Why didn't he tell me?" she asked, distracted for a moment from the main question.

TJ shrugged. "I think he wanted you to be proud of him," he said. "He was ashamed to admit that he'd gotten himself into this situation. It even took him a while to tell *me*."

"Did anyone else know?" Nina asked, taking in what TJ had just said. Did her father adjust his behavior for her the same way she did for him? Didn't he know she'd be proud of him no matter what?

TJ shook his head. "I don't think so," he said. "And your father wanted to keep it that way. He didn't want to sell the houses—the real estate market had tanked, too. His only other option was declaring bankruptcy. But the public humiliation, the way people would talk, the way they'd look at the hotels . . ."

"My dad couldn't stand the idea of that," Nina said, slowly.

"Exactly," TJ said. "That's when he came to me with the plan. He needed a second signature on the checks."

Her father's pride had led to this. And she'd benefited from his crime. Her father had taken nearly three million dollars from the corporation. She wondered how many dinners and dresses and car rides and who knows what else that money had bought her. She felt a throbbing in her temples.

"No one else ever found out?" Nina asked.

TJ sat down. "Not that I know of," he said. "Once the stock market started making money again, we stopped. Your father actually lowered his salary after that. I think he was trying to make amends, pay the money back in better times. And he told me to legally disband Manxome Consulting earlier this year, when the cancer came back."

Nina couldn't believe what was unfolding. She heard Jane in

her mind and realized that if something came out about this, even after the election, being with her could be a problem for Rafael. It could taint him as a politician, dating someone whose family was involved in an embezzlement scandal. *Embezzlement.* The word made her skin crawl.

"Maybe I should talk to Ned about selling my shares," Nina said out loud. "Let this be someone else's problem."

TJ shrugged. "You could," he said.

"Does Aunt Caro know?" Nina asked.

TJ shook his head. "I never told her." He cleared his throat. "Tim doesn't either, of course. I'd appreciate if you didn't—"

Nina closed her eyes briefly. "I won't," she said. Out the window she could see the top few floors of The Gregory on the Park, and the lights from Los Tortolitos on the roof. It was why her father chose this office space, this office, so he could see his hotel while he worked. She couldn't rage at her father, punish him for his decisions, but TJ was still here. "I think you need to step down," she said, serious, controlled. "You can retire. We can figure out a way to make it work for the company, but I can't have someone running this corporation who makes decisions like those."

TJ looked down. Nina tried to feel bad, but anger crowded out her sympathy. She resented that she'd been put in this position. Even if she sold the company, she needed to know that it would be taken care of. That she'd be leaving it in good hands. It was her name on there. And she didn't want to let the employees down either, people who were counting on the Gregory hotels for their livelihood.

She waited for TJ's anger, for his own resentment to bubble to the surface. But instead TJ said, "You're right." And he looked almost relieved. Nina had given him a way out. "I'll announce my retirement this week. And tie up loose ends this month. You know Tim wants to—"

"I know," Nina said, cutting him off.

TJ looked at her and then got up from the table. "I should get back to my office," he said. "I have a call in five minutes. I'm . . . I'm really sorry, Sweetheart."

NINA STOOD, STARING AT THE DOOR, wondering what to do now. She looked up at the small sketch of Caravaggio's *Narcissus* hanging above the door frame. If her father needed money, he could have sold that. Or any of the pieces in the house in the Hamptons. But her grandmother had never sold any of the art in her collection after she'd bought it, and he hadn't either. And he wouldn't, because it would have shown financial weakness, Nina realized now.

She wondered whether he'd bought *Narcissus* years ago to remind himself to keep his vanity in check.

Clearly it hadn't worked.

67

WHEN GENE DROPPED HER OFF IN THE COUNTRY THAT
night, Nina took in a lungful of chilly air. After the day she'd had,
being out of the city felt good. She needed time to process, to
breathe, to decide what to say to Rafael. She knew she had to tell
him about her father's crime—she wouldn't be like her dad, keeping secrets from people she cared about. But she was afraid of
what that would mean. Maybe he would turn around and leave.
Maybe this thing between them would be over before it really
began. But even knowing a difficult conversation was ahead, the
idea of seeing him again, being close to him, thrilled her.

Nina walked into the house and flicked on the light. There
were some olives in the refrigerator. The remains of the bottle
of wine she and Tim had started. She couldn't help but think
about how she'd agreed to marry him the last time she was
here. How she'd found her mother's letter. She'd been a different person than she was now.

As she walked up the stairs with her overnight bag, Nina
decided that it was time for her to take over the master bed-

room. Partly because the house was hers now, and partly because she didn't want to have to think about how she and Tim had had sex in her bedroom. Didn't want to think about Tim at all, if she could help it. She already felt terrible about what happened between them. Ashamed. And guilty. But it also felt right.

Had Tim said anything to his parents yet? Had TJ said anything to Caro? She wondered if either of them would call her. Or if they'd go from family to employees to nothing at all.

Nina started unpacking her bag into the dresser and closet in her parents' old room, moving her mom's clothing to one side and taking over the other herself. There weren't many of her father's things there. As she put away her socks, she heard the doorbell ring.

When she got downstairs, Rafael was smiling at her through the window.

Nina opened the door and he stepped inside.

"Nice house," he said, looking around. He put a duffel bag down on the floor. For the first time since she'd met him, Rafael looked unsure of himself. Nervous, almost.

"Thanks," Nina said, nervous herself, leaning in to give him a quick kiss on the lips.

He embraced her, then pulled back and looked at her for a beat, tipping her chin up with his fingers. "What's wrong?"

She leaned against him, pulling strength from his arms, which were now wrapped around her. "Remember how I told you I found out some things about my dad? Some surprises?" she said, her head nestled against his shoulder blade.

"Mm-hm," he said, "like this house."

"Right." Nina breathed the musk and spice of Rafael's cologne. "Well, I found out one more secret today. At the office."

She felt his body tense, as if he were physically steeling himself for the news.

"What is it?" he asked.

Nina pulled away. Sat down on one of the kitchen chairs. "I don't think it'll come out. But if it does . . ." She was staring at the torn cuticle on her thumb. She couldn't face him. "My father embezzled money from the Gregory Corporation. And TJ—the CEO who had a hand in it, Tim's dad, actually—is retiring. I told him he had to."

Rafael took a deep breath. Nina looked away from her cuticle. "Whoa," he said, shaking his head, sitting down beside her. "What was your father thinking?"

"Pride," she said. "He was saving his pride."

"That's crazy," Rafael said, still shaking his head.

Nina bit her lip. "He started to pay it back, kind of, but that doesn't change anything." She took in a breath, knew she had to face this. "If it ever gets out," she said, "I could be a liability. Mac would say you shouldn't date me. Ever." Every muscle in Nina's body was coiled tight, waiting for his response.

He didn't hesitate. Rafael leaned in and kissed her. "My political ambitions don't trump my happiness," he said. "I was happy being a lawyer. I could be happy doing a number of different things. But I'd never be happy knowing I was the kind of man who abandoned a woman because of something her father did. What your father did doesn't change how I feel about you."

Nina slid closer to him and pressed her lips to his neck. "I think you might be the best person I have ever met," she said.

"If I am, it's because you bring out the best in me," he said into her hair.

Then Nina took his hand and led him up the stairs.

68

WHEN THEY STEPPED INSIDE THE MASTER BEDROOM, the bed so obviously the centerpiece of the space, Rafael said, "You know, we don't have to sleep together tonight."

Nina tilted her head up and kissed him again. This time, the kiss was soft, a thank-you and an invitation all at once. "We can do whatever feels right," she said. "We don't have to worry about how things will look up here—there's no one but us." Nina was floored by this man. This man who could accept all of her, who could forgive the baggage that she brought. Would reinvent his dreams for her.

"How freeing," Rafael said, stepping farther into the room.

"I know," she answered, running her fingers along the top of the dresser. "I understand now why my mom liked it here so much. It's like a secret hideaway."

"This was your house when you were a kid," Rafael said, picking up the photograph of Nina as a newborn asleep on her mother's chest.

"Sort of," Nina told him. "It was my mom's—my dad bought it for her. We stopped coming after she died."

Rafael came up behind Nina and ran his hand down her arms, his fingers fluttering against her skin.

She rested her head against his chest and closed her eyes.

"Se te están pegando las pestañas," he said, tucking her short hair behind her ears. It was just long enough to stay put.

Nina smiled. She hadn't heard anyone use that phrase in years. Literally, *your eyelashes are sticking together.* Her mom used to say that when Nina was young, trying to stay awake past her bedtime, fighting sleep even though she was about to pass out. Hearing it, she realized how tired she was. "I'm exhausted," she said, stifling a yawn.

"I'm pretty beat, too," he answered, resting his chin on the top of her head. "It's late. Maybe we should turn in for the night."

Nina let the feeling of closeness, of intimacy, melt through her. She imagined what it would feel like to be wrapped in his arms, under the covers. Then she stepped away from him and turned her head. "Would you mind unzipping me?" she asked.

Nina felt his warm fingers graze her neck as he grabbed hold of the zipper pull.

She wasn't sure if she should take her dress off in front of him, but then Rafael walked across the room, hung his suit jacket on the back of the rocking chair, and started unbuttoning his shirt. She could see the azabache dangling from the back of his collar. In response, Nina slid her arms out of her dress and let it fall to the floor, slipping off her heels as she stepped out of the pool of patterned satin. She was wearing nothing but a nude bra and white lace underwear.

"So that's what you look like," Rafael said, taking off his pants.

When he was free of them, standing in front of Nina in a pair of gray boxer briefs, she echoed his words. "So that's what *you* look like."

Nina could feel a heat thrumming deep inside her, a heightened awareness of Rafael sharing her space, breathing her air. After what she'd told him, after what he'd said . . .

"Bedtime?" she asked, climbing under the covers in only her underwear.

"Bedtime," Rafael answered, climbing in next to her.

Nina turned out the light, so grateful to be with him, so glad that her day was ending like this. The room was inky black— there was no ambient light to filter through the windows. It took a while for Nina to be able to see the outline of Rafael's profile next to her. Soon his long eyelashes came into focus, his sharp nose. She reached out, tracing his body from his shoulder down to his hip.

Rafael responded by running his fingers down her torso, too.

Nina rolled herself sideways, so she was facing Rafael.

"This feels like a big deal," she said, confessions coming easier in the darkness.

"I was just thinking the same thing," he told her. "I feel like I'm about to lose my virginity all over again."

Nina laughed. "Who was she?"

"Brenda Caruso," he said. "The summer after my senior year of high school. We both worked scooping ice cream at Coney Island the year the Brooklyn Cyclones started playing at MCU Park. We had sex under the boardwalk, like that song by the Drifters."

A wave of jealousy washed through Nina. "Can we do that?" she asked.

"Well," he said, "maybe not at Coney Island, but I'm sure we can find a quiet boardwalk somewhere. What about you? What was your first time like?"

"I'm boring," she said. "It was my college boyfriend, Max. We met during freshman year and had sex in his dorm room while his roommate was away for the weekend. It was the first time for both of us. He pretended he wasn't nervous, but we admitted to each other later how afraid we both were that it would be awful, that we would be awful, that we'd disappoint each other."

Rafael shifted closer to her. She felt the mattress dip as he moved. "Is that what you meant before when you said this is a big deal? Are you worried we'll disappoint each other?"

That was almost what she was worried about. "Maybe," she said, moving toward him.

Rafael bent forward and kissed the top of her head. Nina closed her eyes.

He kissed each eyelid.

"I'm actually worried that I'll disappoint *you*," she whispered. "Or I'll do something or want something that you . . . that you'll think . . ."

He kissed her lips. "Never," he answered.

He kissed her again, harder, and this time let his kiss slide down to her neck. Then his hand was in her hair as he ran his tongue along the length of her collarbone, his fingers trailing along the bottom of her jaw. She turned her head and caught one of them between her lips and he closed his eyes. "You are so damn sexy," he said, opening them again, looking up at her.

Rafael slid his finger out of Nina's mouth and she half smiled. "It's nice to feel this kind of desire," she told him.

"It *is* nice," he said. "It's been a long time since anyone wanted me like this."

"That's not true," Nina said. "I wanted you. I just kept it quiet."

"I've wanted you, too," Rafael said as Nina moved her hand down his body. She could feel him getting harder against her fingers. She kissed him.

Rafael kissed her back just as insistently and reached under the covers, slipping his fingers inside her. She moaned, then licked her fingers before putting them back on his erection.

The two of them rocked against each other's hands, the pleasure of it making them shiver. But Nina wanted more than hands.

"Can we?" she asked, rolling to her side, guiding him toward her under the covers.

Rafael nodded in response and Nina wrapped one leg around his hip while sliding onto him. "Oh," they both breathed in unison.

It felt like they were made for each other. The shape of his body, the angle of his hips, the length of his torso—the way they each knew intuitively what the other person wanted, needed.

When she came, Nina's body shook with a feeling so intense she didn't know if she could call anything she'd experienced before an orgasm. Or maybe she needed to create a new word for this sensation—this feeling of pleasure so all-consuming that there wasn't room for anything else.

After Rafael came a few moments later, he and Nina lay against each other on the bed.

"Remember that thing you were worried about?" he said, as he caught his breath.

"Mm-hm," Nina answered.

"Truly no need to worry about that ever again," he said. "There is no way you could ever be disappointing."

And in spite of everything else that had happened—and whatever else was yet to come—Nina Gregory fell asleep with a smile on her face.

69

THE NEXT MORNING, DESPITE HOW LATE THEY WENT to bed, Nina and Rafael woke up early.

She looked over at him in the bed next to her, his hair rumpled, his mouth curved into a grin. She had the overwhelming urge to kiss him, so she did.

"Well, that's a nice start to the day," he said, his voice gravelly from sleep.

She'd been worried it would feel strange to wake up next to someone who wasn't Tim, but it didn't. It felt natural. Like this was where she was supposed to be.

"I can drive you back," Rafael said, his hands reaching out to caress her breasts.

Nina shook her head. "I'll take the train," she said, luxuriating in his fingers on her skin. "We're being extra careful. Jane and Mac would have me drawn and quartered if someone spotted us together."

Rafael slipped his hand to Nina's waist under the covers. "I'd never let them," he said. He pulled Nina closer and curved his body around hers. "I'm so glad you interviewed to be on my campaign staff, and even gladder you quit."

"Same," Nina told him, then she squinted at the clock. "I think we have some time before we need to head back to the city. We could go for a run, or—"

Rafael silenced her with a kiss. "Or we could do this," he said.

Nina couldn't help it, she blushed.

And Rafael kissed her cheeks where they'd turned pink.

70

AS THEY WERE GETTING DRESSED, RAFAEL SAID, "AT least we won't have to stay hidden for too long. The election's over in three and a half weeks." He knotted his tie. "And then you'll be dating either the mayor of New York City or a lawyer whose dream crashed and burned." He looked at her. "Will you still want me if I lose?"

"No question," she said, but as she pulled a navy camisole over her head, she wasn't thinking about what would happen if he lost. She was thinking about what would happen if he won. Dating the mayor of New York City would mean living in an even brighter spotlight. Unconsciously, her body stiffened.

"What is it?" Rafael said.

"Nothing," Nina told him, she wasn't going to think about that. Not now. "We should finish getting dressed and head back to the city. I've got a new job now. I've gotta get up to speed."

"Buena suerte," he said, wishing her luck as she bent to slide her feet into her heels.

"Gracias," she answered.

And when she stood up, he kissed her again.

HALF AN HOUR LATER, Rafael dropped Nina off at the train in Cold Spring, and she waved good-bye from the platform. "I already miss you!" she called through his open window as he drove away.

Even in the chilly air, her body was still vibrating with the heat of him, and her muscles were sore from what they'd done together. He'd made finding out about her dad's embezzlement tolerable. He'd taken her out of that world, away from everything, and made her feel loved and understood and appreciated.

Her phone pinged. Nina looked down expecting Rafael. It was Tim.

I was thinking, the text said. *This is all a huge mistake. I missed you last night. I miss thinking about the future we were going to have together. I know I said not to contact me, but can we talk again? I can accept the new Nina—or at least most of it.*

Nina stared at the screen. She didn't miss him, not in the way he missed her. She'd slept with another man and felt better than she had in longer than she could remember. There was no way she could respond that wouldn't hurt him, so she told him the truth.

I'm sorry you missed me, she wrote back, just as the train pulled up to the platform. *But I've been thinking, too, and I think this was the right choice.* Then she added: *Will you let me know when you've told your parents?*

Tim didn't respond.

She understood. She deserved his silence. She deserved

worse. He'd thought she was his forever, and she'd let him believe that. She'd become a person he didn't recognize. She just hoped he'd remember the good things about her, too. That ten months of dating wouldn't kill thirty-three years of friendship forever.

71

BACK IN THE GREGORY CORPORATION OFFICES, WITH-
out Rafael there to distract her, Nina felt the weight of her father's actions again. But it was an odd sensation, because there
was nothing she could do to fix it. Nothing she could come up
with, at least. She'd contemplated paying the company back,
but to do that, she'd have to admit to what her father and TJ
did and that would hurt the corporation even more than her
father had. So instead she decided to tackle a problem she could
do something about: She'd look for candidates to interview for
the CEO position. As she started sorting through her father's
ancient Rolodex, Melissa buzzed. "Caroline Calder wants to
see you," she said. "Are you available?"

"I am," Nina answered, wondering if Tim had told his
mother about them yet, if that was what Caro wanted to talk
about.

When Caro opened the office door, her face gave nothing
away. "Want to take a walk?" she asked. "I spoke to my husband this morning."

Nina could see Caro's fists clenched. She was upset, even if she wasn't showing it.

"Sure," Nina said, standing up. "Let's go."

The two women walked out of the office and took the elevator down to the ground floor.

"Central Park?" Nina asked, orienting her body north.

"As good a place to talk as any," Caro answered.

They walked quickly, Nina waiting for Caro to speak. When they were two blocks from the office building, Caro finally said, "So it seems like your father and my husband made some unfortunate choices." That was what this was about. Not Tim.

"That's one way to put it," Nina said, wondering what TJ had told her, whether he'd given her the whole story.

Caro turned, and Nina could see tears shimmering in her eyes. "God, they're such idiots. It's not just the illegality and the secrecy and the impropriety of it all. It's the fact that their goddamn egos were more important than morals. More important than anything, really."

So he'd told her everything.

Caro had put words to what Nina hadn't quite figured out how to say. "Yes," she said. "I know. And how do we get out of this mess? What do we do to fix it? Can we?"

"I don't think we can," Caro responded. "I think we don't say anything. We're the only ones who know."

The women had reached the park and walked in through the Artists' Gate, making a left on the park's footpath. Nina thought about that, about keeping this secret her whole life. About asking Rafael to. She'd have to. They'd have to.

"You were right to tell TJ to retire," Caro continued. "If anything comes out, TJ will take the fall. As he should. I told him as much. But hopefully it won't come to that."

Nina's heart felt battered. So much had happened over the past six weeks. She thought about the person she was, the life she was living on primary day, and it seemed so foreign to her, like that woman was someone she'd once read a book about long ago. There was so much she wanted to say but she didn't know how to express. At least not now. Maybe she'd call Leslie later. Leslie would help her figure all of this out.

"Are you taking the day off today?" Nina asked Caro, as the park drive turned north. "Want me to walk you home?"

"We can go in that general direction," Caro answered. "But I think I might stay at the hotel tonight. This isn't just about the company for me. I wish he'd said something. That he'd told me so I could've talked him out of it. That he trusted me."

Nina should've realized that sooner. Honesty. Partnership. The two things Caro valued most had come crashing down around her. "You can stay at my dad's place if you want," Nina offered. "It's empty."

"Thank you," Caro answered. "I'd prefer that. Fewer questions." She shook her head. "When you've been married to someone for nearly forty years, you think you know him. I guess that's not always true."

Bikers and joggers were whizzing by, women with baby carriages—a couple of men pushing them, too. Nina often wondered what stories people had tucked inside them as they went about their day. No one would expect that she and Caro were having the conversation that they were. Anyone who saw them would probably assume they were mother and daughter, out for a stroll.

"While we're talking about secrets," Nina said, thinking about it for a split second before following her heart and asking.

"Do you know what happened the day my mom died? I found a letter in the house upstate that my mom had written, talking about my father's affair."

Caro turned to Nina with a look of alarm on her face. "Oh, Nina. I'm so sorry you had to find that out."

"So you knew," Nina said.

"I did. Your father thought you'd never need to know. He felt terrible about it."

Nina shrugged. "It's the least of my problems at the moment."

They walked by a playground, and the sound of children laughing floated toward them on the breeze.

"I don't know how much you read," Caro said, "but your father was having an affair with a British gallery owner he'd first met when he studied at Oxford. Veronica something. I can't remember her last name. But she'd moved to New York after a divorce to open a gallery here."

Nina could see her father being attracted to an Oxford-educated gallery owner. Like with her mother, he was interested in intelligence when it was paired with something slightly more bohemian. "Was he going to leave us for her?" Nina asked, feeling for a moment like the small child she once was.

Caro stopped walking and looked squarely at Nina. "He would never have left you, darling. Even if he and your mother divorced, he never would have left you. In spite of whatever flaws he may have had, your father loved you more than anything in his life. And from what he said to me afterward, he'd told Veronica as much when she suggested he get divorced, that they split their time between New York and London, that he build a Gregory Hotel there. He'd said no, but she stopped by with a Christmas present on her way home to England for the holidays anyway. And that changed everything."

Caro started walking again, and Nina followed. "It changed everything," Nina echoed.

She wondered what her life would've been like if her father hadn't had that affair, or if Veronica hadn't dropped the Christmas present off. What if Nina herself hadn't put it under the tree. Or her mother hadn't decided to go to the country that evening.

"Your father never saw her again after that," Caro said. "He felt too guilty."

Nina couldn't imagine what that must've been like. The guilt he must've been carrying for decades. She'd felt a piece of it when she broke up with Tim. Whose mother she was talking to right now as if she were her own.

"If . . ." Nina started, not quite sure of where to go next. "If Tim and I stopped dating," she said to Caro, "would you . . . would you still be . . ."

"Oh, darling," Caro said, "of course. We're family. Are you and Tim still going through a rough time? I'd hoped you'd worked things out after the fund-raiser. I remember when my sister passed away, everything TJ said and did was wrong. For months. If you don't want to talk about it, we don't have to—if it seems too strange. But if you do, I'd be happy to listen and offer any advice I can."

"I broke up with him," Nina said quietly. "Yesterday morning. He wants us to be the same as we always were, but . . . I'm different now."

Caro stopped walking. Nina stopped, too, waiting for her to say something. Anything. Caro's face was blank, until she looked at Nina's open, pleading eyes. Then she gave her a rueful smile. "If you were my daughter, I'd say, 'You need to go after what makes you happy.'"

Nina hugged Caro. And as the older woman's arms tightened around her, Nina felt tears overflowing her eyes. Caro had forgiven her. She loved her anyway. Through her tears, Nina let herself imagine that her father would have, too.

72

THAT SATURDAY MORNING, THE THIRD OF THE MONTH,
Nina put on one of her old black dresses, her grandmother's
pearls, and her mother's diamond studs. *I need your resolve,
Mom*, she thought as she slid her stockinged feet into a pair of
black pumps.

When Caro had called last night to say that she was going
to stay in 21-B for a while, the two women decided that the
Gregory brunch the next day would be just them. Nina asked
Gene to pick her up, and then get Caro, so they could enter
together.

"Good morning, darling," Caro said, as she got into the car,
her eyes covered by a pair of large tortoiseshell sunglasses. She
slipped them off once she got inside. Her makeup was impec-
cably done, as always, but that didn't disguise the puffiness
under her eyes or the raw spot on her lip beneath her lipstick.
She must've been picking at it. Nina could never, in her life,
recall Caro doing that.

"You don't have to come today," Nina said to her. "I can call Pris. I'm sure she'd be happy to have brunch with me."

Caro gave her a sad smile. "Do I look that bad?" she asked.

"No one would know but me," Nina said. "But if you want to go back and—"

"No," Caro said. "I'll be fine. And I'm not leaving you alone for this. I can't stop thinking about your mother and what she would think of it all."

The car stopped in front of the hotel, and Gene put it in park, exiting his door to open theirs.

"What would she have thought?" Nina asked.

Caro sighed, putting her sunglasses back on before getting out of the car. "I don't think she would've been surprised."

The brunch was just as bad as Nina had imagined it would be. From the moment she walked in, guests wanted to shake her hand, give their condolences, tell her a story about the hotel, or her dad.

But she was able to squash down her tangled emotions and keep her head up. In piercing her father's myth, she'd found strength. In finding his flaws, she'd learned how to grow. With that knowledge, she was able to be the gracious hostess, the bereaved daughter, the role everyone expected her to play.

Neither she nor Caro touched their food. But they made it through.

As they left the hotel, Caro gave Nina an uncharacteristically tight hug. "You need me, you call," she said. "Do you hear me, darling?"

Nina nodded. "I do. And if *you* need me, *you* call. Okay?"

Caro pressed her lips together and nodded. Nina could tell that behind her sunglasses, she was trying hard not to cry.

73

A FEW NIGHTS LATER, NINA WAS ON THE PHONE WITH Rafael, walking through her apartment, wandering from room to room. He'd just gotten home from yet another fund-raiser.

"This sneaking around is killing me," he said.

Nina circled through her living room.

"Me too," she said. She imagined what it would be like to walk hand in hand with him in Central Park. To sit next to him at a bar, enjoying a glass of wine. To have burgers and concretes at the Shake Shack in Madison Square Park.

"Where would you want to go?" Rafael asked. The sound of his voice made Nina crave his presence; talking on the phone was an exquisite kind of torture. "If we could go out right now. This minute."

Nina thought about it.

"Maybe a museum," she said. "We could look at paintings together, and then sneak off into a dead-end hallway and make out like teenagers."

Rafael laughed. "I didn't know many teenagers who made out at art museums."

"I did," Nina said, thinking about how she and her high school boyfriend had kissed at the MoMA just outside the room that held the Jackson Pollocks.

"Of course you did," Rafael said.

Now Nina laughed, stopping in her dining room. "What's that supposed to mean?" she asked.

"Just that you're a classy broad, Miss Gregory. Totally out of my league."

"Not true!" she said.

She heard Rafael sigh on the other end of the line. "Palabrecita, I'd so love to look at art and then make out with you right about now."

Nina paused at the de Kooning hanging on her wall, the one she'd bought as a thirtieth birthday present to herself. It gave her an idea.

"Actually," she said. "I know somewhere we could do that and no one would see, if you're willing to take another long car ride." She thought about what Tim had said right after her dad died about using power, using money to make someone you loved smile. Maybe he was right about that.

"What are you talking about, Palabrecita?" Rafael asked.

"The house upstate isn't the only house I inherited," she said, cringing at how that sounded. "My grandmother collected art, and a lot of it is out in the house in East Hampton. We can go. I'll book us a car if you want. Or we could meet out there, if you'd rather drive yourself. Or I can drive, actually. My dad's car is in a garage not far from you."

Rafael was quiet for a moment. Nina wondered which part

was taking him so long to process. The prospect of a long car ride? The second house? The fact that it was already ten p.m.? "What the hell," he finally said. "Let's do it. How about you grab your father's car and we meet near the FDR? If it looks like some photographer is following me, I'll let you know and we can come up with a backup plan."

"Has it been worse?" she asked. "The photographers?"

"Not great," Rafael said. "But this late, they usually leave me alone. We can talk about that on the ride out. Or at the Gregory Museum."

Nina laughed. "It's not a museum," she said. "Maybe I oversold it. It's just a house."

"Uh-huh," Rafael responded. He was laughing, too.

Nina loved making him laugh. She felt his laughter in the very core of her.

"Okay, see you soon," she said.

"Until soon," he answered.

74

WHEN THEY GOT OUT OF THE CAR AT THE GREGORY estate, Nina grabbed Rafael's hand and started walking toward the house. And then realized he wasn't moving at all. His head was tilted up. "This place is incredible," he said.

Nina tried to see the house through his eyes. It wasn't anything like the one upstate. This was a real Georgica Pond mansion. Seven bedrooms, nine bathrooms, a pool, a tennis court, beach access, a boat slip. It had always just been her summer house; Nina was used to it. But when she put herself in Rafael's place, maybe it was kind of incredible.

"Come on," she said, tugging his hand. "It's even better inside."

She hadn't given Richard a heads-up that they were coming, so the house wasn't set up the way it usually was when Nina arrived, with flowers on the tables, music on the sound system, and the refrigerator filled with food.

Nina flipped the lights on. "It's nicer during the day," she told Rafael, "when the sun comes through the skylights."

Rafael looked around, taking it all in. The art on the walls, the statue in the corner, the grand staircase that led to the second floor. "It's plenty nice now," he said. "The whole apartment I grew up in would fit in this foyer."

Nina could tell Rafael hadn't really thought about it before—how much money she actually had. "I hope this house doesn't change the way you look at me," she said, tightening her grip on his hand. "I'm still me."

Rafael turned, looked her up and down, and smiled. "Yup," he said. "You look exactly the same to me." And then he leaned over and kissed her. "Is it time for the making-out-like-teenagers part of the night?" he asked.

Nina pulled away. "I promised you art," she said. "A proper date."

"That's right," he said. "Art. A date." He slid his hand into the waistband of her jeans, into her lace underwear. "Is there more than just in this foyer?"

"The art's all over the house," she said, her lips against his neck.

"Bedrooms too?" he asked, sliding his finger inside her.

"Bedrooms too," she confirmed with a gasp.

They left a trail of clothing as they went, jackets in the foyer, sweaters on the stairs, shoes in the hallway, until they stumbled into the bedroom closest to the staircase.

"Whose room is this?" Rafael asked, looking around at the whitewashed wood, the painting of Venice hanging across from the bed.

"Guest room," Nina said. "We call it the Grubacs room. That's who the artist is." She waved her hand toward the painting. "See, we are getting to look at art together."

Rafael looked at the painting, then back at Nina. "I'd rather look at you," he said, tugging her into bed.

Nina ran her fingers up his chest and around his shoulders. "Me too," Nina said. "I'd rather look at you." She kissed her way down his stomach and then unbuttoned his pants and pushed them down along with his boxer briefs. Her mouth was on him, her legs up on the pillow next to his head.

As she ran her tongue up and down, she felt him unbuttoning her jeans, pulling down her underwear, and then his mouth was on her. Her body was guided by instinct, awash in pleasure. Far too soon, she felt herself climaxing, her muscles constricting around Rafael's tongue at the same time that the salty taste of him filled her mouth. She rolled away from him and swallowed, then propped herself up on her elbows. They were facing each other, and she was smiling. Rafael wasn't, though. His face looked . . . she couldn't tell how it looked.

"What is it?" Nina asked. She was worried all of a sudden. It was the house. It was her. She'd done something wrong. Wanted too much.

"Truth?" he asked.

"Truth," she answered, scared to hear it, but knowing she needed to. "Always truth."

He sat up, away from the pillows. "I'm . . . I'm afraid," he said.

Nina cocked her head sideways. She didn't know what to make of that. "Of me?" she asked.

He shook his head. "Of losing you," Rafael said. "Of you breaking my heart. Seeing you in this house . . . I don't know how I'd ever be able to keep you."

"What do you mean?" Nina asked.

Rafael sighed. "Do you know the story of my divorce?" he asked.

Nina was trying to follow his train of logic. She was

supposed to know how his brain worked—it had been her job. But now, she wasn't sure where he was going. "Something about a helicopter?" she asked.

Rafael smiled. "That's the part everyone always remembers. I did take her on a helicopter ride around Manhattan for our third anniversary, but it was because I knew I was losing her. I knew she wasn't happy. And when we talked the next morning, she told me there was someone else."

"Oh," Nina said, moving so that her head was next to Rafael's. So she was holding his hand. "I'm so sorry."

"It nearly destroyed me," Rafael said. "I took leave from work. I drank too much. I watched *Law and Order* marathons. I felt like an idiot. Like a failure. And I couldn't figure it out. How could she do that to me?"

Nina listened, her heart breaking for Rafael, angry at this woman who had hurt him so badly, but jealous, too, that he'd cared so much about her. And then wondering if in the future, Tim would be telling someone the story of their relationship, and she would be the villain, the woman who had hurt him like that.

"I blamed the other guy. That asshole for taking her from me. But then I realized, her affair wasn't the problem. It wasn't the disease, just the symptom. And then I was able to take a step back and see all the problems in our relationship. All the infections that were brewing deep in its vital organs. And I got past what she did. I got over it. But I don't want to have to do it again. Now that I've seen the world you grew up in . . . how could I ever think I could make you happy?"

"First of all," Nina said, "the two of us being happy together has nothing to do with the way either of us grew up. And second of all, infections can be treated, can be healed. We'll just have to be on the lookout. Make sure we catch them early before they have a chance to spread."

Rafael grabbed Nina's other hand and faced her. "Can you promise me we'll do that?" he said.

Nina took her right hand out of Rafael's and held it up, palm out. "I promise," she said. "I don't want you to be afraid of me."

"I don't want to be either," Rafael said.

She kissed him. The top of his head first, then his nose, then his lips, so glad that he was still there. So glad that she hadn't scared him away. He was the eye in the middle of the storm. He was her strength, her center, her fuertrado. "I was going to take you to my room," she said. "But it's down in the other wing of the house. How about if we sleep here tonight?"

"Works for me," Rafael said. "As long as I get to wake up next to you."

Nina climbed under the covers. "I promise," she said again.

Rafael fell asleep in her arms, and she watched him breathe. He had a glamour, she realized, just like her father. The confidence, the charm, the megawatt smile. Inside he was just as broken as everyone else. Maybe even more so.

She thought about her dad. His affair wasn't the problem, it was a symptom. There was something deeper there. Something that made him act that way. That was the case with Manxome Consulting, too. It was just a symptom of a different kind of disease. He felt the same pressure she did, Nina realized, inherited along with the family name: to appear to the outside world as if everything were perfect, even when it wasn't. To swallow your own feelings. To be afraid of failure, not because you wouldn't recover, but because of what everyone else would say. Pressure like that, it could break a person in so many ways. And it had broken her father. Nina knew it now.

With that realization, the anger she had been feeling toward him dissipated. She couldn't accept what he'd done, but she could at least try to understand his actions, put them in context. And make sure she didn't end up the same way.

Nina leaned back against the pillow and, with her arms still around Rafael, she fell asleep.

75

THE NEXT DAY, AFTER AN EARLY-MORNING RIDE HOME from the Hamptons, dropping Rafael off first so he could make his breakfast meeting, Nina was back at her apartment, getting ready to head to the Gregory Corporation offices.

She had to start preparing for the board meeting where TJ was going to announce his retirement and she was going to talk about some changes she wanted made at the hotel. Because she wasn't going to sell. She realized on the ride back that morning that she'd never be able to sell her family's company. After her night with Rafael, she'd come to terms with who her father was; she loved him in spite of his flaws. And that realization made it easier to make the decisions she wanted to make, to run the company the way she wanted to. She'd talked to Rafael that morning about her ideas: rooftop gardens to supply the restaurants, a partnership with local homeless shelters to donate the extra shampoo and soap and lotion, and a philanthropic foundation that she'd run personally that would funnel money to charities working to support young entrepreneurs as her own silent apology for what her father had done. Vorpal Sword, she'd call it. It didn't have to be named after her. And it would remind her that she could slay the Manxome foes—and any other foes who came her way. That she was of her father, but she wasn't her father. And she didn't have to work in politics to help change the world. That was what Nina had decided in the car. And the decision had felt good.

So she'd made another one, as Rafael drove along the Grand Central Parkway. She'd picked up her phone and Googled Daphne Lukas. Her aunt had passed away three years before from a heart attack.

Instead of sorrow, Nina had felt anger.

Life was so goddamned unfair sometimes. Someone else was gone from her world forever. But at the end of the obituary, Nina saw a line: *Daphne Lukas Harrison is survived by her daughter, Clio Harrison of Denver, Colorado.* It was her cousin. The one she'd never met.

Nina Googled her and found an e-mail address at the Mountain School, a science magnet high school where her cousin taught biology.

"Are you going to e-mail her?" Rafael had asked.

"I need to think about it," she'd answered, leaning into him.

He kissed the top of her head, his eyes still on the road. "I know I don't get a vote," he said. "But I think you should. Not today, necessarily. But one day, when you feel ready."

Nina had kissed his cheek after that. Maybe she would. One day. When she felt ready.

WHEN CARO CAME BY Nina's office later in the day to say that she and TJ had decided they were going to live apart for a while and asked if she could stay in the apartment on Central Park West until she found one of her own, Nina made one more decision. She texted Tim, told him that if he wanted to talk about his parents, if he needed a friend, she was still there for him. He didn't respond, but Nina didn't blame him.

76

THE FRIDAY EVENING BEFORE THE ELECTION, NINA was in Rafael's apartment on Central Park North for the first time. They knew they shouldn't, but there was too much to do this weekend to sneak upstate or out to the Hamptons, and Rafael said he couldn't bear being away from her for another night. So she came in with folders filled with paper in her arms as a cover, and even then, went in through the building's back entrance. Luckily, there'd been no photographers waiting there. They mostly camped out in the front, when they staked out his place.

Rafael's apartment was in a new building on 110th Street, and the wall facing the park was made completely of windows, tinted for privacy. It was amazing to Nina how many beautiful views there were in New York City.

"Want a drink?" Rafael asked her as she walked into the living room. There was a bottle of red wine already in his hand. "I sure as hell could use one."

"How come?" she asked, dropping her bag and the folders next to a guitar leaning against the wall and taking off her coat.

He uncorked the bottle. "My poll numbers are down."

"What?" Nina turned to him after hanging up her coat. "Do you have the breakdowns?"

He handed her the bottle of wine and then pulled a folder out of his briefcase. "Here," he said. "I'm down in the older male demographic. Older white men, if you want to drill down. Mac says it's the tax thing I talked about in the last debate. It'll pay for universal pre-k, but you know—taxes are a touchy issue."

Nina looked at the numbers. "Older white men?" she repeated.

Rafael nodded and poured two glasses of wine, handing Nina the first and taking a sip from the second.

"Did you and Mac talk about using the Irish side of your identity to combat this?" She and Rafael had discussed it a bit since it had first come up, even though Jane and Mac were clearly against it. They decided it wasn't worth messing with a good thing, since he'd been far enough ahead in the polls that a win was likely. But it wasn't anymore.

"We actually did," Rafael said. "He's worried I'll lose other demographics if I incorporate that side of my identity."

"What do you think?" Nina asked, sipping her own wine.

"Deep down? En mis tripas?" Rafael asked.

"Yes, in your guts," Nina said. "God, that sounds so much better in Spanish."

Rafael laughed. "In my guts, I think you're right. I think I should win or lose as myself—all of myself. And if we do nothing, if we just cross our fingers and hope, the polls have me losing by two percentage points. So what's the risk?"

Nina leaned over and kissed him, and he tasted like red wine and determination. "Well, polls aren't always right, but it's your campaign, you're the boss."

"I know," Rafael said. "I'm just so afraid to let all of them down. My team. They've put in so much time, so much passion. They believe in me, all of them. And I don't want to mess it up—for them even more than for me."

"You won't," Nina said. She'd been getting used to seeing this vulnerable side of Rafael, ever since their trip to the Hamptons. It made the relationship seem balanced, somehow. She needed him. He needed her. "I believe it—en mis tripas."

Rafael smiled at her. "By the way," he said, "I'm cooking tonight."

Nina raised her eyebrow. "You are?" she said. He'd been her sous chef up in the country and out at the beach a few times over the past weeks, late at night, when his campaign obligations were done for the day, but he hadn't made anything for her on his own.

Rafael picked up a plastic bag. "I bought ingredients on the way home," he said, "to make picadillo. My abuela's recipe."

Nina agreed to be his sous chef this time and started chopping peppers at his request. Half an hour later the two of them were sitting at the kitchen table with steaming plates of picadillo in front of them.

"This is delicious," she said, after she took her first bite.

"Gracias," Rafael said. Then he paused. "Now you say it."

"How come?" she asked.

Rafael smiled at her. "Because I think the way you speak Spanish is especially sexy. That hint of a Castilian accent? Makes me crazy."

"Delicioso, gracias," Nina said, giving him what he wanted, her *c* more like a *th* than an *s*.

"How did I get so lucky?" he asked her.

"How did *we* get so lucky?" she answered.

LATER THAT NIGHT, Rafael lay in Nina's arms. Even though he had a king-sized bed, they took up maybe three feet of it, the way they slept, twisted around each other, their legs scissoring, woven tightly together. Rafael said that when he was in bed with her, it was the only time he could sleep through the night.

77

THE NEXT MORNING, NINA USED THE SERVICE EXIT TO leave Rafael's building while he walked out the front door. They were lucky she had, because the same photographer who'd ambushed them at the Dublin Pub was there taking Rafael's photo in his workout clothes. Nina got home and saw it on Twitter: *Rafael O'Connor-Ruiz Calms His Pre-Election Jitters with a Run in Central Park*. That, she realized, would be her life with him if he won. Pictures in the papers. Her clothing analyzed in the *New York Post*. She knew now wasn't the right time to talk to Rafael about her worries, so she called Leslie.

Leslie had been as supportive as ever when Nina caught her up on everything that had happened. Breaking her engagement to Tim, sleeping with Rafael, Rafael's willingness to be with her in spite of what her father had done. Nina had told Leslie about that, too. It felt wrong, keeping anything a secret from her best friend. And Leslie had been outraged at first, like Nina had. But now that Nina had made her peace with her father, Leslie had, too.

"Auntie Nina!" Cole's voice came over the phone in an excited shout. "My mommy says we can come visit you soon! We're going to see all the dinosaurs."

"That's awesome, sweetie," Nina said. "I can't wait. You know what else is in the dinosaur museum?"

"What?" Cole asked.

"The biggest whale you ever saw in your life!"

"I never even saw a small whale," Cole told her.

"Well, then it'll be your lucky day when you come. Your first whale will be enormous."

"Can we go tomorrow?" Nina heard Cole asking Leslie, no longer paying attention to Nina on the phone. "Or maybe today?"

"Maybe in a few weeks," Leslie said. "How about you go draw a whale for Auntie Nina and we can send it to her?"

Nina heard the phone clatter to the floor.

Then Leslie picking it up.

"Hey," Leslie said. "I was thinking maybe we could come for Thanksgiving this year. Since it'll be your first without your dad."

Tears pricked her eyes at her friend's words. "I love that idea," Nina said, sitting down on the couch in her living room and wiping her eyes. "I've mostly been ignoring Thanksgiving, but I think it's time to face it."

"It'll come anyway," Leslie said.

"Like death and taxes," Nina said.

Leslie laughed. "Just with more gravy." Then she said, "So what's up? How's your secret hunk of a boyfriend doing?"

Nina sighed. "He got paparazzi'ed this morning."

"Ugh," Leslie said.

"That'll be my life, Les, if I'm with him. Even if he's not

mayor now, he's a politician. He'll keep running. He says he'd be happy doing something else, but I don't know if that's really true. Or at least how he'd be happiest."

"And?" Leslie asked. Nina could hear her washing dishes on the other side of the phone.

"I hated it so much when I was a kid and we were in the newspapers and magazines the year my mom died. And my mom hated it, too. I can't help but think it's part of what messed up my parents' relationship. What if it does that to me and Rafael?"

Leslie turned off the water. "Listen, Neen. I've never seen you as happy with anyone else as you've been with Rafael. And you're older now—and much tougher—than you were at eight. Plus you've grown up in this world in a way your mother never did. You've got tools she never had. And you're going into it with your eyes wide open. What's the alternative? Stop dating Rafael?"

When Leslie put it that way, the paparazzi didn't seem so bad. Nina thought about how she felt when she was with Rafael—desired, adored, needed. And loved for every aspect of who she was. She didn't want to give that up. "You're right," she said. "Thanks for talking me off a ledge."

"What else are friends for?" Leslie said. Nina imagined her smiling. "And . . . for whatever it's worth, I think you'd make a great mayor's wife."

Nina laughed. "You're ridiculous," she said.

"And that's why you love me," Leslie answered.

As the conversation went on, Nina thought about all the people she loved. Leslie was happy that Nina and Rafael were a couple, and Caro had come around, after the three of them had lunch together. But Nina still hadn't heard a word from Tim. And as much as she adored Rafael, as much as she wished she could shout about her relationship with him to everyone she met on the street, it still made her sad that the decision had to be an *either/or* instead of an *and*.

78

ON ELECTION NIGHT, NINA WAS STANDING WITH RA-fael at campaign headquarters. They were in the conference room off the elevator lobby, just the two of them, and Nina was helping him get ready. There had been a media blitz starting the previous afternoon. Spots on all the local stations, on the radio. New speeches in English and in Spanish, talking about both sides of his family. Targeted ads flooding every social media platform. Rafael was interviewed on practically every website in the city.

They didn't know it if had worked—wouldn't know until the votes were counted—but they were optimistic. Or at least try-ing to be.

Nina resisted the urge to run her fingers through Rafael's hair, since it was stiff now with hair spray.

"Are you ready?" she asked as she fixed his collar.

"Are you?" he asked.

"Ready as I'll ever be." She was so nervous she hadn't been able to eat all day.

He smiled and kissed her cheek to avoid another lipstick fiasco.

"You didn't forget your azabache today, did you?"

"Never," Rafael answered, patting the collar of his white button-down. "But if I lose, it's okay, too."

"Of course it is," Nina said. They'd talked about it last night—what would happen if he won, what would happen if he didn't, when they would go public with their relationship either way. Slowly, they thought was the best way to do it: a date or two out in the open, then more, then something posted on his Twitter account. Let people get used to it. It meant keeping things a secret a while longer, monitoring their time together, but they could be patient.

"Do you know about the theory of the multiverse?" Rafael asked, wrapping his arm around Nina's waist.

"Is that like in *Back to the Future*, where there's a second 1985?"

"Kind of," Rafael said. "It's the idea that every time something important happens, a new world is created based on each potential outcome. There's a world where I went to law school and another where I didn't. A world where your grandfather bought a hotel and another where he didn't. A world where your father never met your mother in Barcelona."

"One where my mother didn't die. Or my father didn't have an affair."

"Exactly," Rafael said, fiddling with his tie pin. "I read about that concept after my dad died, and I found it comforting. I liked the idea that there was another universe out there—maybe more than one—where he was still alive. And if I lose this election, there will be another universe where a different version of me won. But if that Rafael doesn't have a chance to be with you . . . well, I don't envy him the win. He can have it."

"There *is* something kind of comforting about that," Nina said, turning toward him and smoothing his lapels. It was hard not to touch him. "We're just living one version of the present, but the other ones are out there. They all would've happened, regardless of the choices we make."

"That's precisely it," Rafael said. "They'll all happen anyway, but we get to live this version."

He kissed Nina's forehead. Maybe, she thought, she should stop wearing lipstick.

There was a knock on the conference room door, and then Jane called, "The results are in."

Rafael walked out the door first, Nina a few minutes behind. The rest of the team was gathered around the television set in the corner.

"Here it comes," Mac shouted from the other side of the office.

Rafael walked closer to the television.

"Ninety-four percent of the vote has been counted," the newscaster said. "And the race is . . . still too close to call."

Everyone groaned. Mac walked out of the room.

"It's okay if I don't win," Rafael said, almost as much to himself as to everyone else. "If I lose, there's another Rafael in another universe who won and all of you were part of it."

Jane looked at him as if he were speaking a language she'd never studied.

"He's talking about the multiverse," Nina tried to explain.

"Breaking news!" said the newscaster. "Ninety-six percent of the vote has now been counted, and we can declare a winner in the race for Gracie Mansion!"

Nina felt the room take in a collective breath and hold it. Their media push could've changed everything. Or nothing at all.

"And the next mayor of New York City is . . ."

"You're killing me!" Jorge yelled at the screen.

"Rafael O'Connor-Ruiz!" the newscaster shouted.

Jane started crying. Nina felt tears in her eyes as well—tears of shock and relief and happiness.

Rafael crossed the room in two giant steps and kissed Nina, dipping her backward.

"We're still supposed to be a secret," she said as she tried to pull away. Cell phone flashes went off.

"Remember how I ran as my whole self?" he said to her quietly. "And I won? Well, part of that is that I'm dating you. And I want the world to know." Then he kissed her again.

"Can I post this?" Samira asked.

Rafael quirked an eyebrow at Nina. Slowly she nodded.

"Post away," Rafael said. Nina knew this would be all over the Internet in about five seconds, but she didn't care. Whatever came next, she could handle it. They could handle it together. They were partners. She felt Rafael's tears on her cheeks—and wondered if he kept kissing her so no one would see him cry.

She pulled away from him, just a centimeter, so their lips were no longer touching, but their noses were. "I love you," she whispered, so quietly that even in a room full of people, only he could hear. It was the first time she'd told him that. The first time she realized it was true.

"I love you, too," he said.

Then he wiped the tears off his cheeks and faced the room to thank his staff before they headed over to the victory party, where Nina would meet his family for the very first time. She wished her father were with her, her own piece of family, but Caro was meeting her there instead. Priscilla and Brent, too. Family by choice instead of by blood.

79

A WEEK AFTER RAFAEL BECAME THE MAYOR-ELECT OF New York City, and a week after the world found out that he and Nina were a couple, the Vorpal Sword Philanthropic Foundation got its official 501(c)(3) designation and was open for business.

"How do you want to celebrate?" Rafael had asked Nina a few days before, while they were having dinner in Nina's apartment. "My schedule's insane, but it looks like I've got an hour and a half on Saturday. Maybe we can do something then?"

Even in the midst of all of his meetings, Rafael made time for Nina whenever he could. And she loved it.

"Have you seen the people taking trapeze lessons along the Hudson?" she'd asked back, as he refilled her water glass.

"I actually have," Rafael said. "Though I've never done it myself."

"Me neither," Nina said, "and it scares the hell out of me, but I want to do it. Let's celebrate this weekend by flying on a trapeze."

When Leslie and Pris heard what was happening, they wanted to be part of the celebration, too—Leslie said she'd take the whole week of Thanksgiving off and come to Manhattan early with Cole and Vijay. And Caro said she'd love to fly, as long as she wasn't too old. Nina assured her that she wasn't. And then called Tim and left him a voice mail inviting him as well. He hadn't called her back.

"I don't mind if you want to invite TJ, too," Caro had offered. "I know he misses you." The two of them were talking, trying to find a way back.

But Nina hadn't been ready yet. "Maybe for Thanksgiving," she'd told Caro.

When Nina got to Pier 40, she looked up at the ladder she'd have to climb, the platform she'd have to jump off.

"Maybe this wasn't my best idea," she said to anyone who was listening.

"Are you kidding?" Leslie answered, Cole in tow. "This was absolutely your best idea. Well, after starting a charity with your family's money. We're gonna fly, Nina!"

"I'm gonna be a superhero!" Cole said. He was wearing a T-shirt he'd made himself with a big lopsided *C* on the chest and had already had what he declared was the very best day ever because he got to meet the NYPD detail that traveled with Rafael.

Rafael left the officers behind and came over to put his arm around Nina. She noticed a few people surreptitiously snapping a picture of the two of them, but she didn't mind. She and Rafael had decided that they wouldn't hide anything. They'd be themselves, be open with the media, live their lives authentically in the spotlight and hope that authenticity would make them real to everyone—no façades, no glamours. And if they were criticized, so be it. It made living a life on display easier when you weren't trying to hide anything, when you were simply being yourself.

"I love you," he whispered into her hair.

"More than words," she answered him.

And even though she did, she loved him more than anything, she still loved Tim, too. And missed him. She looked around, hoping that he'd show up, even if he hadn't called her back.

"He's not coming, darling," Caro said softly, realizing who Nina was looking for.

Deep down, Nina already knew that. She felt a shiver of sadness blow through her, until Rafael rested his hand on her hip. "Are you ready?" he asked.

She looked at him, squaring her shoulders, raising her chin. "I am," she said. "Let's fly."

Nina climbed up the ladder, her heart racing. *I can do this*, she told herself, even though her hands didn't want to move to the next rung. Her feet wanted to stay put, too. She'd faced so many things in these past two months—losing her father, losing Tim, taking over a corporation, starting something new from scratch, being in a public relationship with someone she loved so much that sometimes she was gutted by the power of it. She could handle this, too.

When she got to the top of the platform, one of the people working at the trapeze school handed Nina the bar.

"Hold on tight," he said. "And on the count of three, jump!"

Nina's heart raced even faster; it was like every molecule of her DNA was telling her not to jump.

"You can do it, Palabrecita!" she heard Rafael yell. "Super-héroe!"

"Go, Nina, go!" It was Pris.

Nina looked down at her friends—her family really—and smiled. And then she jumped, soaring over Manhattan, happy, strong, and free.

And as Nina looked out over the city she adored, time stretched. She thought about the past and the present and the future and decided that, regardless of the sadness she'd experienced, she was glad she lived in this universe.

It was a beautiful day to be a New Yorker.

Poetry Note

THE POEM "JABBERWOCKY" BY LEWIS CARROLL IS REF-
erenced throughout *More Than Words*. It's a poem that is important to Nina's father—and to Nina herself. She grew up
hearing about it. I did, too. Like Joseph Gregory, my grandfather had a boat that he kept docked in East Hampton (though
his boat was much smaller than the one I imagined the Gregorys sailing on). And it was also called the *Mimsy*, though it
wasn't named for the line in "Jabberwocky"—it was named for
my grandmother, who herself was named for the line in "Jabberwocky." My grandmother, Mildred, was nicknamed Mimsy
from the time she was born because her own father was a huge
fan of Lewis Carroll. And, perhaps because of the provenance
of her name, she was, too. I still have the copy of *Through the
Looking Glass* that she bought for my father when he was a
child, which contains "Jabberwocky"—and a pronunciation key
for the nonsense words therein. When I was thinking about a
poem that I wanted to run through the heart of *More Than
Words*, this one came to mind because of the story I always

imagined when I read it—a boy, a son, sent out alone to slay some unimaginable foe and given love only when that deed was accomplished. I imagined that was how Joseph Gregory would have felt as a child, worthy of love only when he achieved what was expected of him; that's why I had him connect so deeply with "Jabberwocky." As for my great-grandfather, I'm not sure what he saw in the poem, though I wish I could go back in time and ask him.

Jabberwocky

'Twas brillig, and the slithy toves
Did gyre and gimble in the wabe:
All mimsy were the borogoves,
And the mome raths outgrabe.

"Beware the Jabberwock, my son!
The jaws that bite, the claws that catch!
Beware the Jubjub bird, and shun
The frumious Bandersnatch!"

He took his vorpal sword in hand;
Long time the manxome foe he sought—
So rested he by the Tumtum tree
And stood awhile in thought.

And, as in uffish thought he stood,
The Jabberwock, with eyes of flame,
Came whiffling through the tulgey wood,
And burbled as it came!

One, two! One, two! And through and through
The vorpal blade went snicker-snack!
He left it dead, and with its head
He went galumphing back.

"And hast thou slain the Jabberwock?
Come to my arms, my beamish boy!
O frabjous day! Callooh! Callay!"
He chortled in his joy.

'Twas brillig, and the slithy toves
Did gyre and gimble in the wabe:
All mimsy were the borogoves,
And the mome raths outgrabe.

—*Lewis Carroll*

Acknowledgments

I SPENT NEARLY TWO YEARS WRITING *MORE THAN WORDS*, and it has morphed more than any project I've ever worked on. The setting went from Washington, D.C., to Ithaca, New York, to New York City. The characters had different professions, different sexual orientations, different roles in each other's lives. Some characters who started out dead in one draft ended up alive in another, and vice versa. And some characters were deleted from one draft only to crop up again in a later draft in a slightly different form. I wouldn't have been able to write this book without the support of a huge community of friends and family who talked to me about the story, read various versions of it, and understood when I disappeared into my work.

This book was written after my father died in a car accident and while many people I care a lot about were fighting cancer. They and all the people who love them were in my heart while writing this story. The character Leslie was named after my remarkable high school Spanish teacher, Leslie Walker, who lost her battle with cancer in September 2016. And while Joseph Gregory and my father, John Santopolo, are very different men, they both loved their daughters dearly and had a penchant for driving classic cars. This book is dedicated to my dad because he showed me how powerful the love between a father and daughter can be. And how much losing a beloved father can change someone's world.

More Than Words never would have been finished if it weren't for Miriam Altshuler, my superhero of a literary agent, who is also a dear friend. Thank you, Miriam, for being there whenever I needed an encouraging word, a dose of reality, a person to vent—or to cry—to, and someone to champion me and my work; you are truly one of the best people I know. And Tara Singh Carlson, thank you for pulling out your editorial warrior skills for this one. At this point, I'm pretty sure you were born, alongside Wonder Woman, on Themiscyra, with your own lasso of truth, bracelets of submission, and Amazonian sword, used to slay unwieldy manuscripts. Thank you, too, to the team at Putnam who worked tirelessly to promote *The Light We Lost* while I was writing and who designed, copyedited, marketed, publicized, and sold both my books with such care. Thank you especially to Ivan Held, Christine Ball, Sally Kim, Helen Richard, Leigh Butler, Tom Dussel, Kate Boggs, Alexis Welby, Ashley Hewlett, Stephanie Hargadon, Madeline Schmitz, Ashley McClay, Brennin Cummings, Jordan Aaronson, Kelly Gildea, Katie Punia, Sanny Chiu, Anthony Ramondo, Monica Cordova, Ben Lee, Andrea St. Aubin, and Maija Baldauf. And thank you to the folks at Penguin Young Readers, too—especially at Philomel Books—for being so awesome and supportive while I wrote and promoted and juggled everything. Thanks, too, to Reese Witherspoon, Emma Roberts, Karah Preiss, Danielle and Carly at the Skimm, and all of the authors, reviewers, publishers, and readers all over the world who embraced my first book so fully.

I also want specifically to thank the people who read drafts of *More Than Words* and the ones who provided information I needed along the way. Thank you to my writers' group— Marianna Baer, Anne Heltzel, Marie Rutkoski, and Eliot Schrefer—for all of their helpful feedback on multiple iterations of this story. Thank you to my friends Talia Benamy, Gillian Engberg, Sarah Fogelman, Kimberly Grant, Nick Schifrin, and Ruby Shamir, who so graciously offered to read a version or two of *More Than Words* and provide their insights into love, loss, politics, New York, and so much more. Thank you to my sister Alison May, who went on a research trip with me, offered her medical expertise, and gave me notes on the story, too. Thank you to Rebecca Bloom and Eleanor Coufos for answering my questions about Brearley and Bronx Science. Thank you to Matthew Grieco for making sure I got my *Jeopardy!* facts straight. Thank you to Tom Barron, Robyn Bender, Jordan Epstein, and my grandfather Larry Franklin for teaching me about how businesses work and proper—and improper—accounting practices. Thank you to all of the folks I worked with as a volunteer at Hillary for America—especially the wonderful HardCorr team—for showing me what strong, powerful, and passionate people are involved in politics. You are all so inspiring. And to everyone else whom I asked random questions at parties or dinners or on Facebook about Spanish phrases or politics or business or New York City in the '80s and '90s, thank you for answering (thank you especially to Christina Diaz Gonzales, who taught me the phrase "se te están pegando las pestañas").

And, as always, thank you to my family—especially my mom, Beth, and sisters, Ali and Suzie—for being my anchor.

We are stronger together, and I'm so glad we have each other for support in times of challenge and in times of happiness. And to Andrew Claster, whose love makes me want to be the very best version of myself: I love you more than words and am so glad we exist in the universe where you and I get to be together. Thank you for being you.